After graduating, Amanda Robson worked in medical research at The London School of Hygiene and Tropical Medicine, and at the Poisons Unit at Guy's Hospital where she became a co-author of a book on cyanide poisoning. Amanda attended the Faber novel writing course and writes full-time. Her debut novel, *Obsession*, became a #1 ebook bestseller in 2017. She is also the author of four more domestic suspense novels: the *Sunday Times* bestselling *Guilt*, *Envy*, *My Darling* and *The Unwelcome Guest*.

Also by Amanda Robson

Obsession
Guilt
Envy
My Darling

THE UNWELCOME GUEST

AMANDA ROBSON

avon.

Published by AVON
A division of HarperCollins*Publishers* Ltd
1 London Bridge Street
London SE1 9GF

www.harpercollins.co.uk

HarperCollins*Publishers*
1st Floor, Watermarque Building, Ringsend Road
Dublin 4, Ireland

A Paperback Original 2021

First published in Great Britain by HarperCollins*Publishers* 2021

A catalogue copy of this book is available from the British Library.

ISBN: 978-0-00-843059-7

Typeset in Bembo by Palimpsest Book Production Ltd, Falkirk, Stirlingshire.

Printed and Bound in the UK using
100% Renewable Electricity at CPI Group (UK) Ltd

MIX
Paper from
responsible sources
FSC
www.fsc.org
FSC® C007454

This book is produced from independently certified FSC™ paper
to ensure responsible forest management.

For more information visit: www.harpercollins.co.uk/green

To mother-in-laws everywhere.

1

Saffron

I look across the breakfast table at my husband, Miles, and the reasons I married him move towards me with certainty. We are in tune, both physically and mentally. Why do I ever doubt him? It's not Miles I have problems with, but you, Caprice. His mother. A frail and lonely widow, with kind eyes and a swan-like neck? Or the mother-in-law from hell with a witch's cackle for a laugh? Whichever, you have infiltrated our lives.

You were living in the self-contained annexe that abuts our house, built especially for you. But you have decided it no longer suits. It's suddenly become too poky, so you've moved in with us. And you're here, at breakfast time, sitting next to me, cracking the top of your boiled egg with sledgehammer ferocity.

As my husband frequently points out, you are still a beautiful woman. I like to reply *for your age*, just to remind us both that I am young and you are old. Youth is more powerful than age, I hope, for our relationship has become a battle.

Over the years I have tried so hard to make you like me. But it was difficult from the start. You made it quite clear I wasn't your sort of person the first time we met, when Miles invited me to your family home for Sunday lunch. A painful affair in your large, medieval hall of a dining room, which looked out onto a garden that never ended. It blended into the horizon, dripping with thousands of pounds' worth of showcase flowers.

Rupert, Miles' father, was still alive then, presiding at the head of the table carving a succulent joint of beef.

Miles sat opposite me. A low-slung crystal chandelier dangled between us. His eyes glistened into mine, trying to encourage me to relax. Aiden, Miles' younger brother, was sitting next to me. The silence in the room was suffocating.

After a while, you leant towards me. 'Well, Julie,' you said.

Julie. Miles' ex-girlfriend, and now Aiden's current squeeze.

'It's Saffron,' I replied, with what I hoped was a wide friendly smile.

'Well,' you coughed. 'Sa . . . a . . . a . . . ffron. Tell me how you two met.' Too much emphasis on the *a*. Long and slow. As if my name was difficult to pronounce.

I couldn't tell you the truth. No mother wants to hear her son was seduced at a party when he was drunk and then didn't leave his new girlfriend's room for over a week because they were smoking dope and having experimental sex. So I just smiled and explained that we met at college.

'Oh. Are you at the poly?' you asked.

Aiden and Miles both laughed.

'Polys don't exist anymore. Haven't for almost twenty years. You know that, Mum. They're new universities now. Cambridge poly is Anglia Ruskin University,' Aiden said through a mouthful of homemade Yorkshire pudding.

'Is that where you're studying, Anglia Ruskin, dear?' you asked, with a strong false emphasis on the word *dear* that made me squirm inside.

'No. Actually I'm at the old university; Trinity College with Miles.'

Your lips tightened. 'A bluestocking, then?'

'She doesn't exactly look like a bluestocking, does she?' Rupert trumpeted from the end of the table.

Annoyed by this attempt at a compliment, you thwarted your husband with your eyes. The room fell silent again, interrupted only by the scraping of knives and forks across fine china. After a while you leant towards me again. 'Now, *Cinnamon* . . .' you said.

After a heavy Sunday lunch of roast beef with all the trimmings, followed by apple pie, which settled like lead on my stomach – I was already well on the way to being a vegetarian and subsequently a vegan – you asked me to help clear the table and wash up, while Miles' father invited his sons to admire the new dahlia border in the garden. A sexist division of duties. A throwback to the 1950s. But, on my best behaviour with the family of the man I was besotted with, I didn't comment or complain.

As we were loading the dishwasher I saw the men walking along the path at the side of the house, past the kitchen window.

Rupert's voice crashed towards us. 'Your girlfriend's a pretty filly. Taut and muscular like a fine racehorse.'

Sexist again. My stomach tightened. So he thought I was pretty. Despite the sexism of the comment, that pleased me. But I sensed your body stiffen with envious displeasure. I guessed that, as far as you were concerned, it was unnecessarily flattering.

We continued our chores. You washed the pans and I dried, racking my brains for something to say, wanting to fill the airwaves with friendship and conversation.

'It's a lovely area. How long have you lived here?' I tried.

'All my life.'

'So you were brought up around here?'

'That's what "all my life" means, yes.'

The silence expanded. Ask open, not closed questions, I told myself. 'Where do you work? Tell me about your job,' I persisted.

You stopped washing up, pulled off your rubber gloves and stepped towards me, pouring your angry eyes into mine. 'I'm a wife and mother. It isn't a *job*. It's a privilege and a pleasure. I would have thought a girl like you with brains sprouting out of your ears would have realised that.'

2

Caprice

'Have a good day at work, dear,' I shout as you leave. 'I'll tidy up, and then I'll take the children to school.

'You're welcome,' I mutter beneath my breath as the front door bangs shut.

You never really thank me for all I do with the children. Difficult to work with, getting through nannies like cannon fodder, you are coming home from work early tonight to interview yet another one. In the meantime, I take the flak and help you out. And recently your ingratitude has ramped up a notch. Since I could no longer bear being cooped up in the poky annexe at the back of the house like a factory-farmed chicken, and insisted on moving into the guest suite of the house I paid for in the first place, you have been even more sparing with your thanks.

Saffron, why, when he had a homemaker for a mother, did my son choose to marry you? A selfish career-obsessed woman?

I sigh inside and begin to clear the breakfast table. I wouldn't mind so much, but you are such an intellectual snob, looking down your nose at me because I went to secretarial college. You may have a double first in philosophy from Cambridge University, and have set up your own boutique law firm, but you live in an intellectual bubble; no empathy with real people. You talk to Miles endlessly about politics and legal issues but you never ask my opinion about anything. I am irrelevant. Invisible.

It's not as if you have any redeeming features. I can't understand why Miles finds you physically attractive. Your clothes are too masculine. Sharply tailored trouser suits for work. Jeans, Doc Martens and T-shirts riddled with designer holes for home life. I have to admit, you have long bleached blonde hair, which is nicely conditioned, and pretty cheekbones. But why do you spoil your face with thick horn-rimmed glasses? Haven't you heard of varifocal contacts?

Table cleared, dishwasher loaded and rumbling, I take off my apron and walk towards the playroom. Even though you have washed and dressed the children, and given them breakfast when you got up at 6 a.m., I expect you have left them watching a boring educational programme again.

Upper middle-class children can be as underprivileged as those on benefits. 'Quality time' is a fallacy that deprives in its own way.

3

Hayley

I want this job. It pays well. It's in a good neighbourhood. The agency I'm with informed me that the nannies who've worked here have enjoyed the experience, and have felt cherished and respected by their employers.

When I commented, 'But there's been a high turnover,' the agency boss replied, 'It's just been one of those things. The last two nannies had trouble renewing their work permits. Our government has been tightening up on immigration.'

I ring the doorbell, feeling nervous. A young woman with razor-blade cheekbones and sharp glasses opens the door. She looks a bit like Margot Robbie. I would so like to look edgy and sexy like that. Super-skinny. A real clothes horse. The sort of woman who would look good in anything, even a bin bag.

'Welcome. Do come in,' she says.

I step into this modern mansion. The hallway is laced with thick-pile carpet. A designer dresser built of metal and mirrors stands to the right of me, displaying a crystal vase bristling with flowers: lilies, roses, agapanthus and delphiniums. They fill the air with scent. A spiral marble staircase with a curved mahogany handrail coils upwards from the back of the hallway. Impressionist paintings adorn golden rag-rolled walls. I drink it all in to write about in my diary later. The diary I'm keeping to show my mother when I get home.

'I'm Saffron. How do you do?'

Saffron. Even her name is interesting. Her voice is deep and husky. Deep, but not masculine. Saffron oozes style and femininity.

'I'm Hayley,' I reply, shaking her hand.

'Are you from New Zealand?' Saffron asks.

I nod my head. As soon as I open my mouth everyone guesses where I'm from. My English boyfriend tells me my vocal cords are as soft as guitar strings and that, like all New Zealanders, I sound as if I am talking through my teeth.

'Whereabouts in New Zealand?' Saffron asks.

'Queenstown.'

'We've been there for a holiday. It was fabulous. How could you bear to leave?'

'Every young New Zealander craves some time in England.' I pause. 'New Zealand is small. Parochial. There's more to life than sharp-edged mountains and life-threatening adventure.'

My insides tighten. Actually, I miss our small cosy family bungalow full of finely stretched enthusiasm. My cheery father and brother who spend their days strapping people to bungee elastic. My thin, worried mother who works stoically at the local supermarket.

Saffron puts her head on one side and her lips burst into a wide smile. 'Do come and sit down.'

I follow her into the drawing room, which looks like a film set. It has a large curved window adorned with tumbling white damask curtains and matching window seat. This white extravaganza frames a view of a tennis court and a swimming pool. Am I dreaming? Have I arrived in Hollywood?

'Please sit down,' Saffron says, smiling across at me.

I sink into a silk-covered antique walnut chair, to the right of the fireplace. Saffron sits opposite me and leans forwards.

'I'm sure you've read our job description. We need help, from 9 a.m. to 6 p.m., five days a week.' She pauses and crosses her shapely, slender legs. 'Our elder son Ben is eight years old. He attends a private school, City of London Freemen's. Its name is

7

a bit confusing.' She smiles. 'It's not in London, but Ashtead, not far from here. His younger brother Harry is six. He's still at the local C of E Primary.' She pushes her glasses further back against her nose. 'In term time, we need them taken to school and picked up, and for them to be looked after until 6 p.m., when either Miles or I will be home. If they are ill or it's the school holidays, we need them cared for full-time.' She leans back. 'Does the package we sent to the agency seem suitable to you?'

I smile slowly. 'It does. Very much so. And I love working with this age group. I expect you've looked at my CV. The last children I looked after were the same age and we got on so well.'

'Look, Hayley,' Saffron says, sitting back, frowning in contemplation. 'I've read your references. You come highly recommended, but are you available? I need someone to start quickly.'

I take a deep breath to slow down my reply. I mustn't sound overeager. It will make me seem desperate. But this is by far the best opportunity I've had since I arrived in the UK. So far I've only had a few temporary appointments at homes where the regular nanny was on holiday.

'Well, I could move some things around ... That way I could start on Monday,' I say hesitantly.

'Great stuff.' She gives me a wide beaming smile. 'Well, I'll show you the accommodation. You can meet the children and we can take it from there.'

She stands up, and I follow her back into the hallway. An older woman is now attending to the flower arrangement on the dresser, cutting stamens from the lilies. When she sees us she straightens her back and rubs it, watching me through sad grey eyes.

'Let me introduce you. This is my mother-in-law, Caprice,' Saffron says. 'Caprice, this is Hayley, who's considering coming to work for us.'

Caprice nods her head at me, and carries on trimming the lilies.

8

I follow Saffron up the spiral staircase, along a landing decorated with a combination of modern art and landscapes, through a mock-Georgian doorway, into the nanny's accommodation. I exhale in admiration, as I look at a boudoir with a curved window that drips with what must be thousands and thousands of pounds' worth of rich red-and-gold-striped silk. There's a four-poster bed with red silk curtains and a matching counterpane. A four-poster bed? Silk? For the *nanny*? My breath escapes from my body like a waterfall. I have to get this job. I will never find a better one in the UK. Not only is the room I am standing in lavish in its soft furnishings, it also has a generous sitting area with two armchairs, a two-seater sofa and a fifty-inch TV. And there's a kitchenette with a minifridge, microwave, kettle and hob. I am practically salivating.

'There isn't an oven,' Saffron apologises, 'but you're welcome to use the main kitchen whenever you want.'

'It's fabulous,' I gush.

Even if the children are monsters, I determine to fall in love with them as we move across the bedroom to the bathroom. It has the full complement: toilet, bidet, shower cubicle, ornate basin with a cabinet and full-length mirror. An extravagant claw-footed bath. A black and white marble floor.

'It's so lovely. I've never seen accommodation as special as this.'

Saffron smiles proudly. 'I chose the décor.' Then she shakes her head and her face tightens. 'But Caprice doesn't like it. She says I should have chosen a floral pattern for the bed.'

Caprice. The woman downstairs. The mother-in-law.

'Come and meet the boys,' Saffron continues, suddenly keen to move on.

Please. Please, God, let me get on with the kids, I pray silently.

I walk downstairs with Saffron, and together we step into the playroom, where two skinny blond boys are sitting on the sofa watching TV. So like Saffron, they look as if they have been cloned from her, no man involved. As soon as we enter the room they jump off the sofa and run towards us.

'Mummy, Mummy,' one of them squeaks.

Saffron bends down and takes them both in her arms. When they have all finished hugging, their eyes turn to me.

'I want you to meet Hayley, your new nanny,' Saffron says, smiling.

My stomach leaps. New nanny? Am I employed already? They stand wide-eyed, staring up at me.

'Would you like me to read you a story?' I ask.

'Can we have *The Gruffalo*? Granny says it's too babyish for us, but we love it.'

Granny. Caprice, again? She seems to have a lot of influence in this house.

'I can't see why not. What do you think, Mummy?' I ask.

'Great idea,' Saffron replies as she switches off the TV.

I settle on the sofa, between the boys, and start to read. I love reading out loud. I was into amateur dramatics when I was younger, so I enjoy putting as much expression as I can into every sentence, and playing with my voice. The boys, one each side of me, snuggle against me as if they've known me forever. Saffron stands watching us, a fond smile playing on her lips.

Once the story is over, Saffron prises the boys away from me, and we step back into the hallway.

'Thanks for coming to visit,' Saffron says. 'I'm definitely offering you the job. If you're interested, I'll send the contract to your agency tomorrow. You could move in on Sunday, and start work on Monday. That would be great for us.'

I am so thrilled I feel like taking her in my arms and hugging her. Just as I am trying to stop myself from doing that, I see a man walking towards us. A man with foppish brown-blond hair and broad shoulders, smiling a high-wattage smile. My stomach rotates.

'This is my husband, Miles.'

4

Saffron

I'm sitting on the train to work when a woman with square shoulders sinks down next to me. She presses against me, squashing me. Making me feel claustrophobic. I lean away from her, against the carriage window, contemplating the late payment from my client, Sasha Reznikovitch, who promised the money three weeks ago. We chased her and she agreed to send it by BaccS, last Monday. It still hasn't arrived. We need to chase her again.

My law firm, Belgravia Private Clients – BPC – is a high-turnover outfit with only three members of staff. Me – the only lawyer; Ted Beresford-Webb, a friend from my school days who acts as my financial and office manager; and Julie Walsh, my PA. Julie was Miles' first girlfriend and is Aiden's ex-wife. And we have three clients. Three high-net-worth clients, demanding access to legal advice 24/7, which is why they pay generously.

For a second, as I sit on the train, worrying about cash flow, I regret leaving the magic circle law firm where I trained. I was a senior associate, aspiring to be a partner one day. But then I remember the excitement that tingled through me like electricity when my major client, Aristos Kaladopolous, began talking me into leaving to set up my own firm. Promising to bring all his legal issues to me lock, stock and barrel, if I did. He kept his word. And, so far, it has worked like clockwork.

Hard-working clockwork. Working around the clock more often than you, my dear mother-in-law, would like. I know you think I'm an absentee parent, Caprice. You frequently remind me, with your eyes. With your waspish comments. It is rich coming from you, a woman who has never contributed to family finances. A woman who does not understand the importance of earning money. A woman who married a wealthy man and expects money to flow towards you, like a river. Don't you know that river would stop flowing if it wasn't for aspirational individuals like me? Aspirational individuals like your husband, whose hard work you took for granted?

The train jerks to a halt and I look out of the window. We've arrived at Vauxhall. People begin to decant onto the platform like ants. The mass next to me eases away, and for the first time in half an hour I feel as if I can breathe without concentrating. I sigh as I stand up. Now I must battle with the tube.

Having survived the journey, I walk along Ebury Street, Belgravia, with its fine Georgian architecture, and any doubts about my choice of career vanish. Once again my body solidifies with pride. I am proud of my independence. Proud of what I have established.

Into the building. Up in the compact lift. Left out of it, through an ugly modern glass fire door, into BPC's half of the third floor. Julie is sitting behind a wide imitation marble plastic counter, typing. Her face is partially obscured by a large flower arrangement. She stretches her neck above pinks, chrysanthemums and alstroemeria to say, 'Good morning.'

'Good morning,' I reply.

I look across the room. Ted has arrived too. His thick hair damped and scraped back, neat and tidy as ever.

'Still no news from Sash,' he informs me with a grimace.

'Well then, why don't you chase her?'

An instruction, not a question. He nods his head. I walk across their office, through another glass door, into mine.

My office is too tidy. There's a dearth of the usual scattered papers. No large cardboard boxes filled with files of documents at the moment. No Post-it stickers plastered around my computer screen and desk to remind me of urgent tasks. I'm not as busy as I'd like. My favourite shipping magnate, and major client, Aristos Kaladopolous, is on holiday, breezing around the Greek Islands on his superyacht. A blue and white plastic monstrosity, complete with a helicopter pad, three launches and an army of jet skis. His new wife is keeping him occupied, so, disappointingly, he hasn't become involved in any legal spats for eight weeks.

I tap my fingers on my desk. My stomach tightens. We need Sasha Reznikovitch's money, ASAP. She is an oligarch's daughter, who dances with the Moscow Royal Ballet. And we need some more work to come in. Maybe I should try and take another client. But then, when I'm busy I can only just manage as I am.

The telephone rings and I pick up. My brother-in-law Aiden's amiable voice chirrups down the line. 'I'm in the area. Do you have time for a quick lunch?'

There was a time when it was Julie he would have popped in to see.

'As a matter of fact I do, yes.'

And my spirits lift. Aiden is pushy and bombastic. But he is good company.

Three hours later, we meet in his favourite restaurant, Boisdale's. Old English. Oak panelling and oil paintings. Stiff white table-cloths. When I arrive Aiden is sitting at a table in the corner, waiting for me.

Aiden. Miles' younger brother. So like Miles, but not as good-looking. Aiden's face and body have been softened by an overdose of adipose tissue. Missing Miles' patience and kindness, he is edgy and raucous. But what Aiden has missed in serenity and looks he has gained in financial success. We are comfortable, but Caprice has boosted our finances big time. Miles has a lecturer's salary and let's face it – although I haven't told my family yet, my business is on the line.

13

Aiden is an entrepreneur. His business, selling innovative grease traps for London pubs and restaurants, turns over ten million a year. He has a mews house in Chelsea, a chalet in St Moritz, and a villa in Barbados (the expensive end).

Today he sits opposite me, lowering his chin, widening his well-cushioned jowls.

'How's life going for my favourite girl?' he asks, leaning across the table and putting his hand on my arm.

I know why I'm his favourite girl: because he is in competition with Miles. I guess, and have guessed for years, that Julie, despite marrying Aiden, always secretly preferred her childhood sweetheart Miles. They split up when he left home to go to Cambridge. Almost immediately, she took up with Aiden, when he was on a weekend exeat from Charterhouse.

Before he put on weight. When he still played a lot of sport.

I suspect she took up with Aiden to claw back Miles' attention, but Julie's ploy didn't work. He and I met during our first term at Trinity College Cambridge, and have been an item ever since. So even if she hoped to, Julie never had another look-in with him.

Julie and Aiden got engaged and married a year before we did. Their wedding day was lavish and fun. They had the works; no expense spared. Church bells. Choir with Aled Jones-esque soloist; heart-breaking, jaw-dropping. Reception at Hampton Court Palace. Sit-down meal that deserved a Michelin star. Wedding favours. Toast after toast.

But less than a year later, a week or so before Miles and I tied the knot, Julie turned up at our house, announcing that she was leaving Aiden. She knew I was away on a business trip – I had spoken to her on the phone that very morning. Allegedly she was asking Miles for shelter and advice.

I always wondered whether there was more to it than that. Did she come to tell him how she felt about him, hoping he wouldn't marry me?

14

After talking to Miles, she left Aiden, didn't come to our wedding, and went home to live with her parents. Only after our wedding did she then return to her husband. Was it because she had failed to entice Miles away from me? It is something I will never know the answer to. Miles says the conversation he had with her that night is confidential, and he is a man who always keeps his word.

When Julie finally left Aiden for good, over five years ago, I became Aiden's challenge. His revenge against his brother for being the one that his woman wanted. If he could bed me, he would. A stag thing; wanting to rut his competition's mate. Despite the fun I have being with him, the disingenuous nature of his attention always annoys me. Not for the first time in our relationship, he places his hand on my arm.

'Please stop touching me,' I snap.

5

Aiden

I'm at my favourite restaurant. And you are sitting opposite me, drinking sparkling mineral water while I nurse a large glass of Bourgogne Aligoté. It has been a huge burden to me, falling in love with my brother's woman. I put my hand on your arm and squeeze it; in empathy, in camaraderie. But you wince. Your body stiffens.

'Please stop touching me,' you snap.

'Sorry. I didn't mean anything by it,' I reply, pulling my hand away. Your eyes narrow almost imperceptibly. But as I know every movement of your volatile face, I can tell you think I did mean something. 'Look, Saffron,' I continue, 'I just want to know how it's going for you now that Mother has moved into your house.'

You sigh and shake your head. 'I try so hard to get on with her, but it is time to admit to you that I don't find your mother easy.'

'Well, I already know that.' I laugh. 'Do you remember your thirtieth birthday, when you told me that Mother always excludes you? She dotes on Miles, but not on you? You said you would have room for her in your heart if only she would let you into hers.'

You squirm awkwardly in your chair. 'Did I say that?'

'Yes.'

You frown. 'I don't remember. I try not to complain about

your mother. It's not really fair on you, or Miles.' You take a sip of mineral water. I watch your voluptuous lips adhere to the glass as you drink. My heart palpitates.

I smile inside, remembering how squiffy you were that night. We walked around the garden together, in the moonlight, as I had contrived to have a private conversation with you about my relationship with Julie. I put my arm around you and you didn't seem to mind. I shouldn't have – you were very drunk. But then, it was worth it. I still remember the warmth of your sweet, sweet body close to mine.

You shake your head. 'I have no recollection of saying that.' You take another sip of mineral water. Another purse of your generous lips. You put the glass on the table and sigh. 'But it's true. I would have loved to have a close friendship with a warm mother-in-law. My relationship with Caprice is not what I envisaged.' Your eyes hold mine. 'I have plenty of room in my heart for love.'

My chest tightens. 'I know you do.'

The waitress arrives with our food. A colourful vegan concoction for you and rare calf's liver, so undercooked that blood oozes across the plate, for me. You glance at the blood and your eyes narrow again.

When you have stopped wincing at my food, I continue. 'We are both minimised by Caprice. A very poor second to her favourite: Miles.'

You pick up your fork and push lentils and vegetables around, like a cat toying with them, not ready to eat yet. 'I know she dotes on him, but I have always been under the impression she also dotes on you.' You sit staring at me, fork in the air.

'No. No,' I reply. 'She makes me feel excluded too.'

A slight grimace. A shake of your head. 'You're right. I was telling a white lie to try to protect you. The truth is, Caprice's world centres around Miles. No one else matches him. No one else is good enough. It's a sadness we both have to face.'

17

6

Caprice

It's Friday morning and I'm driving my grandsons to school. Yet again. Listening to *Harry Potter*, narrated by Stephen Fry. Yet again. I sigh inside. *Harry Potter*. Unrealistic. Irreligious. A divisive influence. But you are impressed by it, aren't you, Saffron? And so your sons have become addicted to this turgid nonsense. Despite your Oxbridge education, you don't seem to have noticed it's badly written. I mentioned that to you last week, on a rare occasion when you were attempting to cook, and your shoulders stiffened.

'J.K. Rowling is brilliant. Top-end literature. So creative. So thought-provoking. If you can't see its attraction like the rest of the world, half your brain must be missing.'

You have quite a mouth on you don't you, Saffron? Always condescending towards me, just because you did an obscure degree at an old, rather than a new, university. By the way, I know the difference between old and new universities now. Do you remember me being belittled about that when we first met?

But despite my opinions, I am prepared to be flexible. When the children asked me to download *Harry Potter* to my iPhone, so that they could listen to it on the way to school, I agreed. So, unfortunately, I'm having to suffer owls and Hagrid, wizards and muggles, wands and quidditch. Stuff and nonsense that makes me want to vomit. I love my grandsons. But I do feel they miss out on so much of what matters in life, because of you, Saffron.

They need to be sent to a decent boarding school, like Aiden and Miles were. But you dug your heels in, didn't you? Just when I had talked Miles into accepting my suggestion, you fought back. You forced him to refuse my offer to make sure both my grandsons were offered places at Charterhouse.

Instead, you have insisted that they attend local day schools. The one Harry goes to is a C of E primary, which you insist can't be bettered for a child of his age. It isn't even private and so I worry he's in danger of mixing with the wrong kind of peer group.

At least before too long they'll both be at the City of London Freemen's — a good solid private school. But I'm only being honest when I say its name just doesn't have the same ring to it as Charterhouse.

We're stuck at traffic lights. I change the angle of the rear-view mirror so that I can look at my grandsons. So neat-featured. So dainty. So vulnerable, with angelic blond hair and stick-like arms and legs. Clones of you. You have infiltrated and overwhelmed my family's genes. But never mind. Whatever they look like, I still love them. With a bit of luck as they get older their faces will become stronger. More Jackson. Less Filby. For even though you have taken my son's name and now call yourself Saffron Jackson, you will always be Saffron Filby to me.

We pull into the side road by Harry's school. I switch off the car engine and sigh with relief as Hagrid is silenced.

'Please can we listen to it for five more minutes,' Ben begs.

'No, Ben. We need to drop Harry off now, otherwise you'll be late and your form teacher Ms Frankfurt will tell you off.'

'Mummy would let us,' Ben says.

'Mummy isn't here,' I reply.

'Franki would let us,' Harry tries.

Franki. Their last nanny.

'Franki isn't here,' I reply.

19

'Daisy would let us,' Ben pushes.

Daisy. The nanny before last.

'Daisy isn't here,' I say, voice sharp.

Then I soften. 'Come on, I'll buy you some chocolate buttons to eat on the way home, if you get out of the car right now.'

So young, bribery still works. And you are strict about chocolate, Saffron, so it's a real treat. You frequently remind me not to buy it for them, rabbiting on about diabetes. Rabbiting on about their teeth. But I take no notice. What harm can a little chocolate do? Life needs to be fun.

So, chocolate promised, I open the car door, and they edge out of the car onto the pavement. Eager little hands hold mine as we walk towards St Peter's Juniors. As soon as we reach the playground Harry dashes off to join his friends. Ben and I return to the car to carry on our journey. This time, thankfully, without *Harry Potter*. That is our agreement. After dropping off his younger brother, Ben sits in the front passenger seat and *Harry Potter* is over for the day.

Sitting in the front is another secret treat. You only ever let the children sit in the back, for safety reasons. Despite not spending much time with your children, you are a stickler about certain things. I start the ignition and we set off.

'When can I tell Mummy you give us lots of chocolate?' Ben asks.

'Never. You promised, remember. Otherwise I won't be able to give you chocolate again. It has to be our secret.'

He wriggles in his seat. 'I don't like lying to Mummy.' His voice sounds plaintive.

'It isn't lying. It's just not telling her something,' I snap.

He shakes his head. 'Granny, it feels like lying.'

'How many times have I asked you not to call me Granny? It makes me feel old.'

We are stationary in a line to turn right. I look across at him and see his eyes pool with tears.

'But . . . but . . . I think I love my mummy too much. She's my favourite person. I want to hug her forever and tell her every thought in my head.'

The traffic moves, so I pull my eyes away from him to concentrate on the road. Ben might have passed an entrance exam to an academic day school, but he really needs to tighten up on his people observation skills. It just shows you how academic intelligence isn't all it's cracked up to be. How can he love Saffron more than anyone in the world, when his father is someone as generous and kind as my son Miles?

Fortunately, we do not have to continue this conversation any further. We have arrived in the school car park and it's time to drop him off. He opens the car door and sidles out.

'Bye, Granny, thanks for the lift.'

My stomach tightens. Doesn't he ever listen to a word I say?

Ben and Harry Jackson now deposited at their places of education, it's time for my compensation for doing the school run. The school gate mums have invited me to join them for their once-a-week catch-up. Coffee at a local café. They are real mums. Even though they can't afford to send their children to the most prestigious private schools, I admire them because they're mums with time for their families. You are so irresponsible in comparison. With my help you could afford a top-end school like Charterhouse, but still you rail against it. And you don't make it up to Ben and Harry by being there for them. Your children have the worst of both worlds.

I step into the café. Wooden tables. Wooden floors. Rustic but modern. I look across at the young mums, sitting together on two brown leather sofas. Cradling their mugs of coffee, heads back laughing. And suddenly, from nowhere, Rupert's loss hits me. I was young once, like them, looking after my children, in charge of my family unit. Adored by my husband. I thought my life would be like that forever. And now it has gone. And Rupert has gone. His face moves towards me in my mind's eye, and I

21

want to reach out and stroke his cheek. Pull him towards me and kiss him.

I bite my lip to stop tears falling, before turning around and walking out of the café. I'll feel stronger, more able to cope with company next week.

7

Hayley

The Brits are having an Indian summer. It's mid-September, and yet it's twenty-five degrees Centigrade. My legs burn beneath my black jeans. Not how we Kiwis imagine the UK. And, during this almost tropical weather, I'm moving in to my new home. To my new job. I've told all my friends on Twitter, Instagram and Facebook.

Fresh off the bus, I walk along Lexington Drive, weighed down by my overloaded rucksack. Everything I possess in the UK is on my back. Tired of moving from one temporary job to another, camping in strange houses, I'm so excited to be settling in one place, where I will be comfortable and relaxed.

I walk past the modern mansions, open-mouthed all over again. Houses big enough for twenty people to live in. Houses with tradesman's entrances. Stone porticoes. Heavy front doors of antique oak and mahogany. Ornate door-knockers. Protruding security cameras, turning towards me as I pass manicured gardens and Range Rovers parked neatly in generous drives next to low-slung sports cars and family run-arounds. Houses that whisper – *look at me, I'm rich*.

Despite my heavy bag, I almost skip towards number 20, the one at the far end of the road. The one where I'm going to live.

I arrive and stand back to admire my new home. This mansion is set further back from the road than the others. It has a wide circular drive with a pond, and a fountain in it. The house is three storeys high, with six large windows on each floor. It has a fine old yew hedge bordering the garden, with shiny black railings in front of it. A large fir tree stands to the right of the drive. It's magnificent. I hope they light it up at Christmas.

A large gold lettered sign, 'Wellbeck House', is attached to the railings, by the front gate, next to the entrance buzzer and a large security camera. I push the buzzer. A male voice, which sounds a little like a Dalek's, answers, 'Hello, Hayley. I'll buzz you in.'

I hear a grinding sound, and push the gate. It's heavy. I open it slowly and step into the driveway.

My feet crunch across stone, past the pond with its fountain. The front door opens. Miles Jackson, you are standing on the doorstep smiling at me, large brown eyes twinkling into mine. My stomach rotates. You are so good-looking. You have strong features. A proud chin and nose. Light brown wavy hair. Intense eyes I would love to lie next to. You're an intellectual. An academic, according to my agency notes on the family. I expect your students drool over you, don't they?

'Welcome,' you say, stepping away from the doorway.

I follow you in. The house unfolds before me, even more impressive the second time. I notice a photograph on the dresser next to the flowers. You and Saffron, standing together, beaming into the camera, wearing mortar boards and holding degree certificates. You must have met at uni. Meeting too young – one of the signs of an unsuitable relationship. I push that thought away. The first rule of my nanny agency is never, ever to flirt with the man of the house. Try it once and you're off the books.

'Can I get you anything? It's really hot today. Would you like a cold drink?' you ask.

'I'm fine thanks. I'll just unpack and then I'll come and get a glass of water.'

'Let me show you to your room right away then,' you say. 'Saffron's already shown you the nanny quarters, hasn't she? I know you said you liked them.'

'I did indeed.'

'Well I'm sorry but she's out today with the boys at a friend's house. But at least you can settle in in peace.' You pause. 'I'll come up with you just to make sure everything is OK.'

We walk up the spiral staircase together, side by side. Your presence makes me feel uncomfortable. Because I daren't let my eyes rest on you too long, I'm over-aware of everything around me. The thick-pile burgundy carpet. The golden rag-rolled walls. And for some strange reason I feel myself breathing too fast, too deeply.

We arrive in my sumptuous quarters, red silk an even richer ruby than I remembered. Four-poster bed, larger. Claw-footed bath more tempting.

'Thank you, it's fabulous.' I smile.

'I've put clean towels in the bathroom,' you say, brown eyes gleaming. 'And a large beach towel. The cover is off the pool if you fancy a swim.'

I look at you, the perfect man, standing in front of me, and just for a second, I think I've died and gone to heaven. Then I think of your wife, Saffron, and my brain becomes curdled with envy. Guilt supplants envy. What am I doing, admiring another woman's husband? Especially when she's been kind enough to employ me.

8

Saffron

It's date night. Our new nanny, Hayley, is babysitting, as you are out playing bridge this evening, Caprice. And I'm sitting opposite your treasured son at Red Peppers in Esher, sipping a cheeky Rioja and picking at sesame quinoa. As Miles does not share my dietary habits, I watch him devour a steak burger on sourdough, with sweet potato fries. The heady stench of meat pushes towards me, making me feel slightly nauseous. I try to ignore it.

'So what do you think about my theory?' I ask.

He smiles. 'The one you always harp on about? That Aiden fancies you, because he's in competition with me?'

'Yes.'

'We've been through this so many times. I can't blame him having the hots for you. But why should it be anything to do with being in competition? He finds you attractive. Period.'

'But why keep pushing it?'

He has a sip of wine, holding my gaze with his. 'He doesn't much, does he? Do I need to beat him up?' His tone is mild, and I can tell he isn't taking me seriously.

'It's always there,' I insist. 'An undercurrent. Come on, Miles. You know he came and took me to lunch, again, a few days ago. He put his hand on my arm. I told you.'

He shrugs his shoulders. 'Wasn't he just being friendly? It's hardly making a pass is it – putting a hand on someone's arm?' A frown ripples across his forehead. 'Or maybe it is these days.'

I lean back in my chair. 'Women know when a man wants them. It's instinct. Sometimes it's hard to explain.' I pause. 'And I'm sure he's jealous of you.'

He shakes his head slowly, and eats the last sweet potato fry. 'I suppose Mother and Father always got on with me more easily. Aiden and Father clashed because they were both alpha personalities. Mother always doted on me. She had always been surrounded by feisty lively men: her father, her husband, her brother. She always seemed to prefer my peaceful personality to Aiden's cheekiness.' He pauses as he tops up our wine. 'I do think he felt it from time to time.' He takes a sip of wine. 'And I suppose brothers do sometimes fancy the same physical type.' He frowns again. 'But he's not evil. Give him a break.'

'I never said he was evil. Just that he makes me feel uncomfortable,' I say, trying to stop my voice from sounding snappish.

And my stomach tightens because if Miles thinks brothers fancy similar women, does that mean he still feels more for Julie than he admits? Is that why he's so tolerant of Aiden's attention towards me?

'My mother makes you feel uncomfortable too,' my husband points out. 'Not everyone who makes you feel uncomfortable fancies you.'

'Don't be ridiculous, Miles. Comparing your mother to Aiden isn't comparing like with like.'

I take a mouthful of quinoa, and think about you, Caprice. And I'm back on my wedding day, swathed in silk and lace. You were the only guest who didn't congratulate me. The only person who didn't tell me I looked nice.

I think of you yesterday, when I returned from work, skulking about in the kitchen, tidying up the herb and spice rack.

'You always have it in such a mess, dear.'

Dear. The way you say that word still annoys me. You over-emphasise the *d*, and then swallow the rest of it.

You turned your head from the spice rack and smiled a dead

smile. 'Before you go to the playroom to see the boys, I could do with a quick word.'

I sighed inside, took off my coat and hung it on the coatrack by the back door. Bracing myself for whatever criticism was coming next. I sat down at the kitchen table and you sat opposite me. As well-groomed as ever, with your sweeping doughnut of a hairstyle. You have come a long way since your humble beginnings, after marrying a wealthy man. Acquiring a strong and expensive sense of taste. Your ladies' captain of the golf club look. Elegant. Casual. Designer branded. Chinos and blouses. Scarves and lightweight tailored jackets. Pale tasteful eyeshadow. Pale tasteful smile.

'I'm worried you're too strict with Ben and Harry,' you announced.

'What's the matter this time?' I asked.

'They're not having enough fun – and I'm worried about their diet. They're thin as sticks.'

And I knew you had been taking them to McDonald's, and bribing them with chocolate again.

Before I could reply with my habitual answer about diet – *of course they can have an occasional McDonald's or chocolate treat; everything in moderation, is what I believe* – you stood up and walked to our wedding photograph, on the kitchen dresser. You picked it up and cradled it close to your face, studying it intently.

'You were pretty when you were young, weren't you?'

You have known me since I was eighteen. I'm forty now. This is the first time you have ever said anything nice about my appearance. Forty is a sensitive age. The modern definition of middle age. So you gave me a compliment in retrospect.

Pretty when I was young.

Implying I have lost my looks. I want to look all right even if I live until I'm eighty. So I locked myself in the downstairs cloakroom, put my head in my hands and cried. After all the

28

unpleasant things you have said and done, this was the first time I had allowed you to make me cry.

But I've moved past it now. I know you said it on purpose, but I have forgiven you. I won't allow sensitivity and vanity to reduce me to tears again. You have issues because you miss Rupert and envy me my time with Miles. I mustn't forget that I am the lucky one here.

9

Miles

You look so attractive in the candlelight, so quirky in your Indian print T-shirt and dangly earrings. No wonder Aiden likes you so much. You're warm, you're good fun. He's lonely.

I'm so glad my younger brother has become so successful with his business. I always put him in the shade academically, and even though he was sporty, on all the teams, Mum and Dad despaired of his exam results and his teachers' comments. Look at him now, with his flat in Chelsea, his chalet in St Moritz, his villa on Barbados. My parents had nothing to worry about. Except perhaps his plumpness. Typical sportsman; eating like a horse, even when no longer active, and so piling on the pounds, damaging his once athletic figure.

Despite stellar financial success, it's a pity he hasn't had more luck in his relationships. Things didn't work out with Julie, but I'm sure he'll meet someone else. Someone like you, Saffron. He doesn't mean any harm. He just needs friendship right now.

You shake your head and your silky hair caresses your shoulders. You smile at me and I watch your Julia Roberts lips stretch across your face. Every time I look at you, I know I'm lucky.

But then a shadow moves across my mind. Is Aiden still jealous of me, after all these years, despite all his money?

Perhaps.

10

Caprice

I met my husband Rupert the day I stepped into his office, as his temporary secretary. I wanted the job to become permanent. My mother had recently died of breast cancer. My father's wood yard was struggling. I needed some cash to help pay our bills.

Rupert Jackson's office was untidy, the desk strewn with piles of paperwork, empty coffee cups, full ashtrays, dead packets of Benson and Hedges. Machinery manuals littered the floor. I wove a path between them to approach his desk as he stood up to greet me.

He wasn't a good-looking man. His heavy nose was hatchet-shaped, and his eyes bulged slightly. His most appealing features were his full head of copper-coloured hair, and his cheeky grin. I'm not really sure how, with such a heavy-featured father, Miles became so good-looking. It must be my genes he has inherited.

'Welcome,' Rupert said, in a strong Yorkshire accent.

Welcome, sounded more like a punch in the air, than a word. I was a sun-ripened southerner, used to people who spoke with drawling vowels, wondering what this Yorkshireman was doing setting up a business in West London. He leant across his desk and shook my hand, his palm strong and warm against mine.

'What can I do to help?' I asked.

'You can start by tidying up this office.'

I emptied the ashtrays and washed them. Opened the window to air the fug of cigarette smoke. Picked up the rubbish and arranged the manuals in alphabetical order on the windowsill. He began talking on the phone. Arguing with someone about a shipment of drill bits. Shouting through his straight, wide teeth. His accent seemed stronger than ever. He slammed the phone down.

'The bastard,' he ejaculated, and looked me in the eye.

We both laughed. 'So you don't like him, then?'

'I love the bastard really, I just need him to pull his finger out on my shipment.'

I loved his boldness, his audacity. His personality crackled in the air like electricity. When I was around him I felt alive like I did when I was with my father.

I looked after Rupert in the office, and then later when I married him, I looked after his life. I had so much pleasure doing that and bringing up Miles. And tolerating Aiden. Miles, so sensitive, so intuitive, ever since he was a toddler. Aiden, always a cheeky handful. In Aiden the positive assertiveness of Rupert and my father had transformed into a bossy arrogance. An alpha personality taken a step too far.

I remember the day I became ill with appendicitis. Fortunately baby Aiden was sleeping. Miles was only two. I lay on the sofa gripping my stomach, moaning and crying. Miles walked across the room towards me, eyes filled with compassion. He rubbed my tummy and said, 'I'm calling the doctor, Mummy.'

He went to get the cordless phone, picked it up and frowned. 'What's the number?' he asked. I had to rouse myself and look it up in our address book. I managed to dial the doctor myself, just before my appendix burst. An ambulance took me to hospital whilst our neighbours looked after Miles and Aiden. If Miles hadn't encouraged me to phone our GP I wouldn't be around today.

And Miles was super bright of course. I wasn't one of those mothers who boasted at the school gate. I didn't need to. Everyone knew how intelligent he was. He could count to twenty by the time he was two. No wonder he is a professor now.

There are two types of people in life: givers and takers. Miles is a giver. And you, Saffron, are the selfish kind. But Julie is a giver, so like Miles. Julie has the right attitude. Unfortunately for her, she chose the wrong brother to marry. The difficult one. No wonder she left him; he was more interested in making money than spending time with his wife. Not like Rupert, who made money and really, really, loved and cherished me. My mind and body ache for him still.

I suppose it's never too late for things to work out. Maybe one day Miles will see sense and find a suitable life partner. Maybe one day Miles and Julie will get back together. He's only thirty-nine years old. It isn't too late. He just needs a little push in the right direction. The sort of push only a mother knows how to give.

11

Hayley

I moved in two weeks ago and the Jacksons have already invited me to join them for their family Sunday lunch. Apparently Aiden, Miles' younger brother, joins them at Wellbeck House every Sunday.

We're sitting around their ornate glass and marble table, tucking into lamb tagine made by Caprice, who is sitting at the head of the table, resplendent in co-ordinated shades of cream. Her white-blonde hair shimmers to golden, in the sunlight streaming in from the window behind.

Actually, only some of us are eating tagine. Ben and Harry are guzzling chicken nuggets and chips, smothered in ketchup. Saffron has a vegan dish.

'Aren't you going to try the tagine, or my curry?' she asks her sons.

'No, Mummy. I'm fine, thanks,' Ben says.

'What about you, Harry. Would you like a spoonful of what I'm eating?'

He shakes his head vehemently. 'Granny said we could have this for a treat.'

Caprice winces as he says the word *Granny*. Saffron purses her lips.

'The tagine is delicious, Mother,' Miles says.

Caprice beams across at him, almost purring.

'It is. Thank you,' I add, to be polite, but in truth I find it heavy and unsubtle; laden with too much cinnamon.

I look across at Saffron, pushing her vegan curry around her plate with a fork. So slim, so fragile, as if she hardly ever eats anything. Her skeletal figure emphasises the sharpness of her cheekbones and her enormous eyes. Aiden can hardly keep his eyes off her. Why do men seem to admire physical fragility in a woman? Does it make them feel protective?

'How's business, Saffron?' he asks between mouthfuls.

'Good,' she replies with a curt smile. And somehow I sense she doesn't mean it. 'And yours?'

'Profits are up. My main problem is how to enjoy spending them. What do you reckon? New car? Boat? Long, self-indulgent holiday?'

Saffron's eyes light up with envy. Everyone's eyes are glued to Aiden. Except yours, Miles. Your eyes catch mine and my heart skips a beat. Dark topaz eyes. Kind and caring. The children put their knives and forks together.

'Please can we leave the table?' they ask, wide-eyed and in unison.

'Of course,' Caprice replies.

They sidle away. No one asks them where they are going. I guess they've gone to watch cartoons, or play on the Xbox. I think about following them, but don't. They're not my responsibility today.

Saffron's mobile rings. She pulls it from her pocket, looks at it and springs up from the table.

'Got to take this.' She returns a few minutes later and stands by Miles. 'I'm sorry, I have to fly to Athens to see Aristos. It's urgent,' she says.

'When?' you ask.

'Tonight.'

Your face falls. 'How long will you be away?'

She shrugs her shoulders. 'As long as it takes, but I guess for a few days.'

'Where will you stay?'

'Aristos' place.' There is a pause. She grimaces. 'I need to go and pack.'

'I'll come and help you.'

You put your arm around her as you walk away.

As soon as you are both out of earshot, Caprice says, 'I sometimes wonder whether she's having an affair with Aristos.'

'Don't be ridiculous, Mother. Surely after all these years you must realise Saffron isn't like that,' Aiden says.

I take one look at Caprice's eyes, flashing with determination, and guess she doesn't have Saffron's best interests at heart.

12

Caprice

Saffron, your new nanny is an interesting creature. Much more observant, more attractive than any of the previous ones. A little *je ne sais quoi* about her; wholesome in an earthy way. So opposite to you, with her curvy figure and strong square face. Emma Watson looks, but with bigger breasts.

I see in her eyes, as she glances towards your husband, that Miles is a man she wants. But then he is a man any discerning woman would want; gentle, sympathetic, empathetic. Not to mention his looks.

You had better watch out, Saffron. Your arrogance and condescending attitude will lead you into deep water one day.

13

Miles

Early October, Saffron is away again, and I'm left with the children, Hayley, and Mother. The boys are in bed. It took me ages to settle them, reading eons of *Harry Potter*, which I love. But, even so, from time to time when I'm tired I feel as if I need a break from childcare. Hayley has disappeared to her sumptuous boudoir. Aiden has returned to his flat in Chelsea. He didn't stay long after Saffron left.

Mother and I are in the drawing room sharing a bottle of wine. Saint-Émilion. I take a sip. It is so heavy it almost sticks to my tongue. I prefer a lighter red; Mother chose this.

'Don't you get fed up of Saffron abandoning you for another man?' she asks, voice waspish.

'She's doing her job,' I reply.

She leans forwards and her eyes pierce mine. 'Dropping everything for Aristos has been going on for years. Surely she needs to rein him in?'

Silence falls, except for the ticking of the clock on the mantelpiece. I pull my gaze away from hers and cut through the silence. 'Aristos is her major client.'

'But . . . but why does she always have to go at such short notice?' Mother splutters.

If I have told her this once, I've told her a million times. I sigh. 'It's what he pays Saffron for. To be at his beck and call 24/7. He pays her very generously. And that's the whole point of private client work. When the client asks you to jump, you jump.'

Mother's eyes narrow. 'As long as he isn't jumping *her*.'

Anger pulses through me like lightning. 'Mother, how dare you imply that.'

She raises her eyes to the sky. 'Look, Miles, face facts; a job like hers is an excellent cover for an affair.'

'I trust my wife,' I say, voice clipped.

'You trust a woman who is always having to fly off to stay in luxury accommodation all around the world at short notice?' she pushes.

'I repeat, I trust my wife.' I pause. 'And she's not always flying off. Just sometimes.'

Mother sighs. 'You and I have a different understanding of the word *sometimes*.'

I put my wine glass down on the coffee table in front of me. 'Times have changed. Not all relationships work like yours and Dad's. Most women work these days.'

Mother leans back in her chair and crosses her legs. Her eyes fill with tears. 'Don't criticise my relationship with your father.'

'Calm down, Mum.'

'There's work and *work*. Saffron regularly abandons her family,' she continues.

'Abandoning me for another man. Abandoning her family. Is abandon your word of the day?' I ask.

'Today, and every day, when I consider Saffron's behaviour—' she smiles a slow stretched smile '—abandon does seem to be appropriate.'

I take a deep breath. I must be patient. Mother is still adjusting. She lost Dad five years ago and still hasn't come to terms with his death. His massive heart attack was such a shock. She returned from book group to find him dead in bed. Since then she has tried her best. She helps with our children. She plays bridge twice a week, with a group of widows. But life as she knew it stopped.

And just sometimes, she takes it out on me and Saffron.

14

Saffron

As my taxi pulls up at the airport, I admit to myself that I lied. Despite my protestations to Miles, I am pleased to have been dragged away. You are really pulling me down, Caprice. At least when you lived in your own quarters we had some time apart. I am finding it very difficult having you silently preside as head of the family at every mealtime. Spending more time than ever with the children. Altering my sons' attitudes. Feeding them too much unhealthy food. Allowing them to watch cartoons whenever they want, even when they haven't finished their homework. Allowing them to play on the Xbox almost incessantly, so much so I fear they have become addicted to it.

Having a new nanny will help me keep an eye on your tricks. But I need to build up a good rapport with her. I need our relationship to work. Just like I once so wanted ours to work, Caprice. Do you remember when I treated us to a bonding spa day together? It should have been special, but you hardly spoke to me. Luxuriating in the Turkish baths, the jacuzzi. Sitting next to one another wrapped in seaweed. Drinking champagne over a healthy lunch. Nothing I have ever done to try and help us become close has ever made any difference. But since you moved into our home, the situation has become even worse. Any indifference or complacency I ever experienced because of your coldness has transcended into resentment and anger.

As I step out of the taxi and walk across the airport concourse,

I admit to myself that, all in all, Aristos' call couldn't have come at a better time. A day on his yacht will suit me just fine. He's sent the papers I need to read by email, and I've printed them off. When I'm up in the air I'll take a closer look. If everything is OK I'll witness his signature tomorrow.

I sit on the plane. First-class seat, glass of champagne in hand, perusing his latest movement of money through different tax jurisdictions. I think he needs to speak to his investment adviser and spread his money more widely, but this doesn't seem legally complicated. This time he hasn't actually broken the law. I finish my champagne, stretch my legs and sleep.

We land at Athens airport. Aristos has sent a limousine from his fleet to meet me. A surly but smartly dressed man, in a stiff cotton shirt and blazer, is waiting in Arrivals holding up a sign with my name. I introduce myself and he tells me his name is Andros. I fall asleep again as soon as I get into his limo. The next thing I know, we are pulling through the narrow cobbled streets of the port of Monemvassia, where Aristos' superyacht, *The Spirit of the Sea*, is moored.

The tender to *The Spirit of the Sea* is waiting at the dockside, captained by a young man who introduces himself as Yanni. He is wearing senior crew uniform: a peaked cap and a jacket with fancy gold fringed epaulets. Yanni powers up the engine and steers me towards *The Spirit of the Sea*. She looms in front of us, a shimmering oasis of light and beauty, so impressive I catch my breath. The night presses down on me, silent except for the hum of the engine and the lapping of the sea. The engine reduces. As we approach *Spirit*, and pull alongside, two crew appear from nowhere to catch the bow and stern lines. Yanni throws them with casual confidence, making boat handling look natural, as if he was born at sea.

I am helped on board and led to my cabin by another uniformed member of staff whose name I do not catch. He escorts me up a deck, to a cabin on the portside. It is small but beautifully

42

appointed with its own en suite bathroom, resplendent with gold taps and a miniature jacuzzi bath, which doubles up as a shower. Even though it's late I cannot resist sitting outside for a few minutes to admire the view on my private balcony. I look across at Monemvassia castle, standing proud in the moonlight, reminding me why I have always loved Greece. But I'm so tired. I step inside, kick off my shoes and collapse onto the bed.

Two hours later at 6 a.m., I'm on the sundeck with Aristos, attending our breakfast meeting. No one else is present. I look across at my client, over freshly brewed coffee, and freshly squeezed orange juice. He has a large egg-shaped belly, a round head and oval eyes. A child could draw him in a series of rugby ball squiggles. His generous smile, brown eyes and flamboyant curls soften his appearance. Whatever the peculiarities of his shape, he has been through enough women – wives and mistresses.

He pours us both a coffee. 'What did you make of my paperwork?' he asks.

'It's fine. You haven't got anything to worry about. All above board in each jurisdiction. I just need you to sign the relevant papers and that's that. I'll take them back home and post them.'

I stand up and place the papers in front of him, pencil marked where he needs to sign and I need to countersign. It only takes a few minutes. I place them carefully in a folder in my briefcase and sit down opposite him again.

Aristos takes a slug of coffee. 'Do you hate me for making you come all this way?'

I smile my best smile. 'Of course not.'

A waitress in a black dress with a white starched apron saunters across the sundeck carrying a silver tray. She leaves a plate of warm vegan bread rolls filled with roast vegetables on the table in front of us.

I am so hungry after my long journey yesterday, I help myself and take one. The bread and roast vegetables are so delicious, they melt in my mouth. 'When's your flight back?' Aristos asks.

'Not until 10 p.m. this evening. Do you need me to check anything else whilst I'm here?'

'No.'

'You haven't got any new matters coming along that you want me to look at? It has cost you a lot of money to get me here, I ought to make myself useful.'

'You've already been more than useful. Stay on the sundeck, my housekeeper will bring you lunch, and drinks whenever you want. Yanni will take you ashore to meet the car at 17.30 p.m. I have an appointment in town with Maria.'

'Sounds like bliss to me,' I reply, but in fact disappointment skitters inside me.

Maria, his third wife. The reason he has been happier and less litigious lately. Maria is not good for my business profits. Before he met her he was becoming involved in a legal scrap almost every month.

Aristos finishes his breakfast and sidles off to enjoy his day. I do as he suggests and lie back on a sun lounger. The sun caresses my body and lures me to sleep.

I slip into a dream. A dream that seems real, so real. Floating in an azure sea. Unencumbered. I step from the sea, and walk along a white sand beach. Miles and Aiden are walking towards me.

'I'm sorry to say our dear mother, Caprice, has passed away,' they tell me in unison, eyes full of sorrow.

They both take my hand. Miles is on my left, Aiden on my right. We walk along the beach to a small church at the end of the cove. We step inside. It is your funeral, Caprice. Your coffin is at the front of the chapel by the simple stone altar, decorated with a small silver cross. Ben and Harry are standing at the front with Hayley. All your friends from bridge are here. And some of the school gate mums you socialise with. A lady vicar with a bell-like voice presides. Explaining we are here not to mourn a death, but to celebrate a life. The usual stuff. We sing a hymn – 'Now Thank We All Our God' – your favourite. Then some pallbearers who I haven't noticed before appear from a side door and carry the coffin outside.

We stand, heads bowed, as they lower it into the graveyard, behind the church. I can hear waves lapping on the beach. Miles throws a red rose on top of the casket. It bursts open and bleeds.

My body jolts. I sit up on the sunbed and blink. And for a few minutes in the sweet transition between sleep and wakefulness, I really believe that you are dead, Caprice. For a second I feel light with freedom, like I did in my dream, and then guilt permeates through me. What is the matter with me? Why am I dreaming of your death? A death that would devastate Miles. But a death that would set me free.

45

15

Caprice

Tuesday morning. The house is quiet. The children are at school. Hayley is shopping. Miles is at the university supervising a tutorial. And, Saffron, you are standing in the hallway, just returned from your trip to Greece. Dishevelled and tired. Your trouser suit and face equally crumpled.

'Welcome home,' I say with a smile. 'Can I get you a coffee?'

Don't smile back. Don't strain yourself, Saffron.

'Thank you. And then I'll have a quick shower and get straight off to the office.'

You dump your Chanel travel bag in the hallway, the designer bag you use for all your jaunts, and follow me into the kitchen. You sit, tapping your fingers on the table, looking out of the window.

'How was your trip?' I ask as I put the kettle on.

'Fine.' You shrug. 'But it's a long way to go just to get Aristos to sign a few papers.'

Don't ask me how I am, Saffron.

Annoyed at your lack of interest in me, I snap, 'Why do you do it? Why do you pander to him?'

Your face stiffens. 'I'm not pandering. He pays me.'

I pour boiling water into the cafetiere, and place it on a mat on the table near you. I lean across and push my eyes into yours. 'I'm not sure I believe you.'

Your eyes darken. 'Whatever do you mean?'

'Well, to be honest – and honesty is so important in a rela-tionship – I think you're having an affair with him.'

'Are you insane? He's my client.'

'I can assure you I'm observant, rather than insane.'

You clamp your jaw and clench your fist. And I know I have riled you. Good. Since I moved into your house you have been even colder than before. More distant. Don't you feel anything for me, since I lost my husband? You still have Miles. Can't you find any generosity in your soul? I want you to react. I want you to feel something.

I take a deep breath. 'You need to be careful. If Miles finds out he'll take the opportunity to run off with his teenage girl-friend; the only woman he has ever really loved romantically.'

Your eyes blaze. 'What are you talking about, Caprice?'

Not so calm and confident now, are you, Saffron?

I flash my unnerving smile. The smile that you once told me makes you feel uncomfortable.

'I think you need to know that Miles was always infatuated with Julie. It broke his heart when she ran off with Aiden. Let's face it, she's available now. And I heard him on the phone to her last week.' I pause. 'If you're playing around, why can't he?'

16

Saffron

'I'm not playing around, Caprice,' I shout. 'And I know you love Julie, but Miles never did. Miles and I talk about everything. It was the other way round. Julie was in love with him but he didn't return her feelings. Their relationship was over decades ago.'

She gives me a scathing smile. 'You talk about everything, do you?' There's a pause. 'Over decades ago?' Another pause, longer this time. 'You'll soon find out.'

Anger pulsates through me. I storm out of the kitchen, up the stairs, into our bedroom. I strip off and head for the shower. In an attempt to relax, I turn the hot water on full blast so that the flow pummels and almost scalds me. A voice whispers in my head. *You caught him texting her last week and he wouldn't tell you why. If what Caprice says is true would he admit it to you? If you loved another man would you tell him the truth?*

As I dress and leave the house, the words in my head become louder and louder. By the time I am driving to work, they scream inside my mind. *If Miles loves Julie, would he tell you? You need to find out for yourself.*

Walking into the office, a headache pounding across my forehead, my lips stretch into a forced smile for Julie and Ted.

'I need to talk to you, Julie. Please step into my office.'

I march into my office and Julie follows me.

'Please sit down,' I say, tight-lipped.

Julie frowns and slips into my visitors' chair, looking as

appealing as ever with her neat features and shiny shoulder-length chestnut hair. Her simple toffee-brown cashmere dress emphasises her willowy figure. The woman I thought was my friend. The woman my husband might be in love with.

'What's the matter? What's happened?' she asks.

'I need to know why you were texting Miles.'

She smiles and shakes her head. 'It's a secret. I can't tell you why.'

My insides tighten. 'Just between the two of you?' I ask. 'And I am out of the loop?'

'Yes.'

Anger burns inside me. I want to slap her. 'I think he's cheating on me, with you.'

She turns ashen. 'What's the matter with you, Saffron? How can you possibly think that?'

'Quite easily, I can assure you.'

Her eyes widen. 'That's ridiculous. You know Miles and I are only friends. And work isn't the time or place for conversations like this. Come out to my new place at the weekend and we can talk about Miles' and my relationship.'

Miles' and my relationship. Her words spill across my mind like acid. Burning. Scalding.

There is a knock on my office door. I walk across and open it. Ted stands before me, bristling with worry.

'I need to speak to you, right now, in private.'

Julie stands up. 'I was just going.'

She scuttles across the room, eyes to the floor, embarrassed. She pushes past Ted and leaves the office. I return to my chair, hands and mind trembling. Ted enters looking as if he is on the way to a funeral. Body stiff, face elongated. He sits in my visitors' chair. I have known him twenty years and I have never seen him look so intense.

'I received an email from Sasha's accountants this morning. She can't pay us the money she owes us. She's gone bankrupt.'

Sasha, whose father is an oligarch, bankrupt? Sasha, who lives in a palace? Sasha, who swans around in a private jet travelling to fashion shows between ballet performances?

'How can she be bankrupt?' I ask.

'Same as the next person. By spending more than she has, with no control.'

'But . . . but . . .' I splutter. 'We had her credit checked.'

'That was three years ago. And I spoke to our bank yesterday. They said they can't extend the loan.'

I clench my fist and bang it on my desk. 'No. The bank will have to extend the loan. We've worked too hard to go under. I will not allow us to.'

'What do you suggest we do then?' he asks.

'Who've you been dealing with at the bank?'

'Paul Templeton.'

'Get on to his boss, Jane Prescott.' He lifts his eyebrows questioningly. 'I was at Cambridge with her. Mention my name. It'll help.'

Slowly, slowly, he shakes his head. 'The old school tie rigmarole doesn't work these days. Trying to court favour could even work against us.'

'Don't complain – just do what I say,' I beg.

'OK. Will do,' he says as he leaves the room.

I sit, head in my hands, electric waves of panic rising inside me. My husband is about to leave me for his first love. My business is about to sink. I feel as if I'm falling off a precipice.

17

Hayley

I slip out of the house to meet my boyfriend, Jono. Not long off the plane from New Zealand, I met him at Fabric night club in London. I went with Isla, who had been volunteered by the friend of a friend to welcome me to the UK. Meeting me at Heathrow airport and letting me sleep on the floor of her damp basement flat in Earl's Court until I found my feet. Until I got a nanny job with accommodation.

We were dancing to Carl Cox's classic DJ set. She'd given me an E. I was jumping and pumping to the music, when Jono and his mate Vic approached us and began to dance close. Vic became entangled with Isla. Jono was pumping in time with me. Jono gave us all some more E.

At four-ish we took an Uber back to Jono's squat. Wasting time with a man my parents wouldn't approve of really gave me a hit. A wiry man, covered in tattoos and piercings, living in a squat. Underground. Rebellious. Offering me neat whisky from the bottle. Smelling of cannabis, nicotine, and another world that I had never been part of.

The whisky I drank burnt my throat. We didn't make love. We fucked in the solid darkness. Really fucked. Simple. Hard. Relentless. No give or take, just greed and anger. An impulse. A moment. No strings. Nothing complicated. And that is what it is like with us. Two passing ships in the night, enjoying ourselves. No complexity. No fuss.

Today he's standing at the front gate of Wellbeck House, smoking a roll-up. Just nicotine today I think, not cannabis.

'Wotcha, Hale,' he says, as he leans to kiss me.

He stinks. His scent today is nicotine and alcohol, with a faint tinge of motor oil. We walk along the road together, towards the pub. He puts his arm around me and holds me close.

'How's work?' I ask, pulling away from him and walking at the edge of the pavement.

'Same as ever. MOTs. Changing brake pads. Replacing catalytic converters. Sensors. Spark plugs.' He sniffs. 'It's quite boring, you know.' He wipes his nose with the back of his hand.

'Why don't you train for something else, get another job?' I ask.

'Well I'm used to it now. And the mates I work with are quite a laugh.' There is a pause. 'What's it like working with nobs?' he asks.

'Nobs?'

'You know, the rich and the posh.'

'I'm enjoying it actually.'

'Aren't Saffron and Miles Jackson intellectual tossers?'

'I like them. What makes you say that?'

'I looked them up on the internet. She's a lawyer, isn't she? Lawyer-come-punk-rocker from the way she dresses. Looks pretty fit to me. It's him that I'm not sure about. He's on YouTube. Done a TED talk. The talk's crap. It's philosophy. I think philosophy is a load of shit.'

'What a thought-provoking comment. I expect they'll invite you to do one next.'

'Come on, Hale, don't be sarcastic. You know sarcasm is the lowest form of wit.'

18

Saffron

I'm sitting in Boisdale's, opposite Aiden, Caprice's words racing in my head.

Miles was always infatuated by Julie. It broke his heart when she ran off with Aiden.

Julie.

And Julie is so attractive with her shiny chestnut hair, cascading across her shoulders. Her melting chocolate-drop eyes, neat little nose and perfect smile. Clever. Interesting. Funny. One of those people who you are never sure what they are going to say next; whose company is stimulating. I have always liked her. Miles and I usually like the same people. Caprice is the only person we argue about. So the fact that I have always liked Julie is worrying.

'You wanted to see me,' Aiden says, sipping his Bourgogne Aligoté. 'You sounded concerned on the phone.'

'I want to know your version of what happened between Miles and Julie.'

Aiden leans back in his chair, lips toying with a smile.

19

Aiden

I lean back in my chair and look at you, your sculptured face spoilt by a frown.

'Why do you want to know about Miles and Julie?' I ask.

You bite your lower lip, and I wish I was kissing it. 'It was just something your mother said.'

Mother. Causing trouble again. But in this case, trouble that suits her younger son.

'What did she say?' I ask as casually as possible.

You look bereft. Your eyes pool with tears. I want to pull you towards me and comfort you.

'She said that Miles was heartbroken when he split up with Julie. He was envious when she got together with you. That he still has feelings for her.'

Good one, Mother. Why didn't I think of that?

You lean across the table. 'Please, Aiden, tell me – is it true?' you ask, voice cracking.

I take a deep breath, to slow things down. To give me time to think.

'I'm not sure it's fair for me to comment.' I take a sip of wine, holding your eyes. 'What has Miles said?'

You put your knife and fork together and push away your plate of untouched food. I finished my steak and chips ten minutes ago. The waitress sidles over. 'Was the food not to your liking?'

'Fine thanks,' you reply, voice clipped. 'I'm just not hungry.'
She takes our plates away.

'What has Miles said?' I repeat.

'That they split up amicably. They were growing apart anyway. They never really fancied one another so by the time he was about to leave for university, splitting up was an easy decision for them both to make.' You pause. 'But I mean if he was, and still is interested in her, he wouldn't want me to know, would he? That's why I need your take on the situation.'

I swig my Bourgogne Aligoté and put my glass down. 'Look, I don't want to cause trouble.'

You lean further forwards and put your hand on my arm. You don't usually touch me. Electricity jolts through me.

'I'm not asking you to cause trouble. I just want the truth. If Miles was in love with her, he may be attempting to bury his feelings, to protect me.'

I tap my fingers on the table.

'I just need to know what happened between them, I can't just sit and wait to be hurt. The sooner I know, the better,' you push.

Smiling inside, I make a show of taking a deep breath and giving a heavy sigh. 'The truth is, Mother is right. He was deeply in love with her.' I pause for effect. 'She left him, and he was devastated. He's just too proud to admit it.' You lean back in your chair, holding your stomach as if my words have punched you and winded you. 'It made things very difficult between us. He hardly spoke to me for years after Julie and I got together,' I continue.

You sit up straight, swallowing to push back your tears. But one escapes and trickles down your right cheek. You wipe it away with your serviette.

'I didn't realise you went through a patch of not speaking,' you almost whisper.

I finish my glass of Bourgogne Aligoté, and catch the waitress's eye to get her attention. She walks straight over. I wave my glass at her. 'Another large one please.' She smiles, nods, and disappears.

'Why do you think we hardly saw one another, when you first met Miles?' I ask.

You take a sip of sparkling mineral water. 'I just thought it was because you were both busy studying,' you mumble into your glass.

'Think again. Miles couldn't bear to see Julie and me together.'

You look up, azure blue eyes misted with tears. 'But . . . but . . . that was years ago. And we have built our life together. Do you think he still has feelings for her?'

'Love like that doesn't disappear.'

20

Saffron

Saturday afternoon. Worry about Julie, Miles, and my financial problems with Belgravia Private Clients, is making me feel nauseous and tired. And now, when I should be spending quality time with my family, I'm driving down the A3, towards West Wittering Beach. To visit Julie in her new home. I pull off the A3 at Eashing because she told me it's a nice drive through the Downland villages.

Love like that doesn't disappear.

And Belgravia Private Clients is about to go under. Unless . . . unless . . . I get a loan extension and a juicy new client. I need to be pushy and schmooze. But this week I have been far from in the mood. I have spent most of my time sitting in my office keeping away from Julie and fretting. My whole life, everything I have built up, is collapsing around me.

This drive is calming me, though. I have Tchaikovsky's *Swan Lake* turned up full blast to soothe me. I'm on my way to do something about my plight. To find out what Julie has to say. And she is quite right. The drive is pretty. If everything goes wrong for me, perhaps I can move out of Esher, start a new life, further away from London. That's what Julie has done, even though it's a long way to travel to work.

The route takes me through Chiddingfold, with its duck pond and village green. Thatched cottages and Georgian country mansions. Past homes of brick and flint. Past its fourteenth-century wattle and daub pub. Winding through gentle farmland and woods of ancient trees. Northchapel. More brick and flint and characterful pubs. Through dripping valleys of autumnal trees. On to Petworth, the prettiest little market town I have ever seen.

My sat nav guides me to Julie's new home, in West Wittering, just behind the beach. I ring the bell. The door opens and a tall angular man with jet-black hair stands in front of me.

'Hi there,' I say. 'I'm Saffron Jackson. Here to visit Julie.'

'I'm Conrad, Julie's partner. Do come in.'

Conrad? Julie hadn't told me she had a new man. I wonder if I should breathe a sigh of relief. Does a new man mean she's not that interested in Miles? Or is she just a man eater? She always banters with Miles when we meet for drinks in the City. Have I been wrong to dismiss this as easy friendship?

She appears, walking towards me, through the hallway, beaming from cheek to cheek. Wearing blue jeans and a fluffy blue jumper with a large white star on. Her shiny hair glistens and her chocolate-drop eyes welcome mine. She hugs me, engulfing me with her trademark Chanel No. 5 scent.

'Thanks for coming over. We need to talk.'

Panic rises, even though I was the one to instigate this meeting. What is she going to say?

We need to talk. I need to tell you I'm in love with Miles.

Conrad is hovering awkwardly in the hallway. 'Can I get you anything to drink?' he asks.

'I'm fine thanks.'

'Let's go for a walk along the beach, and then come back here for supper. You must stay and eat. Conrad's a wonderful cook.' Julie kisses him. A short sharp peck. Too plastic. Too platonic? 'See you later, darling,' she says.

He disappears upstairs.

Julie and I step along the hallway, through a large dining room into the kitchen where Julie grabs a windjammer and hat from the hooks by the back door. Out into the garden. The salty tang of the sea assaults my nostrils, reminding me of happier times.

Of childhood holidays. When life was innocent. Before sex and love and men contaminated it. The wind that is folding the plants to the ground in this well-stocked garden explodes against my face. I look down at the plants and wonder how they survive. Lavender. Salvia. Phormium. Cordylines. They are dry and bent. But alive. We push through the wind across a fragile lawn and step out through the back gate.

We weave in between the dunes onto the wet sand of the beach. The sea is pale blue with white horses on this bitterly cold but bright October day. The sky above is like a mirror. The horizon a grey line in the distance.

'A walk on the beach always blows the cobwebs away. And we have some cobwebs we need to attend to.' Her voice sounds stern and harsh. 'At least the wind is behind us now, so we can have a decent chat,' she continues.

'I didn't know you had a new man,' I start.

'Nice-looking, isn't he?'

I nod.

'Was he the problem between you and Aiden?' I ask.

'Oh no. Conrad is recent. I only met him a few months ago.'

I take a deep breath and swallow. 'And are you only interested in Conrad? Or is there something going on between you and Miles?'

She splutters. 'I told you in the office there's nothing going on.' She pauses. 'What's the matter? I'm so worried about you. Where on earth is all this coming from? Why are you even asking me this?'

I feel my eyes filling with tears. 'It's Caprice and Aiden. They say you and Miles were in love and that you still are.'

We stop walking. Julie stands looking at me, wide-eyed. For a moment I think she's about to confess, but then she shakes her head and bursts out laughing. 'That's ridiculous.' She puts her hands on my shoulders. 'Miles and I have been just friends for years. Even before we technically split up. Even then it was friendship rather than passion. Whatever nonsense they are making up is a complete lie.'

'But . . . but . . . why would they do that?' I ask, wanting to believe her but finding it hard. 'And why would both of them – quite independently – say the same thing?'

She shrugs. 'It's beyond me. But then again some people are very poor at understanding platonic friendships between men and women. And Aiden might want to get back at me after our divorce.'

We continue our stroll.

'I promise you, nothing is going on.'

'Then why are you texting each other?'

'I can't tell you. It's a surprise.'

'It's certainly a surprise that you are texting each other like a pair of adulterers. What am I supposed to think?'

'That is insulting, Saffron. You need to trust us. What is a relationship if it isn't based on trust?'

'I've been watching *The Crown* on Netflix. I expect Prince Charles tried to keep Diana quiet by making statements like that, too.'

Julie puts her hand on my arm. We stop walking again, and stand, eyes locked. 'Why are you so worried?' she asks. 'We've been friends for years. And you have been with Miles all that time. Why can't you trust us?'

'I've been wondering about this for years. It has been in the back of my mind; niggling me. Why did you run to our house, the night you left Aiden the first time? I know you didn't come to see me, because I told you I was going away on a business trip. Why did you need to see Miles alone?'

'I thought you were going to be there too.'

'But I told you.' My voice sounds whingey and plaintive.

She shakes her head. 'I must have been so stressed at leaving Aiden that I forgot. When I arrived I was surprised you weren't there.'

'I even sent you a text.'

'I never received a text, I promise. I wasn't trying to spend the night with your husband alone. He's been my friend, my sounding board, for many years now. But I wasn't saying anything to him that I wouldn't have shared with you.'

'But Miles won't tell me what was said. As if it was not for my ears.'

'That's just him being too private, too cautious. Because I was upset. In tears.'

'So, leaving Aiden had nothing to do with your feelings for Miles?'

She laughs. 'No way. Aiden became difficult. Too obsessed by money. I thought you'd have realised that. Over the years you've had to spend enough time with him.' Her face is crumpling with concern, as she looks at me. 'Please believe me, there is nothing between Miles and me, except friendship. We do get on well, but we just don't fancy each other. What's got into you? You and Miles are so close. You have such a special relationship. Why are you so worried?'

I'm crying now. Full-blown tears running down my face. 'Caprice told me he's about to leave me, for you. She said she heard you talking together on the phone last week.'

'I haven't spoken to Miles for months.' Julie pauses. 'Look, Caprice is a troublemaking bitch who has got it in for you because you're married to her favourite son, who adores you. She's jealous. Push it away. Don't let her get to you.'

'And Aiden?' I ask.

'Well, he's Machiavellian too. And he's always had the hots for you.'

'I do have trouble with him pestering me,' I sniff, pulling out a tissue and starting to dry my tears. 'But I thought it was because he was jealous that you loved Miles?'

'Where do you get this from? I *don't* love Miles. Our relationship ended over two decades ago. I am in love with Conrad.

Aiden is a bastard who always wants what he can't have and takes what he has for granted. That's why I left him. There's no more to it than that. All he cares about is money, and women he can't have.'

I drive home, after stilted conversation over Conrad's Thai stir-fry supper, still not sure whether Julie is telling the truth. If she is having an affair with Miles, would she tell me? No. Of course not. I would be the last to know. But . . . but . . . she sounded so sincere.

21

Hayley

Saturday afternoon. Saffron asked me to help Miles with the children today but Caprice unexpectedly released me, and told me to take the day off, so I'm sitting opposite Jono in the pub. He is drinking Doom Bar, whilst I sip a large glass of Merlot. The new serpent tattoo on his index finger has become infected. It's bandaged and he winces every time he lifts his pint.

'How's it going at the nobs' house?' he asks.

Not this again. I wriggle uncomfortably in my chair. 'Why are you so scathing of my employers? From what I understand you were brought up in a posh house too, before you became rebellious for the sake of it.'

He grins a mischievous grin. 'Well, the middle class in the UK are oppressive and controlling. No wonder I needed to pull away.'

'You didn't *pull away*. You were expelled.' I hesitate. 'From that school. I can't remember its name. The boot boarding school.'

He laughs. 'Wellington. It's a famous English school.' He pauses. 'And yes, *I* decided not to conform. And then I was expelled, because of that. The sterility of the upper-middle classes is caused by their desire to fit in.'

'Is that why you took expensive elocution lessons, after you were expelled? To sound less posh? To make sure you didn't fit in?'

He scowls and winces as he lifts his pint. To make the pain

and effort worthwhile, he takes three large gulps before he bangs the glass clumsily back down on the table. 'How did you know about my elocution lessons?'

'You told me when you were drunk.'

His face is riddled with embarrassment. 'It's not so strange. Many celebrities have done it. It's not popular to be far back anymore.'

'Far back?'

'You know, using long vowels. Baath. Paath. Graass.'

I take a sip of wine and giggle at the strange way he overeggs his words. 'What celebrities have taken elocution lessons to lose their educated accents?' I ask.

'Mick Jagger, for a start. He's a posh boy really.'

'He hasn't rebelled by moving into a squat.'

Jono shrugs. 'Maybe he did when he was up and coming.'

'When he was up and coming he was studying finance and accounting at LSE. And he was a talented singer-songwriter with an amazing voice and magnetic stage presence, right from the start. I'm not sure you have much in common with Mick Jagger.'

'Don't diss me, Hayley.'

'It isn't dissing someone to say they're not as talented as Mick Jagger. Not many people are.'

'Stop arguing with me, Hayley,' he snaps, then changes the subject. 'Tell me how Miles, the super-wuss, is. Has he made any more boring vids lately?'

I fold my arms. 'You asked me not to diss you. I'm asking you not to diss Miles.'

'Oh, I see. Got a thing about him, have you?'

My face feels hot. I know I am blushing. 'Of course not. No.'

Back at Wellbeck House, head woozy and mouth dry after drinking too much red wine, I step into the kitchen to make myself a hot chocolate and drink some water before I collapse into bed ridiculously early in an attempt to sober up. I couldn't face going back to Jono's tonight.

You are sitting at the kitchen table, nose in a book. 'Hi, Miles,' I say trying not to slur my words as I walk towards the kettle. Trying not to notice your dreamboat looks, your soft melting eyes. Your strong cheekbones that I have watched Saffron stroke, when she was canoodling with you on the sofa and didn't know I was walking past the window. She loves you so much and I don't blame her. If I had you, I would treasure you too.

'What are you reading?' I ask.

'*The Philosophy of Moral Attitude*,' you reply, looking up. Hmm, I think to myself, that's what Jono needs to read. His moral attitude is seriously weird. Drink, drugs, and criticism. Never a nice word to say about anybody or anything. He doesn't even like puppies and kittens.

You smile at me. 'Hayley, you're just the person I wanted to see. I've got a present for you.'

You stand up and walk across the kitchen, towards the dresser. You pick up a gift bag and hand it to me.

'Thank you.' I beam. 'What have I done to deserve this?'

Your smile widens. 'Well, I just saw it and thought you would like it.'

You saw something, thought I would like it and bought it for me. My stomach rotates with pleasure.

I open the bag and pull out my gift. A toy koala. Soft and fluffy and grey with a black leather nose.

'You said you had one as a comfort toy when you were a child. I couldn't resist it when I saw it. I thought you could keep it on your bed and it would make you feel at home.'

I want to pull you towards me and hold you and kiss you. But you are out of bounds.

'Thank you so much, Miles. That is so kind of you – I love it.'

I sink into bed after drinking a pint of water and a large cup of hot chocolate. Red silk engulfs me. I pull my koala towards me, hold it against my naked body and wish it was you, Miles. Then my body stiffens, leaden with guilt for admiring you so much when Saffron is so kind to me. For using Jono for company, when all he will ever be to me is a stopgap. I know I wouldn't feel like that if I was with a man like you, Miles. If I was with a man like you, it would be a forever thing. Maybe, one day, I'll find someone to love.

22

Saffron

Returning from my trip to visit Julie, I step inside the house. It's quiet. Too quiet. And I know Miles isn't home. There's no jazz blaring from the radio; his Saturday night favourite. No aroma of curry to tantalise me. No whistling as he potters around the house.

I leave my coat and handbag in the hallway and step into the kitchen. You are hovering by the kettle.

You turn to me. 'Busy day, dear?'

Dear, with your usual weird emphasis. I know you don't hold me dear.

'Yep,' I reply.

That's all I'm telling you. I wish you would fuck off back to the annexe at the side of the house. Do you remember? The annexe where you're supposed to live. Carefully agreed before you moved in.

'Where's Miles?' I ask.

You purse your lips. You blink. 'He went to the gym. He needed to relax after a busy day with the children. They are in bed, by the way.'

Emphasis on *by the way*. Be careful, Caprice.

'I paid Hayley to look after them, so that Miles could have a rest,' I tell you as I pour myself a stiff G&T.

You give me your critical smile. The one you save for me. 'But he wanted to spend time with them. So I gave her the day off.'

'So which is it, he wanted to spend time with them, or he needed a rest?' I find myself snapping.

Your smile increases. You like it when I snap. You enjoy reporting my misdemeanours to your beloved Miles. I ought to try and control myself. Not allow you to rile me. It's just, with all this Julie business, I've really had enough.

Even though what I really want to say is *Fuck off and get out of my kitchen,* I manage to ask, 'What are you up to this evening?'

'I'm going to have a quiet evening in my bedroom, and watch a film.'

Well then fuck off to do it quickly, I want to retort. I want my home to myself. Without you, Caprice.

Sighing with relief as you leave the room, I flick the Sonos on with a tap of my iPhone. Shostakovich begins to enrich the kitchen. I sit at the quartz table, head in my hands, and breathe deeply. *He loves me. He loves me not. He loves me. He loves me not.* Breathe. Breathe. He loves me. He loves me. He has always loved me. I mustn't envy Julie - my friend and his.

23

Miles

After a busy day with the boys – Mother helping me – when they are settled in bed, I finally escape to the gym. My exhausted mother has retired to her boudoir for a hot bath and an early night. Our squiffy nanny has done the same I think, clutching the small gift I couldn't resist buying her when we visited the toy shop with the boys this morning.

I spend an hour doing circuits – cable chest presses, chin-ups, push-ups, Smith machine squats. Just as I'm about to leave, my phone vibrates and pings. A text from Aiden.

Bored stiff. Any chance of meeting up for a drink?

Saffron, when I left home, you weren't back from your jaunt to the south coast. I called you, I texted you, but there was no reply. Was your phone dead? Out of battery? Or were you without reception? As I step outside onto the pavement I try again. Still no reply. Maybe you have decided to stay overnight. It is a long drive.

Love to meet up. Saffron's away. Fancy some company?

Where shall we meet?

The Cricketers' pub, Richmond Green. Come on the train so you can have a few pints.

Midnight. I'm in the Uber on the way home. I've had more than a few pints. I've overdone it by mistake. I try and text you again, but sending you a message is too confusing for my fingers.

Maybe I should be worried. It's not like you to be uncontactable is it, Saffron? I try to work out when I last heard from you, but I can't remember. The fug in my brain is becoming thicker, tighter. Lights whirl past me as the Uber pushes home through darkness. Streetlights, car lights, lights from pubs and restaurants. They rotate in my mind. Saffron, where are you? Are you at Julie's? Have you come home?

Deposited at the front gate of Wellbeck House, I stall as the gate code eludes me. Then it begins to whisper slowly across my mind. I manage to press it into the control and the gate slides open. I tiptoe across the drive. I don't want to wake Mother, or Hayley or the children. But I do want to wake you, Saffron. I want to wake you, to hold you. To tell you I love you. The key to the front door struggles against my fingers. I fight it and fight it, until eventually it turns. I push the door open and creep upstairs.

Into our bedroom. I snap on the light. My heart fills with happiness. You are here, my angel, my love. But you sit up in bed, wide-eyed and snarling. Like a tigress, with bared teeth. Not the sweet pretty woman I love.

'Where have you been?' you bark.

'Out for a drink with Aiden,' I hear myself slur.

'Why didn't you tell me?'

'I did. I texted you. I called you. You didn't reply. I thought you'd stayed over at Julie's. That's why I went out.' My words are running together. Indistinct. Heavy.

'I wouldn't do that without letting you know.' There is a pause. 'Now you're back, how about telling me why you've been texting Julie?'

'I . . . haven't.'

'Don't lie. I know you have.'

I fall backwards onto the bed. The world turns black.

I wake up with my head hammering so hard that my jawbones ache. My mouth tastes of charcoal embers. I look down and see that I am still fully dressed. You are lying next to me. As soon as you see that I am awake you roll over, on top of me. The pressure of your body against mine makes me feel sick. You begin to thump me, to pummel me.

'What is it, Saffron? What's the matter with you?' I ask.

'You're lying to me. You *have* been texting Julie and I want you to tell me why.'

'I have not been texting Julie.'

The impact of your punches increases. Slower. Harder. More painful.

'Stop it, Saffron,' I beg. 'I'm feeling sick.'

You are sitting on my stomach now. 'So am I. Sick of you. Sick of your lies. Tell me why you've been texting her.'

'No.'

'So you admit you have?'

'Don't be ridiculous.' I push you away and roll off the bed. I pull myself up to standing, so weak I fear I might faint. Nausea overcomes me. I dash to the bathroom and vomit.

24

Hayley

You have a hangover, and so do I, but I won't mention that in my diary. My mother would disapprove of me drinking and working for a family who also overdo it with booze. I've given you ibuprofen and paracetamol. Lemon and ginger tea. You have smiled weakly and thanked me, but the smile didn't reach your eyes. Your eyes have black bags beneath them, which make you look like a panda.

Saffron has taken the boys out to Windsor Great Park, but you weren't feeling up to joining them. Caprice is having a quiet day napping in her room. Instead of having a day with your family you are lying on the sofa in the drawing room watching TV. *The Andrew Marr Show. Politics London. A Very Country Christmas.* When it comes to *Sunday Worship* you finally turn the television off.

I have stepped into the drawing room to check you are all right. I stand looking down at you, wrapped in a furry blanket that belongs to Harry, eyes wide and woebegone. You haven't shaved. You are paler than pale.

'Can I get you anything?' I ask. 'Anything at all I can do to help?'

'You are so comforting.' You smile. 'You can help me by working here forever. What can I do to bribe you to stay and not go back to New Zealand?'

My heart lurches but I laugh. 'You shouldn't have said that. Nearer the time, I might take you up on it. Make you pay for an educational course to extend my visa.'

25

Saffron

Monday, Tuesday, Wednesday, I am trawling through my working week, watching Julie and Miles like a hawk. Being polite but distant. This week I have been keeping my office door open so that I can hear Julie answering the phone, able to keep myself totally aware of who she is talking to. The office supply company. An electrician who is coming to put some new lights in. Today she is looking extra-glamorous. Slightly more make-up than usual. Slightly shorter skirt. Perhaps I should follow her at lunchtime. Perhaps today is the day the lovers will make contact.

Julie emerges from behind the reception desk and saunters towards the toilet. As the door closes behind her I walk out of my office to hover by the reception desk. She has left her iPhone on the counter. It buzzes. I can't help myself. I pick it up. She has a new text.

Promise you won't tell her yet. She'll find out soon enough.
Love Miles x

'Love Miles' and a kiss. Part of me dies inside. I have loved Miles for so long. Trusted him with every aspect of my life. This is too much. My life will fragment without Miles.

No. No, I tell myself. I am an educated woman. A survivor. I can survive without a man. I can survive without Miles. But I stand by the reception counter, staring at this week's flower arrangement of asters and lilies, feeling empty and bereft.

I hear heels click across porcelain flooring. I drop the phone and look up. Julie is walking towards me, flashing her white-toothed smile.

'Are you OK, Saffron? What can I do to help?' she asks.

'Nothing really. I just . . . I just . . .'

Her smile has dissolved. She is staring at me, neck stretched and frowning as she picks up her phone and puts it in her pocket, waiting pointedly for me to go.

26

Aiden

I'm ringing the doorbell of Wellbeck House. Just passing on the way back from a business trip.

You open the door, Saffron, and for once your face lights up when you see me. You are looking particularly good this evening. Dishevelled and sexy. Your tumbled out of bed look really turns me on. I wish it was my bed you'd tumbled out of.

'Oh, Aiden, how good to see you. I could do with some company.'

I step into the hallway and follow you into the drawing room.

'I'm just having a G&T. Can I get you anything?'

'I'll have one too. Thank you.'

I watch you as you prepare my drink at the cocktail cabinet. Your hand shakes a little as you select a crystal tumbler, as you pour the Bombay Sapphire, as you add ice and lime and Fever-Tree. As you turn and hand me the glass, I realise that your dishevelled look is partly because you've been crying.

We sit next to one another on the sofa and sip our drinks. 'What's the matter, Saffron? Where is everyone tonight?' I ask.

'Caprice is in her room watching a film, thank God. Hayley has gone to the pub with Jono.' There is a pause. 'And Miles . . .' You snivel and tears well in your eyes.

'And Miles?' I prompt gently.

'He went to the gym, but his car broke down. He's waiting for the AA to come and fix it. Or so he says.'

'What do you mean, "or so he says"?'

'Oh, Aiden, I'm so worried about Miles and Julie. I think you're right. Love like that doesn't disappear. I know they've been texting each other. But Miles denies it.'

I smile inside and shake my head slowly. 'I did try and warn you, Saffron.'

27

Saffron

Aiden is sitting on the sofa next to me. The gin has gone to my head. I shouldn't have drunk so much on an empty stomach, but Aiden kept topping me up. A film is running on the TV in front of us. I don't know what film. I'm not following it; I can't understand the dialogue. I'm muzzy-headed, as if I'm viewing the world through misted glass.

Miles loves Julie. Julie loves Miles. Miles wasn't at the gym. He is out with her tonight. He is so late back they must have booked into a hotel.

These words keep repeating in my head, growing louder and louder, faster and faster. Aiden is pressing against me. His arm slips around me. He is trying to kiss me.

Miles loves Julie. Julie loves Miles. Trying to kiss me. My mouth is closed. I open it. I'm kissing him back now. It's so long since I have kissed anyone except Miles. It feels good. Different. Harder. Sexy.

We continue to kiss but suddenly I'm not enjoying it. It is too hard, too ferocious. Aiden is not the gentle man I love. I pull away and look up. Miles is standing in the doorway watching us. I see him through a window of mist.

28

Miles

I'm standing in the doorway of our drawing room. Watching you, Saffron. Is it really you? The woman I love, snogging my brother. Stuck to him like glue. It can't be real. But you open your azure eyes to look at me, and my heart stops as I realise it is true.

'Miles, you're back,' you say, slurring your words.

You disentangle yourself and stand up. You walk towards me, eyes glazed. As you move closer you stumble. You are drunk. Very drunk.

'I'm going to bed,' you mumble as you push past me.

29

Saffron

The room spins around me as I stand up and walk towards Miles. Slowly. Slowly. Faster. Faster.

'I'm going to bed,' I mutter.

Slowly. Slowly. Faster. Faster. I am moving through a vortex. I negotiate the hallway, and holding on to the banister, I drag myself upstairs. Fully clothed I collapse onto our bed. Our bedroom is no longer a room, but a lightship taking me into space.

30

Miles

'All right, mate?' Aiden says as he stands up. The shifty bastard. Cocky. Smug.

All right, mate? It's not all right. He is no longer my mate. The world turns red as I step towards him and punch him in the face.

31

Aiden

I fall back on the sofa, writhing in pain. I do not punch him back. I know I deserve this. It was worth it, Saffron, for the feel of your soft, sweet lips against mine.

'Don't blame me,' I yelp. 'You need to talk to Saffron.'

'Don't tell me what to do,' Miles hisses. 'I'll talk to her tomorrow. Right now, she looks as if she's off her head. She must be, to be dallying with you.' He widens his nostrils in disgust. 'Piss off, Aiden. Get out of my house.'

'As long as you don't punch me again, when I walk past.'

I watch his fist clench. 'I can't promise that,' he snarls.

32

Saffron

I wake up in the morning, head pounding, mouth like sandpaper. My body feels heavy with guilt as I remember kissing Aiden. Enjoying the taste of someone different, just for a few seconds, until it felt wrong. Aggressive. Claustrophobic. Pulling away, seeing Miles watching us.

Miles. I put my arm out to touch him, but his side of the bed is empty. The duvet is smooth. He hasn't slept here.

Slowly, carefully, I manoeuvre my fragile body out of bed, by planting my feet firmly on the floor and pulling myself to standing. I've still got my shoes on. Oh my God, I was so off my head. I need to talk to Miles and explain everything. Beg him to tell me what is happening with Julie.

I drag my body to the bathroom. I clean my teeth, smooth my clothes down and brush my hair, then set off in search of my husband. But as soon as I set foot on the landing, I hear Harry calling.

'Mummy. Mummy.' His voice is strident and plaintive.

I step into his Thomas the Tank Engine themed bedroom. He jumps out of bed, grabs my legs and hugs them. I bend down and put my arms around him, but the sudden movement exacerbates my headache and I feel sick. As soon as my hug has satisfied him, I pull away.

'Why don't you go and find Ben? Watch a video in the

playroom. I need to talk to Daddy about something, then I'll come and fetch you. We can have breakfast together.'

'Please may we have chocolate croissants?'

'Yes.'

Harry puts his head on one side and looks at me, wide-eyed. 'Even though it's not Saturday?'

'As long as you let me have a quick chat with Daddy, that's fine, yes.'

I hold his hand and we walk onto the landing together. I drop his hand and bend down to kiss his cheek.

'See you soon.'

He pads off towards Ben's room. I stride into the guest room, where Miles sleeps when he is upset. I find him fast asleep, lying beneath white Egyptian cotton, breathing deeply, slowly, heavily. I sit on the bed, beside him. He stirs.

'Miles, we need to talk.'

He sits up. His face is ravaged. Grief-stricken. The only time I have ever seen him look like that is when his mother told him his father had died.

'We certainly do. What happened?' he asks.

His voice is broken. I gasp for breath. 'I thought you were out with Julie.'

'Why would you think that?' he shouts, the veins at his temples pulsating. 'How many times do I have to tell you, Julie and I were over years and years ago. Before I even met you. You need therapy if you can't accept that.'

'Ask your mother then. Ask Aiden.'

'What have they got to do with it?' he hisses through clenched teeth.

'Your mother said you were infatuated with her. She told me you were on the phone to her last week.'

His body stiffens. He shakes his head. 'My mother wouldn't make up lies like that.'

'Wouldn't she?' I ask. 'So I'm the liar, am I? At least I know where I stand.'

His lips tighten. 'And what did Aiden say?'

'That love like yours and Julie's never disappears.'

'He didn't think that when he married her.'

'That sounds bitter. You do still care about her.'

He raises his eyes to the ceiling. 'And all this nonsense is your excuse for kissing Aiden?'

'I was very, very, drunk and obsessing about the fact that you didn't love me.'

'It's all an excuse. You looked as if you were enjoying it.'

I put my hand on his arm and he stiffens. 'I wasn't.'

He pulls away from me. 'You're lying. Please don't touch me. If you weren't enjoying it, why were you doing it?' He shakes his head. 'You know I've always told you I couldn't cope with infidelity. How could you do this to me? And with my brother. I feel bereft. Betrayed by both of you.'

'Please forgive me, Miles. I love you so much.'

'This has broken my heart, Saffron. If you must know, Julie and I have been texting because a friend of hers is a high-profile jeweller. Julie has arranged for her to commission the solid silver collar necklace you always wanted, you know the one, with circles like dollars linked together, and matching earrings, at a substantial discount. We were lying about the texts because we wanted it to be a nice surprise.'

He pulls a box out from a drawer in the bedside table and hurls it at me. I step aside. The box smashes onto the floor. Thousands of pounds' worth of designer necklace spills across the floor in front of me. The necklace that I have seen at jewellery fairs and craved for so long.

'You don't trust me, and now I don't trust you.' He pauses for breath. 'I don't want you near me. Get out. Leave me alone.'

33

Caprice

Miles is shouting. Saffron is shouting. One of them mentions Julie.

'Get out. Leave me alone.'

The noise is coming from the guest room, which means they didn't sleep together last night.

Good. Good. The seeds of envy that I planted are putting down some roots at last.

34

Miles

'I don't want you near me. Get out. Leave me alone.'

Your shoulders fall. Your face diminishes. 'I love you, Miles. More than anything in the world. Please forgive me. Please tell me we can move on from this.'

Part of me wants to hold you and say, *Yes. Of course we can move through this. We love each other more than anything. And that means we can get through anything together.* But I can't. My body and my mind ache with your betrayal.

'I'm not sure I can ever forgive you. Please leave me alone. Please do as I ask.'

You turn away from me, and leave the room fighting for breath between sobs.

I try to close my mind to your crying. I shower, dress in the same clothes that I wore yesterday so as not to go anywhere near our bedroom. I go downstairs to say goodbye to our children. They are in the kitchen, eating chocolate croissants, with Hayley. How could you do this to them? To our family? Barely aware of where I am, I drive to work like an automaton.

In my office, I try to read an article on moral philosophy. The words on the page vibrate in front of me. The edges of the letters become blurred. All I can think of is you. The day I first saw you, in a tutorial. Your face turned towards me. I had never seen anyone so beautiful. As soon as I saw you I wanted you, with a longing and a passion I had not known before.

On our wedding day, my heart soared with happiness, as I watched you walk towards me wrapped in creamy silk. Your perfect sculptured face smiling into mine as you lifted your veil. Aiden stood beside me, my best man.

Aiden.

I want to punch him again. Pulverise his face.

I put my head in my hands and try and contemplate my life without you, Saffron. That thought makes the pain I'm suffering intensify. I try and imagine who I have ever met who might have made me happier. And the truth is there is no one. There never has been anyone else for me. Whatever has happened between us, I need you. Whatever happens between us, that will always be the case.

35

Saffron

I cannot go to the office. I feel too low to go anywhere today. My life is over. I wish I was dead. I wish I had the courage to kill myself. Feeling as low as this is dangerous. The only safe thing for me to do is stay at home, in bed.

My mobile rings. I do not want to pick up, but when I see it's Ted I force myself.

'I know you're not well, but I just wanted to share the good news,' he says. 'The bank have agreed to extend our loan. Jane Prescott, the contact you suggested, is sending us a letter to confirm it.'

'Thank you, Ted.'

'Feel better soon.'

I put the phone down. Ted's news has not made me feel any better. What I once craved so badly, and would have made me jubilant, seems irrelevant now that I have fallen out with Miles.

36

Miles

I leave work early and drive home. When I open the front door, Mother is standing in the hallway, dressed in pale shades of khaki green, scrutinising our wedding photograph and frowning. She looks up, sees me watching her and puts it down hurriedly.

'Are you all right?' I ask.

She smiles her slow stretched smile. 'Never better. And you?'

Never worse, I think but don't say.

'Your wife is upstairs in your bedroom. She didn't go to work today.'

I dash up the stairs two at a time, and fling the bedroom door open. There is a lump in the bed, topped by your tear-stained face. I rush towards you.

'Let's put the past where it belongs – behind us. I love you. I can't live without you.' I kiss you. 'I love the passion that you feel for me.'

37

Saffron

Miles is here. Telling me he loves me. That he loves the passion
I feel for him. I am holding him against me. He kisses me.
My heart sings with happiness. My life begins again.

38

Caprice

I'm hovering in the kitchen, waiting to talk to Miles. I'm slowly pottering, making fresh coffee in the cafetiere, hoping to catch him alone. Excitement has been simmering in the pit of my stomach since hearing you shouting yesterday morning. I'm waiting to find out when he's leaving you, Saffron. You'll have to move out. I put money into this house and have a charge against it, which I will require to be repaid, if you try to stay living here.

I look out of the kitchen window onto a sunny autumn morning. Wind toys with dying leaves, playing with them as they fall to the ground. A swathe of gold and russet carpets the play area; the swings and slide that the boys so adore.

The boys. Ben and Harry, my grandsons. My stomach tightens. Does the fact that you are their mother give you some sort of legal priority over the house? Despite all the charges I have taken out to protect the Jackson side of the family? You'll not get a penny if I can help it. I'll go and see my lawyer, first thing tomorrow.

You enter the kitchen, with Miles and the children, wearing an outfit that needs to be taken to the charity shop. Mustard-coloured skinny jeans. Not actually mustard, but grubby yellow. They don't look clean. As usual, at the weekend, your feet are ensconced in your heavy Doc Marten boots, which, let's face it, is an old-fashioned look. And you're wearing a T-shirt that isn't a T-shirt, but a piece of plastic. I can see your bra perfectly through it. You have very small breasts. Not a point of interest for most men. You have finished off your attire with a cardigan, too tight to button up, stretching across your back and stick-thin arms.

But, despite your strange refusal to wear make-up at the weekend, you look refreshed. Laughing and smiling at something Miles just said.

'It's Saturday morning. Let's have chocolate croissants again,' you say.

'Yes, please,' Ben and Harry chorus.

Miles has his arm around you. He looks at you, eyes melting like a puppy dog's.

'And then let's go to Virginia Water,' he suggests.

'That would be lovely.'

He moves his head towards you and your lips meet. You kiss. As you pull away I see you mouth, 'I love you.'

'I love you,' he mouths back.

It is so over the top, I want to vomit. Miles looks towards the window. 'Oh I didn't see you there, Mother.' He pauses and smiles. 'Good morning.'

And you, Saffron, don't acknowledge me. My teeth clench. I am not an irrelevance. I am your husband's mother. He wouldn't be alive if it wasn't for me. And neither would your children. I am the root of this family. Remember, remember, you wouldn't even be in this beautiful house if I hadn't given you so much money.

So, my older son has made up with you, Saffron. But not for long. Wait until he finds out about your next misdemeanour. There are only so many issues a man can deal with. Keeping my son, Saffron, is a battle you cannot win.

39

Saffron

Walking around Virginia Water. A family of four, holding hands in a line. Skipping through golden frosted autumn leaves. Stopping by the lake to take photographs. To feed the ducks. Standing beneath the ancient totem pole with its crudely painted angry faces.

'Why are the faces staring at us, Mummy?' Harry asks. 'What do they want?'

'They were painted a long time ago by a tribe of American Indians, and each face represents one of their ancestors.'

'The top one looks like Granny when she's in a bad mood.'

I look up at the top face and think of you this morning, skulking in the corner of the kitchen. You looked so disappointed to see us all together, chatting and laughing. Why do you want to be my enemy? Why did I believe you about Julie? Why, when Aiden comes on to me so much, did I believe him too? You are toxic. Aiden is opportunistic. I will box clever with you both from now on.

40

Aiden

I'm lying in bed with a bag of frozen peas on my face, trying to reduce the swelling and bruising. Working from home because I can't go into the office. I don't want my staff to see me looking as if I've been involved in a pub brawl. I keep running it back, Saffron. The scene with you, before Miles hit me. It moves across my mind on repeat, like waves across the sand.

It was beyond my dreams – you kissing me back, tasting of desire. Just the thought of it gives me an erection. I know you were off your head. I had really laid it on heavy with the gin, disguising the strength of the drinks with an overdose of lime juice. I wince in pain as I push the peas harder against my bruises. Do I feel guilty? A little. Yes. But like a puppy dog who has stolen a joint of meat, the scolding was worth it. For the feel of your body against mine. The electric heat of your kiss.

But I know I need to make amends and apologise. Otherwise I'll never get an opportunity like it again. Throwing the peas onto the floor, I reach across my bedside table, pick up my mobile and press speed dial. You pick up.

'Saffron, I'm sorry. I want to see you. We need to talk.'

'What about?'

'You know what about.'

'I know what I *don't* want to talk to you about. About how you took advantage of me in my own home. Plied me with drink. Almost destroyed my marriage. Broke your brother's heart. He used to trust you.'

'I just want to apologise, that's all.'

'I don't want to see you again. Ever. If Miles wants to keep in touch because you're his brother, I guess I'll have to put up with it. But please, please, leave me alone right now.'

41

Saffron

Ted's pointed features are buried in a frown when I enter the office. I stop at the reception desk in front of Julie.

'Good morning Julie. We need to talk. Please put any calls on hold and come with me into my office.'

Her usually cheery face crumples. Does she think I am going to sack her?

'Of course.'

I step into my office, hang up my coat. The second I sit down, my door opens and she is walking towards me. Shoulders back, mouth in a line. Bracing herself for bad news.

'Do sit down, Julie. I just need to apologise.'

She raises her eyebrows, surprised. 'What for?'

'Hasn't Miles told you?'

'No.' There's a pause. 'I mean, told me what?'

'That I now know why you were texting one another. I behaved so badly, when all you were doing was organising a fabulous birthday present for me.'

I feel tears pricking my eyes. 'I'm just so embarrassed and sorry. I should have trusted you. We work together. You are such a good friend to me and to Miles. I should have trusted Miles and not taken any notice of Caprice. Or Aiden. It all got very out of hand – my fears, my emotions. My paranoia. I'm very ashamed of myself.'

Julie stands up, leans across my desk and takes my hands in hers.

'Don't beat yourself up about this. I told you when you came to West Wittering, Caprice is a troublemaking bitch; Aiden is a bastard who always wants what he can't have. You mustn't let them make mincemeat of you. Your husband loves you more than his life. Your business needs you. *We* need you.'

I stand up and move towards her. She hugs me and Chanel No. 5 engulfs me.

We spring apart at a knock on the door. Ted walks in. 'I've just heard there's a temporary hiccup with the loan.'

My heart stops. 'What?'

'They want more reassurance that we have the potential to pay it back.'

'But . . . but . . . I thought they'd already given us the green light.'

He wriggles uncomfortably. 'In theory, yes. But when they looked at our recent accounts in detail, they decided our outstanding fees give insufficient coverage.' He pauses. 'They want to see all the accounts, since BPC started.' His tired eyes pierce mine. 'We mustn't overreact by panicking,' he continues. 'It'll be all right. Don't worry, our accounts are in apple-pie order. I'll send them over to the bank this afternoon.'

I am breathing too deeply, too quickly. I fear I am about to have a panic attack.

'Look, you two, I'm sorry but I need to relax. Hold the fort. I'm going out for a jog.'

Decked out in my new iridescent purple trainers and skin-tight Lycra, I step outside and begin to run. My body slips into rhythm as I concentrate on efficient arms and legs. And careful breathing. Dodging pedestrians. Trying to ignore the fumes from passing lorries and buses. Into Hyde Park.

There's hardly anyone here. A few mothers pushing buggies. A couple wearing office clothing, holding hands surreptitiously. I run around the lake. The Serpentine sparkles in the fresh late

October sunshine. A kaleidoscope of burnished colour surrounds me, interspersed with soft green waterfalls of cascading willow.

Breathe. Breathe. Push through the pain. My worries float in the air and dissipate. Miles has forgiven me. Julie has forgiven me. And I'll get new clients. It's only a delay in cash flow, I tell myself. The loan will come in.

A stitch piercing my right side, I stop by a bench at the top of the Serpentine. I flop down on it, next to a wizened old man wearing a tweed peaked cap. He is reading a newspaper, and doesn't look up. The silent solemnity of City life.

I catch my breath and set off again along the north side of the Serpentine towards the Bayswater Road. Another circuit of the lake, then back towards Belgravia. Mind now comfortably numb, I warm down by walking slowly back towards the office. I'm hungry. I skipped breakfast, so I step into Tom Tom's coffee bar to buy some falafel.

A man with a wide-brimmed hat is sitting in the corner, drinking coffee. His face is swollen and bruised, as if he has been in a fight. He looks familiar. I double take – it's Aiden.

'What are you doing here?' I snap. 'Why are you on my patch?'

'I need to talk to you. I know you often come here for lunch. I was prepared to wait all day in the hope of catching you. Please sit down, I only want to apologise,' he says, gesticulating towards the chair opposite him.

Reluctantly, I join him at the table. He smiles a slow smile, wincing in pain as he rearranges his bruising.

'I told you on the phone. There's nothing to discuss.'

He leans forwards. 'Look, I'm so very sorry, Saffron. I have real feelings for you, but I have been selfish and allowed those feelings to cloud my judgement.'

I shake my head. 'You've got to stop this, Aiden. You know I love Miles. I will never be with you.'

'Not even if you were a widow?'

My body jolts. Has he been imagining Miles' demise?

'Not in a million years. Even if we were the last two people on the planet,' I reply coldly.

'That's pretty insulting.'

'I need to make it clear.' I pause. 'And you need to apologise. You need to make things right with Miles.'

42

Aiden

I ring the doorbell. Miles answers it in his dressing gown and slippers.

'What do you want?' He glowers.

I swallow and take a deep breath. 'To explain.'

'Come in.'

I step into the hallway. He stands opposite me, face stiff, arms folded. 'Go on then.'

'I'm sorry.'

'Is that all you've got to say?' he spits.

I see his fist clench and brace myself. 'I'm sorry I'm in love with Saffron. I'm sorry that I plied her with an overdose of gin,' I continue.

'And an overdose of lies.'

'That too,' I concede. 'How can I make it up to you?'

'By leaving my wife alone.'

'I can't agree to that. It had never happened before and will never happen again.' I pause. 'Please forgive me?'

He slowly unclenches his fingers. 'I'll try to. After all, for better, for worse, you're the only brother I've got.' The edges of his lips curl up and then fall. 'And most of the time you're a good brother to have.' A shake of the head. 'But you're on your last chance now.'

43

Miles

Aiden leaves. I sink into the sofa in the drawing room and memories swirl around me. I'm back at public school and it's prize-giving day. Pupils are sitting in rows at the front of the hall. Parents, stiff with pride, are sitting behind. The hall murmurs with anticipation. The self-congratulatory gathering is packed into the oak-panelled hall decorated with painted names of previous heads and regal crests. Touches of gold filigree and pillar box red.

The head begins to call the names of the lucky winners. Each pupil walks across the stage to shake hands with the head, who presents them with silverware. Each pupil's prize presentation is accompanied by their proud parents standing to take a photo-graph – and by the rest of the audience's unenthusiastic clapping. No one seems very excited about the success of another person's child. Proud parents rise in minute-long intervals to form a Mexican wave of expensive outfits and hats. Aiden wins the lower sixth prize for cricket. I turn and look back at Mum and Dad, standing, clapping. But Mother has a stiff, wooden, smile-free face.

My year's turn, the upper sixth, arrives.

History – Miles Jackson.

Debating – Miles Jackson.

English literature – Miles Jackson.

Greek – Miles Jackson.

Latin – Miles Jackson.

I stumble across the stage five times, beaming at the audience. Thanking the headmaster. So much silverware, I try to balance it on my knee and place it beneath my seat without clanging it together.

Then I pull myself from the scene. I am no longer in the school hall living through the moment. I am sitting in Wellbeck House fretting about Aiden's behaviour towards you, Saffron.

What happened next on that school prize-giving day? I ask myself. An uneasy feeling comes over me; a realisation that something isn't fair, and there's nothing I can do about it. Then I remember where it came from.

When Aiden won the sports prize that day for his year, for cricket, I watched him swell with pride as he received it, knowing it hadn't pleased Mum, because I had seen her unsmiling face. Nothing pleased Mum except stellar exam results. She over-eulogised academia because she had had very little academic opportunity herself. And sure enough, in the car on the way home for the holidays, she only congratulated me, not Aiden.

'Do you know what the head said to me at the last cricket match?' she asked him.

Aiden shrugged. 'No. How would I know that?'

'If you tried as hard at English and maths as you do at rubbing cricket balls you might have a career in front of you.'

'That's nice. Most encouraging.'

I looked across at Aiden, biting his lip and looking out the car window. Living in my academic shadow must have been hard.

But now I am an academic. And he is an entrepreneur. Far more successful than me. My mother should have always appreciated her younger son more. Are you right, Saffron? Is Aiden hitting on you to get back at me? Or is it worse than that. Is he truly in love with you?

103

Aiden Jackson, we have shared much in life, but I am not sharing my wife. My fist clenches. Be careful, Aiden. Still waters run deep.

104

44

Caprice

Saffron, you fly towards me like a hellcat, claws out.

'Don't ever lie to me again. Don't ever come between me and Miles again,' you shout. 'Otherwise, I'll . . . I'll . . .'

You stammer. You struggle for words. Who would think you're a top-flight lawyer?

'Otherwise you'll what?' I taunt.

45

Saffron

I lie in bed, watching Miles sleeping next to me. Even though he is almost forty, his face in repose looks so young, so vulnerable; mouth slightly open, content in slumber. His thick brown hair spreads across the pillow. I lean across and gently, gently kiss his forehead. Every time I do that I imagine love is energy, and that I'm passing love from my head into his. His precious head, containing so many thoughts and ideas that I cherish.

By what contradiction of fate did a man like Miles burst from your loins, Caprice?

She brought up the man you love. A good man. She can't be all bad, as she managed to do that.

But, Caprice, I haven't found kindness in you yet. I think of you yesterday, taunting me, metallic eyes steady on mine. 'Otherwise you'll what?' you asked.

Have you no conscience? No belief in social responsibility? I've tried to love you, to have a close relationship. Memories come flooding back.

I ached for you when Rupert died. You looked so broken and bereft. Like a baby bird with bones so frail, even the wind might make them snap. Rupert's sudden death had left me grieving too. Aiden, Miles and I came to stay with you to help organise the funeral. Julie had already left Aiden. I made a point of not interfering, to keep in the background; to clean and cook and help with the washing. I didn't suggest a hymn choice, or involve myself in your discussions about the eulogy. Our sons came with us. Ben was three years old and Harry was one. I thought seeing the children might cheer you. But it just harassed you. So I kept them out of your way, allowing them to watch a surfeit of Netflix cartoons in our bedroom. Then you complained about my bad mothering skills; because you thought too much screen time was bad for them.

Breathe, breathe, I told myself. You were grieving heavily. I had to give you kindness and space.

Funerals are always difficult. A rite of passage for the dead that society is obliged to move through, supposedly to comfort the relatives. It's just personal – I know funerals comfort some people but they make me feel even worse. Rupert was good fun. Rupert and I clicked. I knew I was going to miss him. I was feeling sick, gut-wrenchingly sick that day. Goodness knows how bad you must have been feeling, Caprice. Although I was suspicious of your motives, you always insisted you loved him very, very deeply.

Black shiny limos were lined up on the drive, behind the hearse. Miles was shaking as I held his hand and we slipped into the first car together to join you and Aiden. Miles was very distressed by his father's sudden death. My body ached in empathy with him. I wished him peace and solace with all the silent energy I could muster. From my soul. From my heart, my bones, my sinews. Aiden was using bluster and bravado to cover up his true feelings, but I knew he was devastated too. His eyes were hard and staring. Jaw locked. Lips tight.

'Julie's arrived,' you said, pointing across the drive. 'I wasn't sure she was coming.'

She was running towards us, red-faced, wearing a black hat and trench coat. You wound the window down and she leant inside, gasping for breath.

'Sorry I'm late,' Julie shouted.

'Get out of the car,' you hissed at me. 'Julie needs to come with us. She might not know where we are going. You've been here all week. You know the way.'

The car seating had been carefully planned. Close family in the front limousine. Cousins and uncles and close friends in the cars behind. I froze for a second. I didn't want to be separated from Miles. But it all happened so quickly, none of us had time to think about what was happening or to answer back. You opened the limo door and pushed me out.

'Get in,' you instructed Julie.

You always preferred Julie to me, didn't you? You still do. Your last conniving game stemmed from this. When you told me Miles was infatuated with her, you wished it was true. You would have liked her as a daughter-in-law, instead of me.

Julie slipped into my place in the car, and I was left standing alone in front of the house. As it turned out, the other limos were all full, so I walked to the church, arriving just in time for a seat at the back. I wept inside for not being able to sit next to Miles and comfort him at his father's funeral. I had always imagined that we would be able to be there for each other at a time like this.

When I found him again on the way to the burial, he looked ashen. Hs eyes were red and I knew that he had been crying. He held me against him tight.

'So sorry you had to get out of the car.'

'Don't worry about it. I'm not the priority today.'

The wake passed without incident. Tea, sandwiches and small talk. In the evening we watched TV and drank a few glasses of dry sherry, to relax. Caprice, you gave me a brief hug at bedtime and my heart sang. I hoped we'd survived the lows of our relationship and were on the way up.

But that wasn't how it worked out, was it?

A few months later you decided you felt strong enough to tackle sorting out Rupert's possessions. The family were called upon to help. The weekend chosen was planned and sorted, firmly planted in our diaries. A week before, I was at home without Miles, playing with the children, when the phone rang.

I picked up. It was you.

'Hello dear, is Miles there?' you asked.

The strange elongated *deeeaarr*. My stomach tightened. 'He's not around right now. Can I help?'

'Can you get him to ring me later?'

'Yes of course. How are you?'

'Good. Good. Coping,' you replied.

'Well, see you at the weekend. Can I bring anything?'

The line fell silent.

'Are you still there, Caprice?'

'Yes.' More silence. 'I didn't know you were coming.'

'Yes. Yes, of course I'm coming to help.'

'Help sort out *my* husband's possessions?'

I took a deep breath and swallowed. 'I thought there might be something I could do that was useful. It'll be very upsetting, sifting through everything. I could help pack things in boxes to take to the charity shop. Cook lunch and supper. Just be around to give moral support.'

'I don't want you around. I just want my family to myself.'

I have wasted too many hours mulling over our relationship, Caprice. I think, in retrospect, it became worse when Rupert died. I ask myself why – was it because you missed him and envied the fact I still had Miles? Or were you jealous because Rupert was more fond of me than you liked to admit? Any compliments he ever paid me made your lips tighten and your body stiffen.

But we've rubbed along OK, haven't we? I have tried to make excuses for your difficult behaviour and to be patient. Until just recently, when you moved out of your annexe, into our house. You are no longer my mother-in-law but an unwelcome guest. An unwelcome guest I can no longer tolerate.

46

Hayley

You have invited me to join you on a winter trip to Hampton Court Palace. It will be a real highlight for my mother to read about in my diary, Miles. You were given free mid-week tickets. The boys are at school and Saffron is busy. Caprice is too tired to go out all day. There is something wrong with her thyroid gland apparently. Her consultant is balancing the amount of thyroxin she needs. Ramping it up.

So I got lucky.

Swanning around a grand building with a dreamboat of a man. Pretending a man like you is interested in a girl like me. Just for one day.

We are walking along the haunted gallery. My spine begins to tingle as I look out for Catherine Howard running and screaming down this corridor. The tale is that she had been arrested for adultery, and imprisoned in her room, in 1541. She escaped, and was racing down the corridor hoping to find Henry in the chapel, wanting to plead her innocence. She was caught by the guards, restrained and never saw Henry again. A few months later she was beheaded at the Tower of London, aged nineteen. But her ghost is still seen and heard screaming along this corridor to this day.

'Do you believe in ghosts, Miles?' I ask.

'Well, that depends on what you mean by a ghost.'

'You're an academic, so everything you believe will depend on a range of facts bound to confuse me.'

110

You smile your honeyed smile. 'So young and so cynical, Hayley.'

'Come on. Do you think Catherine Howard's ghost comes screaming down here from time to time? Or do you think it's just a story made up to tantalise the tourists?'

Your smile widens. 'I think she's about to blast past us any moment.'

We both laugh.

'Yeah, right.'

'Come on,' you say. 'Enough of buildings and ghosts. Let's go and look at the gardens.'

The gardens are my favourite part. The privy garden, which has been restored to the original garden plan constructed by King William III in 1702, is magnificent. You look out onto it from the back of the palace and it stretches as far as the eye can see and is perfectly balanced.

We walk through acres and acres of gardens until my feet ache. My favourite plants are the dahlias. Planted in July and still full of colour at the beginning of November. Pinks and purples and blues. Some rose-like. Some like camelias. Petals like leaves. Petals like feathers. A blast of structure and colour.

I beam at you. 'These plants are fantastic. When I get home I'm going to join the Dahlia Society of New Zealand.'

'There must be a dahlia society in the UK,' he teases me with his eyes. 'Why don't you join that and stay here?'

47

Caprice

You have been delayed at work, again. There is such a lovely atmosphere without you at Wellbeck House, Saffron. Everyone is so much more relaxed. The boys are enjoying chicken nuggets and ketchup, without a sigh and a look. Miles has cooked steak for the three adults. We are having steak sandwiches with horseradish sauce. Nice and easy. No fuss.

Hayley and Miles seem invigorated after their outing to Hampton Court Palace. They walked for hours in the fresh air, apparently, laughing and chatting. I've not seen Miles look so cheerful for weeks. They showed me the photographs they took on their iPhones, looking like a couple. Oh Miles, if you're not interested in Julie, maybe a real antipodean jewel like Hayley is just the tonic you need to put your life back on track.

I knew as soon as she arrived that she was interested in you. With a little encouragement could I ensure you were interested in her, too?

48

Saffron

My life is engulfing me, overwhelming me. I need to take control or I'll fall into a black hole, an abyss. First, I must handle my business. And then you, Caprice.

I slip out of bed and shower. I'm meeting a prospective client today. A bit OCD about clothes, I stand in front of my extensive wardrobe, arranged as perfectly as a top-end shop display, and try on lilac cashmere. Insipid. Khaki denim. Too casual, and the colour does nothing for me. I shouldn't have bought that dress. In the end I take a punt with a grey suit and crisp white blouse. A bit 'office-boring', but saved by being perfectly cut.

Miles is still fast asleep in bed. I kiss him on the forehead – my favourite place, and tiptoe out, past the boys' bedrooms. Hayley promised to get up early to look after the children today. It's so early even Caprice hasn't woken yet. She is often up before us, preening in the kitchen, making sure Miles and I don't have any time alone with our family in the morning.

I make a cup of Nescafé and stand looking out of the window, enjoying the peace. Staring at the private playpark she has bought to bribe the children. Never missing an opportunity to remind them that she paid for it. Caprice makes sure she keeps them on her side. The children. My children. My stomach feels heavy. What if she breaks up our family? I press my jaws together and swallow. I will not allow her to do that.

*　*　*

My prospective client is waiting for me at The Ned. A former bank in Central London that has been converted into a club and restaurant complex. Anyone who is anybody entertains here these days. He is sitting on a pink sofa by the window, in Millie's lounge. Joshua Cassidy. Twenty-five years old. Professional footballer. Currently injured but due to be back on the squad in three weeks – all being well. Paid the sort of fortune per week that most people don't make in a year.

Maybe he has seen my photo on the BPC website, because he recognises me as I walk towards his table, and stands up to greet me. He leans towards me and shakes my hand. He is wearing diamond stud earrings. And I notice a diamond in the bottom right of his left front tooth, as he smiles. What if it comes out while he's playing? He could swallow it and choke.

He's smaller than I imagined. About five foot eleven – not quite six foot. I thought internationally acclaimed footballers would be enormous; the bigger the better to succeed at sport.

I slide onto the pink sofa opposite him. He pushes the menu towards me.

'I'm a bit tight for time so I've already ordered. Why don't you order quickly so that the kitchen can get us in synch?'

I place the menu on the table in front of me. 'No need to worry about me. I'll just have a coffee and a smoothie.'

Joshua smiles and his diamonds glint in the light from the window behind us. 'I bet a smoothie has just as many calories as breakfast,' he says.

'It's not about calories. It's about what I want,' I reply.

He pushes young brown puppy-dog eyes into mine. 'I like a woman who knows what she wants.'

Twenty-five years old. Cocky. Arrogant. Oh my God. If I was a few years older I could be his mother. I'm not the type to play around. A brick of guilt coagulates in my stomach. Except for my drunken kiss with Aiden. What was I doing? What was that about?

114

A black-suited waiter wafts towards our table with Joshua's breakfast. Almost dancing around us as he places it in front of this overpaid wide boy, who flashes sexism and diamonds. Mashed avocado on toast with poached eggs on sourdough.

As the waiter puts the plate down I catch his eye. 'Please could I have a large Americano with hot milk, and a spinach and ricotta smoothie.'

'Of course, madam,' he drools in a heavy French accent, which sounds as if it has been fragmented through a cheese grater.

The waiter retreats.

'So,' Joshua starts, 'tell me why I should consider using you.'

'Because I would deal with all the things you currently ignore, and which over the next twenty years will make you infinitely richer. You see, you probably only think about today or tomorrow or maybe next week. I think about the future. Your family's future. I have worked in tax and trusts for years in a top magic circle firm. I know how to protect and grow your wealth. Also, I'm experienced at dealing with the routine aspects of legal need, such as conveyancing and divorce. And I specialise in pre-nuptial agreements – something I understand from the media you might be interested in before too long.' I lean back on the pink sofa and smile at him, hoping he won't smile back. I do not want to see his diamond-studded tooth again. 'You get a tailored 24/7 service from me. I am always there when you need me. And you need someone like me.'

'An attentive 24/7 service. I see.' He says this with all the emphasis on the word service, as if he's thinking about sex. I would like to slap him, but I swallow to push away the knots that are tightening in my stomach. I remember his portfolio. I need to be polite. To keep calm. Belgravia Private Clients need this. 'Haven't you been acting for Sasha Reznikovitch?' he asks.

I sigh inside. 'Yes.'

'She's not a good example of your services.'

'Her bankruptcy is a reflection of her behaviour, not my advice. I also act for Aristos Kaladopolous, and James Shoestring.'

He emits a soft whistle. 'They're impressive clients. Would they provide a reference?'

'Of course.'

49

Miles

You have driven to visit one of your two remaining clients, James Shoestring, in his country pile; a not-so-small small-holding in Hereford. He pays the local farmer to run his hobby farm for him, to keep it looking authentic for his occasional visits. The crisis this weekend, I understand, is to ascertain which tax jurisdiction should be nominated to receive the next tranche of his income.

With you away, Hayley and I are taking the boys to Coral Reef Waterworld in Bracknell for the day. Mother is coming with us. She will sit in the café while we swim, and then come for a walk in the surrounding woods with us, after lunch.

We arrive at Coral Reef and park the car, the boys whooping with excitement. Mother marches off towards the café brandishing her *Daily Telegraph*. No doubt ready to attack the crossword with her usual determination.

'See you by the base of the waterslides in about ten minutes,' I say to Hayley as I take the boys by the hand, leading them towards the family changing rooms.

'Fine.' She beams, sauntering towards the child-free area.

Harry and Ben jump up and down pretending to be baby lambs, all the way to the cubicles. I manage to get a big one so that we can change together. Ben stops jumping and changes sensibly. Harry carries on jumping. He is a baby rabbit now apparently.

'Come on, Harry, your turn to get your trunks on,' I say when Ben and I are ready.

But Harry keeps jumping, and giggling. His high-pitched giggle is beginning to give me a headache.

'Don't you want to come swimming?' I ask. 'Would you rather sit and do the crossword with Granny?'

'Don't call her Granny,' Ben and Harry say in unison.

'Why not?'

'She hates it.'

'I didn't know that.'

'She tells us every day.'

Harry puts his head on one side and looks at me. 'I don't want to do the crossword with Caprice, but I can't come swimming because I'm a bunny rabbit.' He pauses. 'And bunnies don't swim.'

'They do,' Ben replies. 'I've seen one on YouTube. Can I borrow your iPhone Daddy?'

I hand it to him. He opens a video of a rabbit, underwater, ears back, kicking its legs, streamlined in the water, like a furry pencil.

'Come on, Harry. We can have a bunny swimming race in the water,' I say hopefully. We have already been twice as long as I said.

'I want to go to the pirate ship. Bunnies like pirates. They like eating them,' he says gnashing his teeth.

'Don't be silly. Bunnies are vegetarian,' Ben replies.

Harry puts his tongue out at his brother. Ben reciprocates.

'Remember what Caprice says. If the wind changes your faces will stay like that,' I say as I grab their hands and drag them out of the changing cubicle. 'Hayley is queen of the bunny rabbits and she's waiting for you by the slide. Let's race there now.'

At last we reach Hayley. I try not to notice her perfectly toasted breasts and hourglass figure tucked into a neat white one-piece swimsuit. To me she looks more like a playboy bunny than a queen of bunny rabbits. The boys run towards her and hug her. She smiles at me, and her brown eyes spill into mine. I pull my eyes away. Men have to be so careful these days.

Maelstrom. Poseidon's Peril. Aqua Splash. Stormchaser. We do all the slides twice. So fast, with their rotating strobe lights of many colours. I feel dizzy. I feel sick.

'Come on, Dad, let's go to the pirate ship now.'

The life-sized plastic pirate ship, *Coralina*, is guarded by water cannons. Bunnies forgotten now, the boys run around pretending they are pirates, having sword fights. Arguing about where to find treasure. I sense Hayley is staring at me. Wondering whether I am imagining it, I glance across at her. Her eyes meet mine and she blushes. Is she blushing? Or is her skin red because it's eighty degrees in here?

'It's hot in here,' I say.

'So take off all your clothes,' she replies with the same intonation as the cheeky song by Nelly that was in the charts years ago.

'I thought you'd be too young to remember that song.'

Frightened she might notice the stirring in my crotch, I push my waist against the hull of the ship and watch a group of teenagers swim past. She comes and stands beside me.

'My mother likes that song.'

Her mother. And I'm old enough to be her father. Even though I felt betrayed when you kissed Aiden, I'm not going to stoop to revenge sex. The last thing I want is to flirt with our nanny and upset you. And you seem upset enough right now. I value my marriage, my relationship, more than anything in the world. I must be careful with Hayley. I must not give her the wrong impression.

119

50

Caprice

I'm sweltering in Coral Reef's café, because it opens onto the over-heated swimming area. Sweat pools behind my knees. It drips down my shoulders and clusters in the small of my back, fastening to my face like a second skin. I'm so bored because I've finished the crossword. The café has a showcase view of the revellers at Waterworld, and so unfortunately I hear the raucous sound of their laughing and shouting. Is everyone enjoying this place apart from me? The heat and the noise press against me – so intrusive, they could be solid objects.

Across the water I see Hayley and Miles standing together on the pirate ship, Harry and Ben frolicking in front of them. I wave across to them. If I can catch their attention I'll gesticulate for them to come out of the pool immediately. My flesh is beginning to cook.

But they do not see me, so I have no choice but to read the newspaper. Again. And check I've got the crossword clues right. As I check the clues my mind plays tricks. For a second I am back in time doing the crossword with Rupert, sitting so close to him that our breath is entangled. I remember the feel of him. His scent of Old Spice mingled with tobacco that was always so reassuring, so comforting. My stomach lurches as I remember the way he would hold me in bed, hug me and love me. Every night and every morning. Old and alone, no one ever touches me now.

I watch you with Miles, taking him for granted, Saffron. Leaving him so often at evenings and weekends to pursue your own life. How is it fair that you still have your man, and I do not have my Rupert?

They are here, at last, walking across the café towards me, faces red and radiant, grinning broadly. Their wet hair slick against their heads like a pod of seals. They look so happy I determine not to complain about how uncomfortable I've been. I just won't come here again. I've heard grandparents complaining about the artificiality of Center Parcs. But Center Parcs cannot be any worse than this, except for the fact you have to stay there overnight.

'Hello, Granny,' Harry says. Ben nudges him. 'I mean Caprice.'

I ignore that mishap. 'What can I get you for lunch? It's my treat,' I say and pause. I wrinkle my nose. 'I've looked at what's available. It's a limp sandwich. Or something and chips.'

'Something and chips,' they reply, almost in unison.

'Well then you've got two choices: fish or chicken nuggets.'

The boys bleat for nuggets. The adults fancy fish. I walk across to the counter, order and pay.

'I'll bring it across when it's ready,' a pale young woman wearing no make-up says. She really ought to do something to brighten herself up.

As I step back towards the table, I look across at Miles, Hayley, Ben and Harry. They are chatting, heads together like a family. A family that has time for one another. A real family.

51

Hayley

'Mmm, thank you, Caprice. That was delicious. Fish and double-cooked chips. Done well, there's nothing better,' I say.

Caprice looks across at me and smiles. She is a good-looking old girl. Smooth skin. Large round eyes. Pale blonde hair, so pale it's almost white, shining in the pool's halogen lights. Tastefully dressed as usual, like a model in a cruise catalogue. Slacks and a blouse. A beauty really. Hard to believe she's nearly seventy years old.

'Caprice,' Ben says pointedly, 'will you take me to the bathroom?'

'And me?' Harry adds.

'I'll go,' I volunteer.

'No. That's fine, dear. I'm happy to go.'

I don't think they need to go to the bathroom. I think they just want to walk their indulgent grandmother past the chocolate machine, without their father knowing. I heard them whispering about it on the way here. They skip off across the café, Caprice trailing behind them.

So it's just you and me, Miles. I look across at you finishing your chips. Your hair is drying in the heat, returning to its usual dark blond. The hair that I would love to run my fingers through.

'How did you meet Saffron?' I ask.

The best way to disguise feelings for a married man is to ask him plenty of questions about his wife.

122

'I fell in love with her at university.'

'I rather guessed that from the photograph in the hallway.'

You grin. 'So you're a detective.'

'Not exactly. Standing together in degree gowns. It's a bit of a no-brainer. I meant more the exact moment you met. What brought you together?'

His face softens. 'We were in a tutorial. Just the two of us. The tutor introduced us. "Miss Filby," he said. And I looked across. Miss Filby was quite simply the most beautiful woman I'd ever seen. As the tutorial progressed I realised she was also the cleverest.' He shrugs. 'We bumped into each other at a party that evening, and we've been together ever since.'

'It's funny how it works so quickly sometimes, isn't it? As soon as you see someone you care about, you just know.'

'You speak from the heart.'

I look into your warm eyes. 'Yes.'

'Do you want to tell me your story?'

'No. Not right now. It's an ongoing situation.'

You raise your eyebrows. 'Well good luck with it then.'

'I need it.'

'Things happened fast between my mother and father too,' you say.

'She misses him – doesn't she?'

'Very perceptive. Yes.'

You lean across the table and put your hand on my arm. My stomach jolts with pleasure. Your eyes cloud. 'She's vulnerable. And we all need to be supportive towards her.'

We are interrupted by Caprice, Harry and Ben coming back. As you turn to greet them you pull your hand from my arm.

'I want ice cream,' Harry demands.

'Say please then,' Ben insists.

'Please. Please. Please.'

'My treat this time,' I say as I leave the table.

I know Caprice saw you touching me. She's looking at me.

123

What is she thinking? She must disapprove of me. If Caprice disapproves of me, I'm stuffed. She's the powerhouse around here.

52

Caprice

You were back so late last night after gallivanting in Hereford, that your family hasn't seen you over the weekend. Not a glimpse. You are a shadow of a mother. A ghost.

Monday morning; 6 a.m. I'm eating boiled eggs and grapefruit in the kitchen, when you pop in for a cup of coffee and a smoothie. You wince in your usual manner as I crack the shell of my first egg. You condescending bitch. How do you expect me to eat it? At 6.15 a.m., you leave. I sigh with relief, crack my second boiled egg, and sit listening to *Today* on Radio 4.

At 8 a.m., the kitchen door opens. Ben and Harry tumble in, school uniforms in disarray; Ben's shirt is hanging out, Harry's shoelaces spill across the floor. They're followed by Miles and Hayley. Hayley looks clean and crisp and sharp. Miles is sporting his casual professor look. Loose-fitting cords, suede boots and a crumpled check shirt. He pushes his generous hair back from his eyes and smiles at me. My world lights up.

'Good morning, Mum,' he says as he lays the table.

'Morning, Granny,' Harry says with a giggle.

I give him my look, my *I'll put you on a spit and roast you* look. Ben sighs sympathetically and shakes his head. He points his finger accusingly at his brother and laughs.

'Good morning, Caprice,' Hayley says, flashing her even teeth as she smiles. Everything about Hayley is even. Balanced cheekbones. Balanced figure. A girl with boobs and hips. 'How's it going this morning?' she asks.

'I've been up a while. I couldn't sleep.'

She frowns in concern. 'What's the matter? I hope you're not feeling ill?'

Miles is helping himself to Dorset Cereal, rattling it into his bowl. He looks up. 'Yes. Are you all right, Mum?'

'Just a bit of back pain. Stuff happens at my age. I took a few ibuprofen and it went.'

'Well, let me know if I can do anything. Get you anything,' Hayley says.

'Thank you.'

'Boys, what do you want for breakfast? The usual?'

They nod. Hayley puts a box of Weetabix on the table and they help themselves. She must be on a diet; she sits at the table sipping a black coffee. I sit watching the bad table manners of my grandsons. Harry isn't holding his spoon correctly. He slurps the milk from around his cereal, sucking it up like a vacuum cleaner. Ben is chomping. There must be something wrong with his teeth for him to make so much noise. I'll be sure to mention this to Saffron, when I next see her.

Miles is staring into the middle of the kitchen, in a daydream. No doubt contemplating one of his obscure philosophical ideas. His research is so obscure and irrelevant. He's lucky to be paid for it. Is that why he puts up with Saffron? Because she's the one who earns the money? I'm sorry he feels the need to stick with her. I have more than enough money to give him. My husband, Rupert, made so much. Surely he knows he doesn't have to put up with a selfish bint for money?

Hayley is glancing across at Miles. She never takes her eyes off him for long. We watch my son finish his breakfast, gulp the end of his coffee, and suddenly snap his focus back into the room. He stands up, pulls the car keys from the drawer behind him, twisting them around his middle finger.

'Come on, boys. Whose turn is it to sit in the front?'

'Saffron doesn't let anyone sit in the front,' I remind him. Just to make sure he realises how difficult his wife can be with anyone who tries to help with the children.

'You don't need to tell Daddy that. You're a spoilsport,' Ben announces.

'Me, a spoilsport?'

'Yes, Granny. You always let me sit in the front so why do you have to spoil it?'

'I rather think it's your mother who's the spoilsport,' I snap.

'Come on, Ben – no one's a spoilsport,' Miles says. 'I'll talk to Mum. I expect she knows you sit in the front. Mums have eyes in the backs of their heads.'

'I love my mummy so much. I just don't want to get in trouble.'

Miles puts his arm around Ben and holds Harry's hand as they leave. 'We all love Mummy and I promise she won't be cross.'

Hayley clears the breakfast dishes and I help her. We listen to the radio in companionable silence. The *Today* programme is still on, repeating itself. Going around in circles. Not really designed to be listened to for the full three hours. But it is a comfortable background noise, part of my daily routine.

When the last bowl is in the dishwasher, and the kitchen is wiped clean, just as Hayley turns to leave, 'Why don't you come for a walk around the garden with me?' I suggest. She hesitates. 'Or are you too busy?' I continue.

She shifts her weight awkwardly. 'Well, Saffron has left a few chores for me.'

I put my head on one side and shrug. 'I'm a chore, aren't I?'

Hayley smiles. 'I wouldn't perceive you like that.'

'How would you perceive me?'

'Well, for a start you're beautiful.'

'No one has said that to me for a long time,' I reply, my heart melting at her kind words. 'Come on, humour me, come for a walk in the garden.'

She nods in assent. I smile and step towards her, threading my arm through hers. We step outside into a warm November day, bright sunlight sharpening the edges of the world around us.

'It's not the best time of year for the garden, but if you take note of what it looks like now, you'll appreciate its summer glory all the more.'

We walk past my poky annexe. How they expected me to live there, I don't know. Saffron must have brainwashed Miles. Left to himself, he would never treat me like that. Past the play area, past the swimming pool now closed for the season. Down the passageway between the swimming pool and the tennis courts, and through the thick line of spruce trees that Saffron insisted on keeping. And then the garden opens out. As we walk, I point out: asters, Japanese anemone, chrysanthemums, carnations, gentian, dahlia and calla lilies.

'But . . . but . . . It's full of colour. I didn't expect that in the UK at this time of year,' Hayley exclaims. 'I loved the dahlias at Hampton Court, but this display is even more varied and impressive.'

'I designed the planting plan,' I tell her, shoulders wide and proud.

'It's amazing,' she exclaims, eyes shining with pleasure. 'It's a pity you can't see it from the house.'

'I know. I told them that when the architect was designing the house, but Saffron overruled me.' I pause. 'Are you interested in horticulture?' I ask.

'Yes. I'm going to take a diploma in gardening in Auckland when I finally return home.' She looks across at me and smiles awkwardly. 'Not that I'm in a hurry. I'm very happy here, in my job. It's just something I'd like to do long term.'

'I'll take you to Wisley one day. It's the best place in the UK to learn about plants.'

We sit on a bench in the corner of the garden. Beneath the shade of a weeping willow, I squeeze her arm. 'I need to tell you something, Hayley . . .'

53

Hayley

Caprice leans forwards, eyes gleaming. 'I think Miles is strongly attracted to you.'

An electric shock runs through me. 'But he seems so in love with Saffron,' I protest.

'His marriage is a sham. He just puts on a brave face.'

'How do you know?' I ask, still cautious.

'A mother always knows.' Caprice smiles. 'I've lived with Miles and Saffron for four years now. I see things. I hear things. Arguments. Discussions. Every day I watch their antagonistic body language.' She pauses. 'And recently, I've seen the way Miles looks at you, with an expression on his face that I've never seen before. You mean something to him. Something new. Something big. I've been mulling over this for a while. I know I'm right. I'm always right about things to do with Miles. It's a mother's duty to help a son live the best possible life. To lead a perfect life, you need a perfect wife. You are perfect for Miles.'

54

Saffron

I go into the office early, before Ted and Julie. Sitting down, I try to clear my head. What a weekend. Visiting James Shoestring's home. James. Retired bond dealer from the City. Lending to those in difficulty with their global investments, he seems to have made more money since he left his job, than he made doing it. But he is such a difficult client. Despite his enormous mansion, I was given a small unheated room to work in. You'd think he could put the central heating on in December. What a skinflint. We had a meeting in his sumptuous dining room, with its de Gournay wallpaper, which he enjoyed boasting about. But I was so cold I wished I had brought my ski jacket. I made a suggestion, and he shouted; yelled at the top of his voice. His face went red. Spittle flew out with his words.

I returned home so late on Sunday night that everyone else in my family was asleep. I slipped into bed, naked, next to Miles, and lay against him, skin on skin. He stirred and kissed me. We made love. I smile inside as I remember. The highlight of my weekend. But after that I couldn't sleep. Worrying about my firm.

I switch on my computer and check my emails. Joshua Cassidy. He's sorry but he's going to pass on me as his private client lawyer. He wants someone younger. More dynamic. More in tune with his persona.

Disappointment skitters inside me. I really need some new work. Ted and Julie have agreed not to take their salaries until the loan comes in. Julie has assured me that she and Conrad are still an item and he is very happy to support her for a while. So this is affecting him too. I suppress the surge of panic rising in my stomach. Turning my mind in on itself, willing the loan to come in. Wishing I was religious and believed that a higher being could help.

55

Aiden

Miles is here, in my Chelsea apartment. Sitting on my black leather sofa, cradling a whisky. Wearing jeans with holes in, and a baggy green jumper.

'So how's it going?' I ask.

'How's what going?' he replies, voice sharp. 'My work? Or my marriage?'

I know I need to be patient with him until he forgives me. I take a deep breath. 'Well everything I suppose.'

He takes a sip of whisky, leans back and crosses his legs. 'As a matter of fact I'm working on vagueness, conditionals and supervaluationism at the moment.'

'What's that?' I ask, feigning interest.

'Are you sure you want to know?'

'Try me.'

'I'm arguing that vagueness produces counter-examples to *modus tollens*.'

'Do I need to understand Latin now?' I pause. 'Is it even Latin? I don't know.'

'Of course it's Latin. You studied it at Charterhouse.'

'I took it for a few years, but it might as well have been Double Dutch to me.'

'Well you are right, it is Latin.' He pauses. 'And *modus tollens* is a deductive argument form. And a rule of inference. Would you like me to explain?'

I do not want him to. But I so want to make friends with him again that I swallow and nod my head.

Miles continues, 'This is how it works. "If P, then Q. Not Q. Therefore not P." It is an application of the general truth that if a statement is true, then so is its contrapositive. The form shows that inference from "P implies Q" to "the negation of Q implies the negation of P" is a valid argument.' He pauses. 'Do you understand?'

'You're joking aren't you? Trying to bait me? Trying to make me feel stupid.'

He uncrosses his legs, puts his whisky down on the table in front of him, and leans forwards. 'I'm sorry. I didn't mean to upset you. It's so complicated I find it hard to explain.'

'Philosophy makes my brain ache. It makes most people's brains ache. But then you were always such an intellectual weren't you? A cut above the rest.' I pause. 'And now you are a professor, you really need to learn how to explain things clearly.'

My voice is rising. I need to be careful. I invited him over to make friends, not to antagonise him.

He hesitates. 'Sorry I expressed myself badly. I really wasn't trying to score points against you.'

I smile uncertainly. 'OK. Well let's just start again.' I pause. 'What about the children? Why don't you tell me about them? How they're getting on?'

His eyes darken. 'You see them every Sunday when you come for lunch.'

'Stop being arsey. I invited you over because I want us to be friends again.'

'You've always been my friend.' Miles pauses, eyes full of sadness. 'I just want you to stop flirting with my wife.'

I lift my shoulders and raise my palms to the ceiling. 'I've apologised. I won't do it again.'

He shakes his head. 'I'm not sure I believe you.'

'If you don't believe me how are we going to move forwards?'

'It's not my fault we're both attracted to the same woman. But I'm her husband, for God's sake. We love each other. You need to forget about her. Back off.'

My stomach twists. 'You don't need to remind me.'

'You need to find someone of your own. Someone special. You had Julie. It just didn't work out. Next time it will. Use Tinder. Whatever. Just make more of an effort.'

I smile. 'OK. Good idea, mate. I will.'

I cannot tell him the truth. I never loved Julie, and she knew. That's why she left me. The only woman I've ever loved is you, Saffron. No one compares to you.

56

Miles

I leave Aiden's flat and walk along the King's Road towards the tube station, dust from passing traffic misting my eyes. How can I hold a grudge against him when I have everything I want? Aiden has everything, and yet, nothing. Life is not built of bricks or possessions. It is far more ethereal. Full of electricity and emotion. Made up of what I have with you, Saffron.

57

Hayley

I know you mean something to him. Something new. Something big. Caprice's voice shouts across my mind. *I'm sure I'm right. I'm sure I'm right.*

Oh, Miles, I have been suppressing how I feel about you for so long. Pushing love away. Trying to be magnanimous. To think about Saffron. To think about your family. Not all out for myself. But now Caprice's words have unleashed the full power of my emotion. It pulses like a tsunami inside me, building and building.

Alone in my designer bedroom, I sink naked into red silk and allow myself to dream. I close my eyes and fantasise. You are lying next to me. Pulling me towards you. Telling me that you love me. Telling me you want me. Telling me that things with Saffron aren't working out.

I lie in bed thinking about you, playing with my clitoris. I experience the best orgasm I have ever had. Panting as I recover. Heartbeat reducing slowly.

Miles Jackson, I've had you in my imagination. Now I want you for real.

58

Saffron

Ted steps into my office, smiling. A real smile that reaches his eyes. The kind of smile he hasn't given me for a long time.

'The bank have granted us a nine-month loan.'

Relief floods through me, warming my blood, my body. I stand up, pull him towards me and hug him. He smells of coconut and musk. I pull away and open the office door.

'Come here, Julie,' I shout.

She scuttles into my office looking worried.

'It's good news. The loan has come through. We're going out to celebrate.'

We're in the cocktail bar at the RAC Club, Pall Mall.

'Here's to BPC. Long may we survive,' I say as I raise my glass. We clink champagne flutes, Julie, Ted and I.

'Thank you for being patient about last month's salary. You've both been so understanding,' I say.

Julie smiles her clean-edged smile. 'It's been worth it, Saffron. I love our team. I love my job. I love our trust. Our friendship.'

And my stomach tightens. I should have trusted her more. I should have believed everything she said about Miles and Aiden. My birthday necklace is hidden in a drawer, I can't bear to wear it, after the way I behaved.

'And I love our team too. Saffron, we've been together since we were teenagers,' Ted says enthusiastically.

I pull my thoughts away from the necklace that I do not deserve to own. I smile inside. Ted and I have been friends almost forever. We were at the same school, same class, same set for English and Maths. We used to walk home together, winding our way along the High Street. Stopping to buy sweets. Browsing in shop windows. We would turn left down the passageway, past the cricket club, towards the housing development where we both lived.

The narrow passageway was lined with gnarled trees, trunks bent like arthritic fingers. The canopy of leaves above entwined together. That was where we shared our hopes and fears. Our secrets. Such close friends, our peer group assumed we were a couple. But we weren't. We told everyone we were cousins. They seemed to need an explanation for our relationship.

This evening, in the cocktail bar at the RAC Club, Ted's eyes shine into mine.

'I told you it would be all right, but you wouldn't believe me.'

'I'll believe everything you both say from now on, I promise.'

We finish our champagne and leave the bar, stopping in the grand hallway of the RAC Club to admire the Christmas tree, stretching up into the stone rotunda above us, a Pantheon-like structure with a giant oval window in its dome. Its elegance and beauty fill me with awe every time I visit, and I have been a member of this club for many years. But it never looks as beautiful as it does in December with a Christmas tree fit for royalty filling it.

We move away, across opulent patterned carpet towards the Brooklands Room, where more Edwardian elegance opens out in front of us. Arched windows stretch from floor to ceiling. Panelling, paintings, pillars, livened up with modern furniture. A masterpiece of simplicity and sophistication.

A waiter leads us to a table by a marble pillar. It doesn't take us long to order and water and wine arrive promptly. Not much later, our starters are placed gently in front of us. Raw courgette and toasted hazelnut salad for me. Smoked salmon for Julie. Chicken liver parfait for Ted.

'We still need another big client,' I say between mouthfuls.

Ted leans towards me. 'We'll get one soon.'

'We will,' Julie says. 'You need to believe Ted and me about that.'

'I'm turning over a new leaf. No criticism. No disbelief.'

59

Caprice

So, Saffron, my plan to make you mistrust my son because of his relationship with Julie didn't work. But I have a new, more enticing project now. How will my son be able to resist the wholesome reality of a beguiling young woman like Hayley?

As usual you are home late, and I'm watching cartoons with the children.

'Would you like to go and see *Frozen 2* next Saturday?' I ask.

'It's for girls,' Ben and Harry reply in unison.

You are out next Saturday; I heard you telling Miles you were going Christmas shopping. I grit my teeth in disappointment. Taking them to the cinema would have just been so easy. All I would have had to do is ply them with sweets, fizzy drinks and popcorn, close my eyes and sleep. But now I'll have to up the ante. What about a trip to the theatre? *The Lion King*? I know they want to see that. And then McDonald's at the back of Waterloo station. Going to McDonald's always seems to please them.

I log into the Ticketmaster website and spend a small fortune on the best tickets in the house.

60

Miles

Thursday night. Curry night. Mother, Ben, Harry and I are tucking into a takeaway. Lamb rogan josh, okra with chilli and ginger, Bombay potatoes, peshwari naan and pilau rice. Hayley is at the pub with Jono. You have escaped home and work, Saffron, for a rare outing on your own.

'Ben and Harry, I've booked a special treat for you this Saturday,' Mother announces.

'What, Caprice, what?' Harry asks, almost jumping out of his seat with excitement. 'Tickets to see *The Lion King*, and then tea at McDonald's.'

The boys jump out of their chairs and race around the table jumping and whooping.

'That's very kind of you, Mother. Now, boys, calm down and finish your curry.'

One more circuit of the table and they obey me.

'Thank you so much,' Ben says as he slips back onto his seat.

'Miles,' Mother says in her instructing tone, 'I need to ask you for some help this weekend. I want you to help Hayley plant some rose bushes that are being delivered from David Austin's in Wolverhampton this Saturday. And keep an eye she plants them properly. I'd supervise myself if I hadn't booked this treat.'

'Isn't it a bit late for planting roses?'

Mother smiles. 'No. Late autumn fall is a fine time to plant. Otherwise I wouldn't have bought them. And Hayley loves plants.

Helping me with this is a real treat for her. So what do you think?'

'Well, I'm not sure. Maybe we could see if there are some tickets left for *The Lion King* so that Saffron and I could come along too?'

Mother stiffens. 'Saffron is going Christmas shopping on Saturday.'

'She was, but her plans have changed.'

'You didn't tell me.'

'She decided to go tonight instead. She was offered a special ticket with twenty-five per cent off tonight, to the late-night Christmas shopping event at the Bentall Centre. I hadn't mentioned it because I didn't think it was pivotal to your plans. She's decided to spend Saturday with her family instead. So what do you think? It would be fun if we all went to the theatre together.'

Mother's eyes are hard. Her chin is jutting out. 'What about the roses?' she asks, voice sharp.

'I'll plant them during the week. And Hayley can have a day off this Saturday. Is that a problem?'

'I suppose not.'

61

Caprice

You came to the theatre, Saffron, and spoilt my special treat with the boys. And you dragged Miles away from his assignation with Hayley.

You don't like fast food, so after the show we visited a plant-based restaurant at the back of Waterloo station. It smelt damp. Not surprisingly, as is true of all vegan cuisine, the food was tasteless. Ben and Harry, even though they loved the musical, were crushed with disappointment about the choice of supper.

So now I'll just have to instigate another plan to make sure Miles gets his opportunity to find happiness with an attractive young woman. You've left your computer in the kitchen. Its metallic surface shines in the sun pouring through the window. I open it and type in your password. I have stood behind you so often as you boot up. Watched where your thin little fingers tap: *1979.* The year you were born. Not very high security. You could have been more inventive, don't you think? A few more taps and I'm into your calendar. Friday 15th November. *Monthly meal out with Julie and Ted.* A regular office social event that you never miss.

I think the boys will be going to a sleepover to one of my school gate chums that night. Just you wait and see, Saffron. You won't have a chance against a young piece of perfection like Hayley, who actually likes children. Your husband resents how often you are away, and your skinny little body is really starting to show its age.

62

Hayley

Friday night. I'm finishing earlier than usual because the boys have gone straight from school to a sleepover at the Chadwicks' house. All arranged by Caprice. Caprice Jackson is quite a socialiser with the school gate mums. She knows so many people.

I pop into the kitchen to fetch a can of Diet Coke and find her sitting at the kitchen table, head in her hands. 'Is that you, Hayley?' she asks without looking up. 'I'm getting a migraine.'

'You poor thing. Can I get you some ibuprofen?'

'I need something stronger than that. My prescription drugs are in my room. I'm going up to bed, I'll take some when I get upstairs.'

She stands up, back bent, leaning towards the floor. I watch her hobble across the kitchen towards the door.

'Goodnight, dear.'

'Feel better soon. Ring my mobile if you need anything.'

A weak smile as she leaves the room. 'Thank you.'

I grab a Diet Coke from the fridge and open it. I take a sip. My phone rings: Caprice.

'Come quick.'

'What do you need?' I ask. 'A glass of water? Some toast?'

'Just you.'

I dash upstairs and step into her bedroom, which is Sanderson pink. Roses and peonies on the curtains, on the duvet. The distressed white bedroom suite is curved and pretty. In the middle of the dressing table, there is a photograph of Caprice and Rupert, entangled together. Caprice looks so giddy and happy. So relaxed. In the middle of this kaleidoscope of pink and florals, and past happiness, the modern-day Caprice is lying on her bed groaning.

'I need you to do me a favour,' she mutters between groans.

'Anything you need. Anything.'

'I was going to the opera with Miles this evening. Saffron is out, *again*, even on a Friday night when she should be spending time with him. So I booked a treat to cheer him up. But I feel so ill, I just can't go. Could you go instead?'

My mouth opens in surprise. No words come out.

'Well come on. Answer me. Can you go instead?'

'Of course. No problem. I love opera. It's very kind of you to suggest I take your place . . . But I'm worried about you. Isn't there anything I can do to make you feel more comfortable?'

'No, I just need to lie down. It'll pass. It always does.' She pauses. 'And I prepaid for a meal at Rules. A special meal – a taster menu.'

'Can't you rearrange or get a refund?'

'No. It was a one-off. On offer. You must go with Miles and enjoy it.'

63

Hayley

'The opera was magnificent, wasn't it?' you say enthusiastically, looking particularly delicious this evening in a tightly cut black jacket lined with satin.

I've already admired it. Hugo Boss apparently. I hope you are impressed with the dress I'm wearing, recently purchased at New Look.

'*Tosca* is my favourite,' I tell you. 'My dad and I flew from New Zealand to Sydney Opera House to see it last year. For my eighteenth birthday.'

'That must have been awesome.'

'It was. And now this. Another special for my diary.'

'Mother booked the taster menu. Is that OK with you?'

'Yes.' I beam.

'It's quite a treat coming here. It's not exactly the sort of food that Saffron likes.'

Is this code? Is this a comment on your relationship?

The waiter approaches our red velvet booth, brandishing a bottle of wine. 'Would you like to try the first wine? It's a Joseph Drouhin Mâcon-Villages.'

'Yes, please.'

He pours some into your glass. You take a sip and nod. The waiter fills our glasses. Another waiter appears, with two plates on a silver tray.

'Your amuse-bouche: caviar and fennel, with red pepper and

creamed goat's cheese on a bed of savoury chilli shortbread.'

He waves each plate in the air before he places it in front of us. 'Compliments of the chef,' he announces twice.

We exchange glances and I bite my lip to suppress a giggle.

The wine and the amuse-bouche are exquisite. I have never eaten in as fine a restaurant as this. It's December, so Rules is already decorated for Christmas, and I have never been in a room as beautiful. Garlands of fir, decorated with red baubles and gold tinsel, are strewn across the ancient panelling. Red seating. Red carpet. I will describe every detail in my diary.

'Do you miss home?' you ask, resting your brown eyes on mine.

This is it. This is my big opportunity. If Caprice is right, and she seems so sure, so definite, I need to give you some encouragement. I take a deep breath.

'Not really. Not when I'm with you.'

A frown ripples across your forehead. 'Well, we do our best to make you welcome. We do enjoy having you living with our family.'

Are you pushing me away? What game are you playing?

'I'm so glad you do.'

Your eyes simmer into mine, and I feel emboldened. You've implied that you want me to stay in the UK on a number of occasions. Why would you do that if you aren't interested? You took me to Hampton Court Palace. You gave me the koala. I lean across the table and put my hand on your arm.

'Caprice told me you have feelings for me. I want you to know, I feel the same way.'

Your frown deepens and you shake your head. You remove my hand. 'Why would Mother think that – say that?'

My body is suffused with heat, and I know I am blushing. I put my hand to my face. It feels like a radiator. I wish the ground would swallow me up.

'But . . . but . . .' I splutter. 'She told me your marriage is a sham. That you are both unhappy. She said you look at me in a special way.'

'If you're developing a crush on me, you'll have to leave,' you reply, your face stiff with anger. 'We'll give you a good reference.' You shake your head. 'I'm very sorry if I've given you the wrong impression. I love Saffron very much. We are happy together. The only feelings I have for you are a paternal fondness. A fondness I have felt for all our nannies.'

64

Saffron

I'm back home after my evening out with Ted and Julie, floating around the kitchen, high on optimism and alcohol. We have been to the pub across the road from our office brainstorming ways to find new clients. My life is on the up. Then you breeze in, Caprice.

'How was your evening?' you ask with a wolfish smile.

'Good. It was lovely, thanks.' I pause. 'And yours?'

'I've been at home. I had a migraine.'

Migraine. The excuse you use, Caprice, when you want to get out of doing something.

'You poor thing. Are you feeling better now?'

'Yes. Thankfully,' you reply.

A short, sharp, convenient migraine. Just as they always are.

'So did Miles go to the opera alone?'

'He took Hayley.'

My insides bristle. 'So you were ill. Who was looking after the children, then?'

'Well, they're at a sleepover with the Chadwicks.'

I frown. 'You arranged a sleepover without telling me? And I could have changed my plans. Gone to the opera with Miles. Hayley could have had her evening off with Jono as usual.'

You shake your head. 'Saffron, when do you ever change your plans? Your diary is robotic.' Your voice is pinched. Waspish.

I breathe deeply to ignore your provocation. 'Can I get you anything?' I ask. 'Hot chocolate, lemon tea, milk with honey?'

A half-smile. 'Do you have camomile?'

'No, sorry.'

'Then I guess I'll have to make do with lemon.'

Make do. I put the kettle on, gritting my teeth. Since you married Rupert, when did you ever have to *make do* with anything? He was loaded. Was that why you fell in love with him?

'They're not back yet. They must be having fun. Hayley is *such* an attractive girl, isn't she? Nice she's having a wonderful treat. And Miles and Hayley get on so well together.'

Is that supposed to rile me? Fearing that my husband will run off with the attractive young nanny? How original, Caprice. You are losing your touch if you can't do better than that.

'By the way, Caprice,' I reply, 'what time should I pick up *my* children, tomorrow, from a family I know nothing about?'

'They're friends of mine, so I'll go.'

The kettle boils. I pour water onto the teabag and leave it to brew. 'You'd better get an early night to make sure you'll be well enough. If you want to go to bed I'll bring your tea up.'

'Thank you, dear.'

Dear. Incorrect as usual. Why does my stomach tighten every time you say it? At least you do as I suggest and leave to go upstairs. Five minutes later, as I am walking across the hallway with your tea, the front door opens.

Hayley and Miles are home, walking towards me. Hayley's face is covered in red blotches. Eyelids puffy. She must have been crying.

'What's happened?' I ask.

'Nothing,' Miles replies. 'We've had a lovely evening, haven't we, Hayley?'

'Yes. But I've got a bad bout of hay fever so I'll be straight off to bed.'

Hay fever? At 11 p.m., December, in Esher? Shoulders down, avoiding my gaze, she scuttles across the hallway.

'I'm knackered,' Miles says. 'I'm going straight to bed too.'

'I'll just take this tea to Caprice and then I'll join you.'

By the time I enter our bedroom, Miles is already in bed. All the lights are off. I undress in the bathroom and sidle into bed next to him. I reach for his hand and squeeze. He squeezes back.

'What happened?' I ask.

'Nothing much. Nothing to worry about. I'll tell you to-morrow evening.'

I don't sleep a wink all night, worrying about Caprice letting the boys go to a stranger's house overnight without telling me. Worrying about what she's up to now.

65

Miles

I hear you breathing shallowly next to me, Saffron, and I know you're not asleep. I know you want to talk. But I don't want an interrogation. I need privacy. Peace in which to think. What did I do to encourage Hayley? I'm a university professor, with students. What if I give them the wrong impression? I've already had a close call once. If it happened again, I could lose my job. And, Saffron, you would never forgive me. Is this Mother's fault, like Hayley suggested? No. I can't believe Mother would be the architect of this.

I want you to know I feel the same way.

What way? I want to scream and shout. Is Saffron right, Mother? Are you always trying to cause trouble between us? Do you hate my wife? But when I'm on my own with you, you always say nice things about her. On our wedding day you told me how pleased you were that I was marrying her.

The evening was a nightmare. After Hayley's revelation I said, 'Let's leave the restaurant – we shouldn't be having dinner together.'

Her face crumpled. 'But I've never been to a restaurant as beautiful as this. And Caprice has already paid the bill. Please, please, can we just pretend I didn't say anything?'

I shifted awkwardly on the velvet sofa. We stayed. Hayley, who hadn't managed her starter, suddenly reacquired her appetite. We ate oysters, roast monkfish, venison. Champagne and elderflower cheesecake. Each dish served with a glass of wine specially selected by the sommelier. Hayley disappeared to the bathroom twice, returning each time with a complexion redder and more blotchy.

At the end of the meal, over coffee and mints, she asked, 'What are you going to do? Are you going to insist I leave?' She paused. 'Are you really going to sack me?'

I looked her in the eye. 'I'm going to tell Saffron. See what she thinks.'

'Please don't,' Hayley begged. 'If she knows, she will definitely want me to go. And I really want to stay.'

'There are lots of jobs out there, and we'll give you a good reference. Don't you think it would be difficult from now on with this, er . . . awkwardness between us?'

'I won't make it awkward. Now I know you're not interested I'll forget about you immediately. I'm a good nanny. Saffron trusts me. Caprice caused this trouble.' She shrugged. 'Why let her rock the boat? I have a boyfriend anyway. You would have been a complication.'

I sat sipping my coffee, unsure of what to say. We all know about Jono. None of us think she is serious about him. Her eyes filled with tears. About to cry again. I felt so sorry for her. It must have been my fault, leading her on by mistake, by being too kind to her. Just like it happened with Kirsty; a slow student whom I was trying to help. She mistook kindness for passion. Hayley is young too. Hayley is innocent. Am I the culpable one?

Guilt and worry tangle together inside me, as I lie next to my wife, thinking about what happened.

'I shouldn't have blown it,' Hayley continued. 'I love Ben and Harry. They are my favourite sort of children. Old enough to hold a proper conversation, and they're so sweet and funny. You and Saffron are such kind people to work for, and Esher is a dream location. My accommodation is incredible.'

She dropped her head into her hands, snivelling, as I checked

Caprice's tab for the bill. I heard her promise 'I'll never pester you again,' several times between sobs.

'Let's talk about it tomorrow evening,' I said. I wanted to sleep on it. I needed time to decide how to deal with this. Dealing with young women obviously isn't my strong point.

Eyes were on us as we left the restaurant. She was crying so much, I couldn't face public transport, so we took a taxi. She cried all the way home while the taxi driver gave me dark looks through the rear-view mirror.

'Is the young lady all right?' he asked.

'She's fine,' I replied, voice tight.

And now, as moonlight slices towards me around the edges of our bedroom curtains, Hayley's words twist and tumble towards me. Favourite sort of children. Sweet and funny. Kind employers. Dream location. Incredible accommodation. I have confused and misled her.

She is a lovely girl who must stay working for us. I determine to handle this with discretion.

66

Hayley

I'm lying in bed, unable to sleep. An owl hoots in the distance. I stand up, open the curtains and look out of the window. It's a full moon, bright and bold in the shadowy sky.

Caprice, were you lying to me? How could you encourage me to make such a fool of myself? Why have you made me spoil my opportunity of working in this environment? I thought we were friends. Why did you play me? Why did I listen? Why did I tell Miles how I felt about him? I should have judged the situation for myself.

67

Miles

After a day at work, unable to concentrate on anything but what I've done to encourage our nanny, I give up pretending to work and go home early. I find Mother sitting at the table in the kitchen with Ben and Harry, drinking a cup of tea and nibbling a Welsh cake. She beams across at me as I stand in the doorway. The children are tucking into chicken nuggets and chips, laden with ketchup. That's all they seem to eat these days, when Mother is looking after them. They are so busy eating they don't look up.

'Miles, how lovely to see you home early.' There is a pause. 'To what do we owe the pleasure?'

'Where's Hayley?' I reply.

Mother's smile broadens. 'She asked for the afternoon off. Said she needed to do some admin.'

I frown. 'Admin. I see.'

Should I confront her about what she said to Hayley? No. Surely Hayley was making it up to cover her embarrassment? Maybe? Maybe not? I can't face an argument with Mother right now. As I pour myself a cup of tea and join them at the table, I worry that Hayley is preparing to fly home. About to complain about me to the agency.

'Well, thanks for taking over, Mother.'

'Anything I can do to help.'

When my mother and my sons have finished eating, I suggest we watch a film, or a cartoon. Something, anything, to pass the time until Hayley gets back, and I can make things right with her.

'Would you like to watch *Cinderella*?' I ask them.

'Boring.'

'*Frozen*?'

'Don't be silly, Daddy.'

'*Bambi*?'

'No. It makes Mummy cry.'

I look across at Mother for help. '*Kung Fu Panda 3*?' she suggests.

'Yes, please,' the boys shriek with excitement.

We meander into the playroom and switch on the TV. The film begins to play. Po, the lead character, is a cartoon panda, fat and ugly with a harsh American accent. The pandas eat noodles and crack obvious American jokes. It's so boring I wish I could fall asleep. But the oblivion of sleep doesn't release me. Where's Hayley? Why isn't she home yet? Saffron has texted. She's stuck at work, preparing a sample portfolio for a prospective client.

Mother and I suffer to the end of the film, bath the boys, and put them to bed. She slips off to her room to relax. I look at my watch: 9 p.m. If Hayley is out for the evening she won't be back for hours. Neither will Saffron. I'm bored. I don't know what to do with myself. I want to fast-forward time, speak to Hayley, speak to Saffron, have a good night's sleep and go to college refreshed tomorrow morning. Back to normal. To get on with my work.

At last, a key turns in the front door. I step into the hallway. It's Hayley, wearing a miniskirt and razorblade heels.

'Good evening.'

'Good evening,' she replies, embarrassed, eyes on the ground.

'Can we talk?' I ask.

She nods her head.

'In the kitchen?'

157

She leads the way. We stand face to face by the kettle.

'I've been thinking . . .' I begin. 'You're right. You are a very good nanny. I'm sorry if I've misled you, or confused you in any way. You must stay.'

68

Hayley

'You must stay.'

I exhale with relief. I put my arms around you and hug you. Then I pull back.

'Sorry. I shouldn't have done that.'

'Just make sure it doesn't happen again,' you say, voice and eyes sharp.

69

Saffron

I return from work late, padding across the hallway, towards the kitchen, to make a vegan snack. There'll be some spinach and butternut soup left from supper. And some pomegranate, hazelnut and asparagus salad. I'm not really hungry. But I know I'm worrying so much about BPC that I'm losing weight. I was skinny anyway, so I must force myself to eat. I open the kitchen door.

Hayley and Miles are hugging, in the corner by the kettle. Entwined together like lovelorn teenagers.

Anger ricochets through my body. I close the kitchen door and creep away, upstairs to our bedroom. I can't bear to see my husband touching someone else like that. Now I know how he must have felt when he caught me kissing Aiden. I undress, clean my teeth and slip between our Egyptian cotton sheets, waiting for him to join me. We need a serious talk.

Half an hour later Miles enters the room. I sit up and snap the light on.

'Oh, Saffron, I didn't know you were back.' He blinks, pushes his hair back from his eyes, and smiles at me.

'Obviously you didn't, otherwise you wouldn't have behaved like that.'

'Like what?'

'I opened the kitchen door and saw you.' I take a deep breath. 'With Hayley.'

Miles' face crumples in embarrassment. 'I can explain. It was a platonic hug.'

'Go on then. Explain.'

'She's attracted to me.'

I raise my eyes to the sky. 'You don't say.' I pause. 'Look, Miles, lots of women are attracted to you. You need to learn to deal with it. It's already happened at college. It won't be the last time.'

'I found her attention difficult to cope with last night. As soon as she was alone with me at the restaurant, she came on to me. I was furious with her. Told her I would sack her. She was so upset. And then she blamed Mother.'

I try not to raise my eyebrows sarcastically. 'Really? What did she say your mother had to do with it?'

'Hayley said Mother told her she thought I had feelings for her and that our marriage was in difficulty. Surely Mother wouldn't say anything like that?'

Anger starts to build in the pit of my stomach. How can he think Caprice wouldn't do that, after the trouble she has just caused over Julie? Why is he so blind to the foibles of his mother? Why can't he see how much she hates me? How much she wants to get rid of me?

'Miles, when will you accept that your mother is perfectly capable of behaving like that?'

'Please, Saffron, let's not argue about Mother right now. I've got enough to handle over Hayley. I'm trying to explain what has happened, why I decided to let her stay.'

I raise my shoulders. 'How you *decided*, without mentioning a word to me?'

'I was about to,' he protests. 'And tonight I told Hayley I wouldn't sack her as I'd originally threatened. So she hugged me.'

'When were you going to tell me?' I shout, opening the bedroom door, and stepping onto the landing. I need some space. I need to get away from him.

'This evening,' he shouts back, the veins in his temples pulsating as he follows me. 'But you came home so late.'

'I saw you together. Do you expect me to believe you?' I slap him in the face.

He reels back, and catches his balance. 'It's true, so I *do* expect you to believe me,' he says, rubbing his face with his hand.

'This time, you're the one who's eroded the trust between us.'

70

Hayley

I'm lying on sumptuous silk, listening to you arguing with your wife. Why is Saffron fighting with you, Miles? Did she see us in the kitchen, when you were only being reassuring and kind? My stomach contracts. Will she make sure I lose my job? If I do, I haven't even got a return ticket to fly home. I've no savings left to keep me going if I'm not earning. Maybe I could take Jono up on his offer, and go to live in his squat.

71

Caprice

The argument I have waited so long to hear is finally ripping across our landing. I smile to myself. I step out of my bedroom and lean down over the banister. I see you swiping your hand across my son's face. There is only so much a man can put up with. Being slapped in the face by a difficult woman is one step too far.

You'll soon be gone, you selfish skinny bitch. You won't get away with this.

72

Miles

I am standing on the landing, face stinging after you have slapped me. Suddenly I am looking at the scene as if from a distance. An aerial view. A photograph. Every time we row, Mother has something to do with it. Hayley caused trouble. Hayley mentioned Mother. Aiden caused trouble. Aiden mentioned Mother. Julie was the centre of the last problem and she definitely blamed Mother. Mother, Mother, Mother, who has always doted on me too much. Maybe I should have listened to you about my mother years ago, Saffron. Maybe it is my mother who is tearing our relationship apart.

'Come on, let's get back into our bedroom,' I tell her. 'Everyone can hear us. We'll wake the boys up next.'

You stand firm, eyes like granite. 'Why should I do what you say?'

I take a deep breath. 'Come on, Saffron. Let me explain. I can assure you I'm telling the truth. It isn't what you think.'

You stand eyeballing me as if you hate me. 'Saffron, I love you. Please give me another chance to explain.'

'OK, OK.'

You walk across the landing and step back into our room. I follow you and close the door. My stomach contracts in embarrassment. Everyone in the house must have been woken up and listening.

You turn towards me, eyes spitting. 'Go on then, explain why you were caressing our nanny.'

'I wasn't caressing her. That's inflammatory.'

'What were you doing then?'

'Hayley has a crush on me, and Mother must have noticed. I think you're right. She must have lied and told Hayley she thought I had feelings for her too. To cause trouble between us. To hurt you.'

'So you're finally admitting your mother has done something wrong?'

I bite my lip. 'Yes, Saffron, I am.' I pause. 'And Mother must have contrived for Hayley and me to be alone, with yet another of her blasted headaches. Hayley then tried it on with me. I rejected her. I threatened to dismiss her, but she was so upset, I decided to give her another chance.'

'And the hug?'

'I've told you already, she hugged me in relief. She didn't want to lose her job.'

166

73

Saffron

'Just admit your mother is a prize bitch who has caused a lot of trouble and I'll forget about it,' I tell him.

'It's true, Saffron. Mother has been a prize bitch.' Miles swallows quickly, as if he's choking on his words.

I shake my head. 'It's not a one-off. Tell the truth. You have got to face facts: she *is* a prize bitch.'

He steps towards me. 'She *is* a prize bitch,' he repeats, voice stronger this time.

I gesticulate for him to come closer. 'Let's go to bed. You can listen to *Tosca* with me.'

74

Miles

'Now you can listen to *Tosca* with me.'

You press the Sonos controller. Maria Callas' voice floats around our bedroom.

You perform a striptease in front of me. Slowly, provocatively, dancing to the opera and removing your clothing.

75

Caprice

Opera music blasts from Miles and Saffron's bedroom. What are they doing making so much noise at this time of night? They need to turn it down or they'll wake the boys. I put my dressing gown on and walk across the landing. I knock on the door. No reply. But I can hear heavy breathing. Breathing. Gasping. Screaming.

'I love you, Saffron.'

More screaming.

Disgusting. Like feral animals. I pad back to my room. I'll talk to them about this in the morning.

76

Hayley

Breakfast time. The boys race into the kitchen.

'Tie your laces,' I snap. 'And tuck in your shirts.'

Caprice, sitting with a plate of cracked eggshells in front of her, nods in approval. I lay the table as the boys tidy themselves up.

'Can I get you anything?' I ask Caprice.

'A cup of camomile tea, please.'

I make her brew.

'Thank you. That's a pleasant surprise. I didn't know we had any,' Caprice says, as I hand it to her.

'Saffron bought some last week.'

I sit at the table and begin to eat my granola. Miles and Saffron enter the kitchen holding hands, and Caprice's body stiffens. I feel hot and know I'm blushing. Seeing Miles, so lovey-dovey with his wife, so soon after my faux pas, is beyond embarrassing. I watch Saffron making her usual bright green smoothie, whisking it with spinach in the liquidiser. At least she is behaving normally. Miles helps himself to muesli, avoiding eye contact with me. Saffron decants her concoction into a large insulated cup and comes to sit next to me.

'Can we talk? Miles is going to take the children to school, so now would be good.'

My stomach curdles. This is it. She is going to fire me.

I take a deep breath, stretch my mouth into a tense smile, and reply, 'Yes. Of course.'

'Let's go and sit in the drawing room,' she suggests, as she stands up, smoothie in hand.

We settle ourselves in antique walnut chairs either side of the white marble fireplace. In this room, which drips with antiques: walnut coffee tables, a crystal chandelier, Indian rugs. A photograph of a young Saffron on the mantelpiece. Thick quirky glasses, even then.

She takes a sip of her smoothie. 'I just wanted you to know how much I appreciate your work here. I'm sorry there has been a misunderstanding. I trust you. I trust Miles. So let's move forwards and forget this. I hope you'll continue to be happy with our family.'

I look into her ice blue eyes. 'Thank you, Saffron.'

At this moment I'm not sure who I love most. Miles or Saffron.

77

Saffron

It's true that you are a real prize bitch, Caprice. First making out that I'm unfaithful, then that Miles is. There is no limit to how low you will stoop to destroy our relationship. Now there is no limit to how much I hate you.

78

Caprice

I'm sitting in my bedroom, when there is a knock on the door.
'Come in.'

Miles' head appears around the door. 'Hey, Mother, do you
have time for a chat?'

I smile my best smile. The one Rupert always loved. When I
smiled like that he would pull me towards him and hug me. My
stomach lurches as I remember his touch.

'All the time in the world for you,' I say. 'You know that.
Always have. Always will.'

He steps inside. Casual today. Jeans. White T-shirt. Such a good-
looking man. So talented. He could have done anything he wanted.
He is musical too. He can sing. Play the guitar. I always imagined
him as a lead singer in a band. With his large eyes and well-balanced
face he has a look of Simon Le Bon about him. How the fans
would have swooned. But he's buried in academia now.

He sits in my floral armchair and folds his arms.

'I'm fed up with you trying to come between me and Saffron.'
His words pierce into me.

'Whatever do you mean?' I ask, wounded. 'I do everything I
can to help this family.'

'You told her I love Julie.' He pauses. 'You told Hayley I have
feelings for her. You insinuate that Saffron is unfaithful.' Another
pause, longer this time. Angry eyes stabbing into mine. 'What
are you trying to do?'

'Being honest. Saying what I think. Honesty is what makes a family. There are three important rules about family life. Communication, communication and communication. Honesty is intrinsic to that.'

'Oh shut up, Mother. You sound like Tony Blair talking about education. It's a repetitive sound bite that doesn't work. It's not communication or honesty. It's lying and destructive.'

My stomach knots. Miles has never spoken to me like this before. 'I'm not a liar. How dare you accuse me of that.'

'Let's put it this way, you're not telling the truth.'

I shake my head. 'It's the truth as I perceive it.'

He laughs. 'If you're wanting a philosophical diatribe about truth and perception, I can give you one, I assure you.'

'I bet you can. But I won't listen.'

He clenches his fist. 'If you try and come between Saffron and me again, I'll . . . I'll . . .'

'You'll what? Kick me out? You can't. I own a large chunk of this house. It's my home.'

'Saffron and I can move to somewhere smaller with you out of our lives.'

'You wouldn't be so cruel. You always promised your father you would look after me if I lived longer than him.'

I put my head in my hands and cry. As I cry, I watch his reaction through the tiny gap in between my fingers. His eyes grow softer the harder I weep. He stands up and walks towards me, face riddled with concern. He pats my back.

'Look, Mother, I'm sure it won't come to that. But please, please, stop causing trouble. I love Saffron. Nothing you can do will tear us apart.'

Miles leaves my room, closing the door softly behind him. I sit up, dry-eyed, and smile. Nothing? Saffron isn't looking after you properly. Of course my next plan will work.

79

Hayley

I'm sitting in Jono's squat, drinking cider, watching him wolf down pie and chips from the takeaway on the corner. It is weird how much he eats and yet he is so thin. His stomach is a bottomless pit. He wipes away the grease from his mouth with the back of his hand.

'Did you fall asleep at the opera with that dickhead? I bet it was a real snore.'

I shake my head. 'I like opera, actually.'

He grimaces. 'Oh, Little Miss La-Di-Dah.'

'What does that mean?'

'Snobby. Up yourself.'

'Do I need to like grunge or death metal to live up to your high musical standards?' I snort.

He grins. 'Yes.'

He reaches across to his iPhone and selects a track from his playlist. 'Break Stuff' by Limp Bizkit pounds out.

'Come on, Hayley, dance with me. I'll show you how to have a good time.'

He pulls me towards him and vibrates to the music, banging his feet on the floor, punching his fists in the air. I gyrate with him, the damp smell of the squat sharpening in my nostrils. They say the sense of smell is the most rapidly adapting sense. That your brain blanks out smells when it is used to them. But my nose hasn't adapted to the stench in this abandoned flat yet. I distract myself by mimicking Jono's foot stamping and air punches. When the track finishes we collapse, laughing, onto his soggy mattress. We rip off each other's clothing. We fuck. Short but not sweet. The usual thing these days. Magnificent orgasm for him. Nothing for me.

Pushing rope-like legs back into his drainpipe trousers, Jono says, 'I just don't want that nancy boy getting any ideas, taking my girl to the opera, wining and dining her and impressing her.'

'Well,' I reply, sarcastically, 'he has a lot to compete with.'

'Sometimes you are such a bitch, Hayley Manville Smith.'

80

Miles

It's Christmas Day. The turkey is in the oven and your nut loaf, with spinach and cranberry, is gently wafting the scent of garlic and ginger around the house. Our favourite Christmas compilation track blasts cheerily from the Sonos. I'm glad Aiden is away at his villa in Barbados. I wasn't in the mood to spend the festive season with him this year.

Bubbles in our glasses, we sit in the drawing room, to open the presents Santa Claus left late last night. His reindeer ate the carrots Ben, Harry and I scattered in the garden. We found their remnants half chewed up on the doorstep this morning. The whisky and mince pies the boys left for Santa in the hallway had also been enjoyed.

'No wonder Santa's so fat, Daddy,' Harry said, 'if he eats and drinks that much at every house.'

Despite his wide girth, Santa managed to squeeze down our chimney and arrange the presents beneath our carefully decorated tree. The tree you and I spent hours fussing over. A real tree of course. We have a real tree every year, and decorate it with unusual silver and gold ornaments, all individually designed.

Mother puts her champagne glass on the mantelpiece. 'Let's get the boys' presents out first.' She bends beneath the tree and starts to pull them out. Ben rips his first gift open. A magic set from Santa. His eyes light up with excitement.

'This afternoon I'm going to give you a show,' he says grinning widely, displaying his gappy teeth.

Harry's next, squealing with delight as he opens a walking, talking robot. He winds it up and it begins to walk across the drawing room threatening to kill us. Mother's lips tighten in disapproval. The presents for the children go on and on. Gravitrax. Lego. More Lego. A Harry Potter knight bus. A David Walliams box set. A telescope. A duelling Stomp Rocket. A baseball bat.

Hayley, who was only too delighted to accept our invitation to spend Christmas with us, as she would have been alone otherwise, is wearing a Christmas jumper and flashing reindeer antlers. I'm not sure she is keen enough on Jono to want to spend Christmas with him, but she didn't have the option. He has gone to Scotland on his motorbike with a daredevil friend whom she disapproves of. If he is worse than Jono, he must be bad. She is stepping around presents and discarded wrapping paper, taking photographs of the children on her iPhone.

You are resplendent in a red silk and lace minidress, so flimsy it could be a nightie, sipping champagne and watching our sons, a smile playing on your lips. Since I had words with Mother this house has been so much more peaceful. It feels like a different place.

'Adults now. Hayley first,' Mother insists, brandishing a yellow Selfridges bag in the air. 'Here you are, my dear,' she says, handing it to Hayley and hugging her.

'Thank you so much. I wasn't expecting you to give me a present.'

'It's my pleasure, for a lovely girl.'

Hayley sits on the sofa and opens it. A Chanel Coco Mademoiselle box set. Perfume. Talc. Soap. Body lotion. The works.

'It's wonderful, thank you.'

'And now you, Miles.' My mother steps towards me and hugs me. She hands me my present from her. I open the gift-wrapped package, tight with ribbons and bows. A Brora cashmere jumper, so soft, slips out. 'Thank you, Mother. It's beautiful.'

'And now you, Saffron,' Mother says, walking towards the tree. She reaches behind the tree and drags out a large present. She attempts to lift it but doesn't manage, and stands rubbing her back.

'Can I help you, Mother?'

'Yes, please, dear.'

I lift the box and hand it to you. It isn't very heavy. Maybe Mother should go to yoga or Pilates to build her strength up. You open your present. A Kenwood cake mixer.

You look across at Mother and smile. 'Thank you very much, Caprice.'

'I know you don't bake, or eat cake. But you've got to start looking after this family sometime.'

You don't say anything, Saffron, but I see the pain in your eyes. And I know the battle has begun again.

81

Saffron

I've got to start looking after this family sometime, have I?

We are sitting in the dining room, having just pulled the crackers I went into Harrods to choose specially. Eating a meal that I cooked for you animal eaters, even though I am vegan. Turkey with apricot and plum, and chestnut stuffing. Homemade cranberry sauce. You have a choice of red wine jus or gravy. I have also provided devils-on-horseback, bread sauce, croquette and lyonnaise potatoes. Roast potatoes. Sprouts with almonds. Carrots in orange sauce and roast parsnips. The wine, which I also chose, is perfect. A rich burgundy. Gevrey Chamberlin 1er Cru Les Champeaux 2003.

Wait until you see the cheese course, and the desserts I have made. And what about all the money I have earnt over the years to support your son and grandsons? Miles' career is just a hobby.

And I have to start looking after the family sometime?

82

Hayley

Saffron is in such a bad mood that she went to bed straight after lunch. Maybe Caprice is right about Saffron and Miles' relationship. Caprice has insisted that she clears the dishes whilst Miles and I play with the children. I started to help, but she waved me away and insisted that she did it alone. So I'm back in the drawing room with Miles, Ben and Harry. Ben is sitting reading the instruction booklet for his box of magic tricks, frowning as he reads, a silky handkerchief and a wand balanced on his knees. Miles and I are helping Harry build his Lego quadrocopter. It's very tricky. We are lying on the drawing room floor, heads together, puzzling over the instructions.

I glance across at Miles' face, deep in concentration, and my stomach rotates. We are so comfortable together. How can he be completely happy with Saffron, when they have so many bitter arguments? The truth is I haven't got over him yet. One day, perhaps, I will finally have a chance.

83

Caprice

Boxing Day, 6 a.m. My back was aching so much all night that I couldn't sleep. Now I'm feeling peaky in the kitchen, brewing coffee. Hoping it will pep me up. Hoping it will help me cope with the day. My morning is not helped by you walking towards me, Saffron, wearing your mini-bathrobe and Ugg slippers. I don't think you should leave your bedroom without getting dressed. It makes you look slovenly. I guess you weren't properly brought up and that is why you are so nonchalant with your own children.

I know it must have been hard for you, being brought up by a single parent. An irresponsible young woman who had allowed herself to get knocked up when she was still in her teens. Even though I also came from a simple background, at least I had two parents who loved each other. I had stability and that is why I am a loving homemaker, in contrast to your coldness.

You haven't even said good morning to me. You never notice me, do you? Pushing your hair back from your eyes as you approach the kettle, you finally condescend to say, 'Oh, hello, Caprice.'

Well done, Saffron. You've acknowledged me for once.

I smile a tight smile. 'Good morning. I've just made coffee. Would you like some?'

'Yes, please.'

I pour you a cup, and hand it to you. You blink sleepily, and start to leave the kitchen. 'Please join me, dear. Sit down. I've got something to show you.'

You turn around and frown, as if joining me is the last thing you want to do. But you do as I request and sit down next to me. I whip my iPhone from my pocket and open my photos. My picture of Hayley and Miles embracing fills the screen. I took it the night after their opera treat. If she asks, I was by the kitchen window, on the way to water the hibiscus I had just planted, when I had my photo opportunity. But the truth is, I was hovering, warmly dressed outside – hoping to catch them together. And I've had it Photoshopped a bit.

'Look at this, dear.'

You take the phone from me and sit studying the photograph. Your lips begin to tremble. And then your fingers. Your face reddens. You turn towards me.

'I know what you did. This is all your plotting, Caprice. What a stupid ploy to resort to the same trick again. I know this was a stitch-up.'

I smile slowly. 'Trick? Stitch-up?' I laugh, a sharp little laugh.

'Yes. It was a hug of friendship.'

My smile widens. 'Do you really believe that? Why don't you look at the photograph more closely?'

84

Saffron

'Look at the photograph more closely,' you say, curving your lips into a thin contemptuous smile.

I stand up and throw your iPhone to the floor. I watch it smash against designer travertine. I move towards you, press my fingers around your throat, and shake you.

'If you behave like this again, it will be you I smash to pieces, not your phone,' I spit.

85

Caprice

I don't know whether to laugh or cry. It's going to be a nuisance sorting out a new iPhone. But, Saffron, wait until I tell Miles you have assaulted me. Bruises on my neck and the remnants of my iPhone as evidence against you. Your intense reaction is far more than I could have hoped for.

86

Saffron

In the privacy of our bedroom, Miles is pushing concerned eyes into mine.

'What happened?' he asks. 'What's Mother done, this time? She told me you'd smashed her iPhone, and attacked her.'

'And did she tell you why?'

'Of course not. That's why I'm asking.'

I tell him, and as I tell him I burst into tears and cry. 'I just can't cope with any more of this. She'll have to move out.'

'But, she's old. She's lonely. She's vulnerable.'

Her contemptuous smile sears across my mind. My ears fill with her comments. I shake my head. 'About as vulnerable as a hippopotamus.'

'Are they vulnerable?'

I laugh. 'No. They're the deadliest of all mammalian man-killers.'

'Are you saying my mother is a killer?' he asks.

'Well, she's certainly killing me.'

Miles frowns. 'Look, why don't we get away for a break? Just us and the boys. We could go skiing for a week, leave Mother behind.'

'A week is nowhere near long enough. I need her to go. I want her to move out,' I hiss.

'Back into the annex?'

'No. To another house.'

Miles puts his head in his hands. 'But . . . but . . . I can't, Saffron, she's my mother. I have to look after her for the rest of her life. She's lost my dad. She needs our support.'

'What about me?'

'I love you both. I have to look after both of you.'

I shake my head. 'You can't have us both. One of us will have to go.'

Miles looks crestfallen. 'I just can't ask my mother to leave.'

He goes downstairs. To spend time with the children? Or to speak to Caprice? I'm too depressed to care.

I curl into a ball and fall asleep. I slip into my constantly recurring dream. The dream that seems real, and so familiar. We walk into the church. It is Caprice's funeral. I stand staring at the silver cross on the altar, transfixed. It rotates towards me, becoming larger and larger. I wake with a jolt. For a second I feel relief that my nemesis is dead. Then I remember. She's alive. With a smashed iPhone, and bruises around her neck, caused by me.

She'll be around for all my life unless I kill her. If I don't kill her, being near her will kill me.

87

Caprice

'Hayley, do come for a walk in the garden with me.'

'Good idea – I could do with a break from my chores. Thank you.'

I link my arm in hers. We walk down the passage, through the trees, and step into my garden.

'It's still colourful and it's almost into January. The worst month for garden colour,' Hayley exclaims.

'Well, I do know a thing or two about plants,' I reply.

I point out Viburnum, and Sarcococca. Sweet-smelling Lonicera climbing up the fence.

'Look at those fuzzy felt-like firecrackers. What are they?' Hayley asks.

'Hamamelis.'

'And the pretty star-shaped pinks?'

'Daphne bholua, Jacqueline Postill.'

We sit in our usual spot, on the bench beneath the weeping willow. It's mild for January, but grey. Misty grey sky with Brillo pad clouds. Drizzle hanging in the air, making my skin feel damp, even though it isn't raining.

'I'm worried about Saffron,' I start.

'Oh, why?' Hayley asks.

'There's been another incident.'

I roll the collar of my jacket down and show her the bruises on my neck.

She inhales sharply. 'Saffron did that?'

'She put her fingers around my neck and tightened them.'

Hayley sits, eyes wide with concern. I reach into my jacket pocket and pull out the plastic bag containing the remnants of my iPhone.

I swing it in front of her face. 'And this is what she did to my phone.'

'Tell me what happened exactly.'

'I said something that seemed to annoy her. Nothing much. I had just made her a cup of coffee and was telling her about my plans for the garden. Where I was thinking of planting some Hostas. Showing her a photo of the flowerbed on my phone. She began to shout – saying how much she hated me living here and was fed up with me taking over the garden. The next thing I knew she grabbed it from my hands and stamped up and down on it, smiling maliciously.' I pause for breath. 'Then when it was destroyed she grabbed my neck and tried to throttle me.'

'Why on earth did she behave like that?'

'Well, I've seen her slap Miles. She's just violent.'

'If she slapped Miles I expect she was provoked.'

I tighten my lips. 'Well, I didn't do anything to provoke her.' I pause. 'I screamed and shouted until she stopped. I can look after myself . . . It's the children I'm worried about.'

Hayley shakes her head in consternation. 'I'm shocked, but I can assure you I've only ever seen her behave with patience and kindness towards the children.'

Seeing that I need to try another tack, I put my hand on her arm. 'I'm just asking you to keep an eye out for any unusual behaviour, that's all. I mean, if she's secretly having a breakdown, she'll need our help, won't she?'

88

Saffron

Ted steps into my office more casually dressed than usual, wearing a two-piece rather than a three-piece suit.

'How's it going?' I ask.

He smiles. 'Not bad, not bad. Eight more months of the bank loan to tide us over. I'm impressed by the list of potential new clients you're planning to target.'

I grimace. 'I didn't do well with Joshua Cassidy.'

He leans towards me. 'Saffron, we only need to catch one.'

'It hurt me, what he said in the email, about wanting someone younger, more dynamic.'

He shrugs and twists his hands so that his palms face the ceiling. 'You win some and you lose some. You mustn't be so sensitive.'

'Talking about sensitive, I need your help with something which is just that.'

'Come on, Saffron. That's fine. We've known each other forever. Try me.'

I stir uncomfortably in my chair. 'I need to know how to use the darknet.'

He stiffens. 'Whatever for?'

'It's embarrassing.'

'Try me.'

'I want to buy some fetish stuff for Miles and me. I don't want the family to ever find out.'

Ted's eyes shine with curiosity. My stomach tightens.

'I do know a bit about it,' he replies. 'I enjoyed my master's in computer science, before I took the plunge and became an accountant. My friend Stan, from the course, is quite a whizz kid, I talk to him about the darknet sometimes.'

'I know you have connections. That's why I asked. I just don't ever want anyone to know about this. I'm so embarrassed. I need to know how to cover my tracks.'

'Why do you need to do that? Why can't you get fetish gear from "normal" sources? It's quite mainstream these days.'

'If Caprice found out, she'd make out I was a pervert. She's always got it in for me. You know that.'

'I can put you in touch with Stan, about covering your tracks. He makes a lot of money on the side, helping people to navigate the darknet. He's a wealthy man in fact.'

I lean across and take his hand. I hold his eyes with mine. 'Thank you.'

'I think it's actually much simpler than people think. You just need Tor encryption to enter it. I'll get in touch with Stan so that he can send you the link. He'll be able to show you how to use it and remain undetectable. But you won't know who you're dealing with.' He pauses. 'And it's a nasty world out there.'

'I'm capable of looking after myself.'

He stands up, leans across my desk and kisses me gently on the cheek. 'Be careful, Saffron. You're my dear friend. You're precious to me.'

89

Hayley

It's February half-term, and Saffron has taken a week off to spend time with Ben and Harry. And even though she has given me the week off too, today she is taking Ben and Harry to London Zoo, and I've asked to go with them, to help. That way Saffron pays for my ticket and my lunch. I will be able to take loads of photos of the oldest zoo in the world and send them back home. My mum has been pestering me to send some photographs of London for a while. London is somewhere she always wanted to visit, but never got the opportunity. And of course I'll be writing a blow-by-blow account for her in my diary.

After today I'm going to spend the rest of the week with Jono. He's promised to take me to both the cinema and the theatre. And to Nando's in Walton-on-Thames. Hardly Rules of Covent Garden with its intimate private booths and uniformed doorman. But at least it is something to do.

But today, Monday 19th February, at London Zoo we are starting with the reptile house. Taking a photo outside. Ben and Harry jumping up and down with excitement. We have watched an old clip of the *Magic Roundabout*, so they're pretending to be Zebedee. 'Boing, boing,' they shout as they jump.

'Let's see the spiders first,' Harry insists.

I shudder inside.

'It's a walk-through exhibit,' Saffron explains as she stands engrossed in the zoo's brochure.

'I'll give it a miss then,' I try.

'No. No,' Harry says. 'You've got to come with me. I want to hold your hand, Hayley.'

Saffron looks at me with concern. 'Don't make her if she doesn't want to.'

'Please. Please, Hayley, please.'

'OK,' I say, trying to push my fear of spiders away. But who can refuse the request of an angelic young child? I mustn't communicate my dread to him. Harry holds my hand tightly. His hand in mine emboldens me. Ben attaches himself to Saffron's. We step inside and are surrounded by ugly pulpy bodies and dangling legs. Some spiders are behind glass. Some are lying in webs which almost brush against our faces. I want to scream. I wince and step back.

A young zookeeper, in a smart beige uniform, walks towards me. 'The spiders in the open are completely docile. They never leave their webs. They're totally harmless to humans. We would never let them roam like this if there was any danger.'

He walks along with us to reassure me. The children seem totally unconcerned.

'Look at the social spiders – this is their house,' he says, pointing to a big wobbly mess of spider silk, clumped together like a mass of ripped-up plastic. 'They are amongst the most unusual spiders in the world. They live together, and even bring up their young together.' We stand looking through the glass into their 'house'. A palpitating mass of spongy bodies writhing together.

'Onwards and forwards,' the zookeeper says with a cheery smile, walking us past a display bathroom. A big black hairy spider appears from the plughole. The sort I most particularly hate.

'Harry, please stay with your mum for a few minutes. I need some fresh air.'

I rush through the rest of the exhibit and step outside. I

breathe deeply. Inhale. Exhale. Fresh air as exquisite as the best champagne. After a while Saffron, Harry and Ben join me.

'We've seen all the spiders now. We're off to see the rest of the reptile house. Please, please come with us.'

Snakes, crocodiles, lizards. Exotic creatures with scaly skin and cold dead eyes. Flashing forked tongues that smell of poison and devilry. Flashing forked tongues that make me tremble inside.

The boys love them. 'Mummy, mummy, can we have them as pets? A snake and a lizard?'

'No way. Hayley would leave us if we frightened her with a scaly pet, and we don't want that, do we?'

'No, Mummy.' They stand looking up at Saffron, shaking their heads.

'Come on,' I say, keen to leave this area. 'Let's go to the gorilla house.'

Gorilla Kingdom is a colony of six western lowland gorillas. A father, mother and four offspring. So hauntingly like humans, with the mother and father caring and children playing.

'This type of gorilla is critically endangered in the wild,' Saffron reads from the brochure.

As we step away, Harry trips and grazes his knee. Saffron wraps her arms around him and hugs him as tears stream down his cheeks.

'Kiss it better, Mummy, please.'

She kneels down and kisses his bleeding knee, so, so, gently. One touch from her lips and he feels better. His tears dry instantly. He beams a sunny smile at her and skips off to join Harry, who is standing engrossed by the tiger enclosure.

How can Saffron possibly be a woman who could hurt her children? All I ever see is love.

90

Caprice

'Granny,' Harry says.

'Don't call me that,' I tell him for the millionth time. My younger grandson has the memory of a goldfish.

'Sorry.' He pauses. 'Why have you got a dog cage? Are we getting a puppy?'

'No. We're playing a game.'

'What is it, Caprice?' my elder grandson wants to know.

'You both take your clothes off, get in the cage, and then pretend to cry. The one who cries the most wins the prize.'

'What's the prize?' they ask, almost in unison.

I show them the stash of sweets and chocolate in my carrier bag. Cadbury's Dairy Milk. Rolo. Twix. Mars Bars. Snickers. Haribo Tangfastics. Gummy bears. Starmix. Giant sour suckers. All their favourites. Whichever one wins, I know they will share.

'And then can we go to McDonald's for lunch?' Ben tries.

'Of course,' I reply with a smile.

91

Hayley

I'm sitting beneath the weeping willow with Caprice, snowdrops tilting their teardrop heads towards us. The first crocuses are beginning to show.

'There's something you need to look at,' Caprice says, pulling her iPhone from her pocket.

She taps her phone so that a photograph spreads across the screen, then hands it to me.

Ben and Harry, naked, locked in a small animal cage. Crying.

'What's this?' I ask, confused. 'Is it a silly game?'

I take a deep breath. 'No. Saffron leaves them like this when she's supposed to be looking after them. She's nuts. She can't cope with them. I've been secretly watching her.'

I shake my head. 'This is outrageous. Ridiculous. It doesn't sound a bit like Saffron.'

Caprice shrugs. 'Look in the back of her wardrobe if you don't believe me. That's where she keeps the cage. Then she goes to the dining room to do paperwork.'

'But she could just put them in front of a cartoon on Netflix while she works,' I protest. 'She doesn't need to cage them.'

'You still don't get it, do you? You must have heard her slapping Miles in the face. She's cruel. She's violent. She puts them in a cage to hurt them and punish them. What do I have to do to convince you she's dangerous?'

I smile politely. 'Aren't the crocuses lovely?' I say in an attempt to distract her.

Sometimes Caprice gets so worked up. As if Saffron would put the children in a cage while she got on with her work. It's obviously a game. I'm very fond of Caprice, but sometimes, just sometimes, I wonder whether her age is affecting her brain.

92

Caprice

I look into your strong brown eyes, Hayley, and know you don't believe me. I need to ramp up the situation. The boys need to look as if they have been hurt. Really hurt. I will make it look as if they've been hurt without truly harming them. I'm an exceptionally loving grandmother. It's for their good in the long run.

93

Saffron

When I told Miles it's you or me, Caprice, I can assure you I meant it. I'm sitting in my office, following the link Ted has sent me, downloading Tor encryption software onto my computer. Next, I need to learn how to use it.

94

Caprice

Miles is away at a conference in Los Angeles for two weeks. So this is it. This is my opportunity. He isn't here, so he cannot be blamed for what is about to happen.

Teatime. I slip cough linctus into the spaghetti Bolognese I've cooked for my grandsons. Easy to do, Saffron, because you are so distracted, checking emails on your iPhone. I use a generous dose, camouflaged with fresh basil and oregano. Cough mixture to make sure that my grandsons sleep well. I gave it to Miles and Aiden regularly when they were babies, to make sure they didn't wake me in the night. I needed my beauty sleep then, just as I do now. And I am still beautiful, of course. More beautiful than you, my wiry daughter-in-law.

I leave the kitchen and go upstairs. You are responsible for feeding the children and putting them to bed tonight. No one else will be going anywhere near them. In the morning, Hayley will wake them up, feed them and take them to school. You'll be up at the crack of dawn, off to see a prospective client. Perfect timing. I smile to myself.

I step into my bedroom to be surrounded by frills and flowers. Time passes with a long soak in the bath. Watching a film on Netflix. Spraying my pillow with lavender.

But I can't sleep. I toss and turn in bed, uncomfortable about what I need to do. Restless until my phone vibrates beneath my pillow at 2 a.m. Already awake, I stretch to tap it off. Relieved to be making a start at last – the sooner this is over the better – I slip out of bed and dress in black slacks and a black polo neck, black tights stretched over my head and face.

Slowly, slowly, I open my bedroom door and creep onto the landing. Tiptoeing across, avoiding the floorboard that always creaks. Past your bedroom. Past Hayley's. Into Ben's room, decorated as a tribute to Manchester United. Red walls, Man United's logo in the middle of each one. I step towards his bed, holding my breath. Asleep on his back, mouth open, arms above his head. Wrapped in his Manchester United duvet. A cheapy from Argos. Not even made of cotton. Why didn't you take him to Harrods? They have an excellent selection from top designers. One day I'll make sure he understands what constitutes taste. Do you want him to grow up to be a football hooligan?

I lean over him. His breathing is deep and even. I put my arms around him and pinch his arm, softly rubbing with my fingers, wincing as I bruise him. Then I move to his bony chest and each side of his waist. He stirs and my heart races. I fear he is about to wake. But he rolls onto his side, mouth still open, and continues to sleep. Feeling sick at what I have done, I creep away, on tiptoe, too nervous to breathe.

Step by step across the landing into Harry's Thomas the Tank Engine utopia, styled by Caprice Jackson. This room is more like it. Slow motion across the bedroom. Harry is lying on his stomach. I lean over him and rub and press his back, feeling more and more nauseous, until the discolouration begins. He doesn't stir, younger and lighter than his brother, thank goodness the hefty dose of cough mixture I have given him has really laid him out.

Back across the landing. Back in my boudoir, I rip off my clothes and pull away the black tights that were squashing my nose. I throw myself into bed and shut my eyes tightly. But now, even though my task is complete, I still can't sleep. I feel so bereft after bruising my grandsons. Then I remember your coldness, Saffron, and I know I have done the right thing.

4 a.m. Moonlight streams around the curtain edges.

5 a.m. An owl hoots. And I tell myself yet again that getting rid of you will be beneficial to my grandsons in the long run.

5.30 a.m. The shower pump thuds.

6 a.m. The front door opens and closes as you leave, Saffron.

7 a.m. Hayley's alarm tinkles in the distance. This is it. My masterplan begins.

95

Hayley

The alarm shrills into my bedroom. Head pounding, mouth dry, I reach across to switch it off. I shouldn't have stayed out so late with Jono doing shots. I drag myself out of bed, feeling sick. Flinging a tracksuit on, walking towards the boys' bedrooms, holding my stomach.

Ben's room first. As I lay his school uniform on his chair, my nausea increases. He slips out of bed and pulls off his pyjama top. I inhale sharply. Bruises. On his chest. On his waist.

'What have you done to yourself?' I ask, swallowing to push back my nausea, moving closer to inspect him.

'What do you mean?' he asks as he picks up his school shirt.

Bruises on his arms too. They weren't there when I took him swimming yesterday, after school.

'Who put you to bed?' I ask.

'Mummy.'

I force a smile. 'Breakfast will be ready soon. See you downstairs.'

I go to Harry's room next. He is sitting up in bed rubbing his eyes. I lay out his uniform and watch carefully as he peels his pyjamas off. Multiple bruises on his back.

I head downstairs to the kitchen, to cook and serve breakfast. Pancakes and syrup, blueberries and strawberries.

'Have you been fighting?' I ask, as I watch them tuck in.

They look up at me, wide-eyed. 'Of course not,' Ben replies. 'Mummy says we mustn't fight.'

After the school run, stomach tight with concern, I step into the kitchen to clear the remains of breakfast. Caprice is sitting at the table doing the crossword. Suave and sophisticated in cream and toffee coordinates. Carefully applied make-up heavier than usual. Eyebrows a little too artificial. Concealer beneath her eyes like plaster.

I take a deep breath. 'I found bruises on the boys this morning that weren't there when I took them swimming yesterday. Saffron looked after them last night. Either she inflicted them, or the boys had a fight,' I blurt.

Caprice purses her lips. She shakes her head slowly. 'I've tried to warn you, Hayley. And now you need to report her to Social Care. Our boys never fight.'

'But you're part of the family,' I splutter. 'If you're concerned, surely it's your responsibility to discuss it with Miles, and do something about it – not mine?'

96

Caprice

'You discovered the evidence, and are able to say the bruises weren't there when you took the boys swimming.' I pause. 'Also, it's awkward for me. Saffron hates me as it is.' I pause again. 'And what about my relationship with Miles?'

A frown ripples across her face. 'I had noticed an atmosphere between you and Saffron.'

'An atmosphere is a polite way of putting it,' I reply.

'Maybe. But then I'm a nanny, so it's best to be polite.'

'You'll keep your place whatever happens. If Saffron can't look after the children, Miles will need you more than ever.'

'If you feel so strongly, you should contact Social Care, not me. You're Miles' mother.' Her voice is begging. Plaintive. Hayley shakes her head and sits looking into the air in front of her. 'I just don't think it's my place to interfere.'

'It isn't interfering. You are the children's nanny. In a position of social responsibility. The authorities will listen to you. If I interfere they'll just stereotype me as a difficult mother-in-law.'

'But . . . but . . . how can I report such a thing when all I ever see of Saffron is kindness personified?'

'But you now know that isn't what's happening behind the scenes. You have visual proof of her abuse. It's really important you take photographs of their bruises right away.'

You sit staring at the floor. Silence descends. After a while you look up, face filled with anguish. 'Maybe I could report it anonymously. Then Social Care could evaluate the situation independently, without asking me to give evidence. They must be expert at that. But I am not taking photographs. That would prove I was the snitch.'

I smile inside. I've won at last.

97

Saffron

Saturday lunchtime, I'm eating American Hot pizza with the children, when the doorbell rings. Miles is still away at his conference. Caprice is shopping at her favourite boutique. Hayley is off somewhere with her boyfriend, Jono. I wasn't ex-pecting anyone. It's 1.30 p.m. Strange time for a visitor to call.

I open the front door. A mousy woman with shoulder-length wavy hair stands in front of me, wearing a cream-coloured trench raincoat and flat court shoes. No make-up. No jewellery. Carrying a large black briefcase.

'Can I help you?' I ask.

'Are you Saffron Jackson?'

'Yes.'

'Married to Miles?' Another nod. 'And you have two sons, Ben aged eight and Harry, who is six.' She flashes a wallet containing a badge. 'Sonia Watson. Social Care. Elmbridge Borough Council.' She pauses. 'Can I come in?'

'Why? What are you here for?'

She takes a deep breath and widens her shoulders. 'We've had a complaint about the care of your children. That someone may be harming them.'

I go cold inside. 'What . . . ?' I splutter. 'As if that could be happening! Who has complained? Who is lying about us?'

She shakes her head. 'Calm down. I'm not allowed to say.

It's confidential. I just need to see your children to ask them a few questions.'

She flashes her badge at me again. A photo of herself with an inky stamp across it. 'I'm just going to phone the council to check your identity.'

Her face darkens. 'It's Saturday. The office is closed.' She pauses. 'If you refuse to allow me to enter your property, I will have to file a report of non-cooperation. That never looks good when we are reviewing cases.'

Fear pulsates through me. Cases? When did my life become a case?

'Do come in,' I manage, trying to push my fear away. Breathe. Breathe. All I need to do is keep calm and show her my happy children.

She steps into the hallway and pulls a pad and pen from her coat pocket. 'Does anyone else apart from your direct family live in this house?'

'Yes. My mother-in-law, Caprice, and our nanny, Hayley.'

She makes notes in a spidery scribble. 'Are you satisfied with your nanny?' she continues.

'Yes. Yes. She's great,' I reply.

She stares at me. 'Great in what way?' she asks.

'Kind. Competent. Reliable.'

'What about your mother-in-law? Does she help look after the children?'

'Yes, from time to time. But she's nearly seventy so we don't like to put upon her too much.'

Sonia Watson carries on making notes. 'Is she good with the boys when she's with them?'

'Yes. Yes. Of course.'

She looks up at me. 'So, who is here today?'

'Just the boys and me. We're having lunch in the kitchen and then we're going to swim in our pool. They love swimming.'

'Where are the other inhabitants of the house?'

208

'My husband is away on a business trip. It's my nanny's day off, so she is out with her boyfriend. My mother-in-law is out shopping.'

'As I explained when I entered the premises, I need to interview your children. Check that they are all right.'

'Of course they're all right,' I reply as I lead her into the kitchen, where the boys are finishing off their pizza. Harry has cheese dribbling down his chin. I get a piece of kitchen roll and wipe his face.

'Boys,' I say, 'this is Sonia. She wants to speak to you. Is that OK?'

'Yes, Mummy,' they say politely. 'Are you a friend of Caprice's?' they ask.

'Is Caprice your granny?'

'Yes, but we're not allowed to call her that.'

'Why not?'

'Because it makes her feel old, so she gets bad-tempered. She wants to be young again. If we call her Granny she glares at us with horrid eyes, and wags her finger. Her fingers are knobbly like a witch's.'

Sonia turns to me, face like stone. 'Please could you leave us. I need to speak to them alone.'

I tremble inside. Who is this woman? What is she doing here? What if she isn't who she says she is? Or maybe it's worse if she is. I step into the hallway and look her up on my iPhone. As soon as I type her name into Google, her photograph and job description appear. Sonia Watson. Exactly who she says she is. And she has an OBE for fund-raising for Childline. Panic rises inside me. Childline. Children who complain they are being abused. Why is she here, focusing on us? I stand by the door, ear pressed against it, straining to listen. But I cannot hear anything except the soft, whispering, background resonance of her voice. Of the children's voices.

Every minute she is in there questioning my children feels like a year. When I finally see the door handle turning, I step back quickly and pretend to be rearranging the flowers in the hallway, like Caprice so often does.

Sonia Watson steps out of my kitchen, pushing her hair from her eyes, shaking her head and frowning. She doesn't look happy.

'Can I have a word in private?' she asks.

I try to smile at her, but my lips don't move. 'Come into the drawing room,' I suggest.

She follows me in and sits on the sofa. I sit on a chair by the fireplace bracing myself for what's coming next.

'I want you, or someone in the family, to take the boys to a GP for a thorough report on their medical condition. It's Saturday today so the surgery will be closed. I'll give you three days.'

'But . . . why?' I splutter. 'What could possibly be wrong with them?'

She frowns. 'As I mentioned when I arrived, we've had a complaint about the care of your children. It was anonymous, from someone outside the household. We have to take all complaints seriously to protect the nation's children.'

'But who has complained? Why would anyone? No one in this household would harm them. They are surrounded by love and kindness.' I pause. 'I love my children more than life itself. I'd do anything for them. I'd give my own life to protect them.'

'You would do anything, would you?' she asks, eyebrows raised, expression as sour as vinegar. 'Well, it's quite simple then. As I said, we just need a medical examination, as soon as possible, to make sure they're all right.'

98

Hayley

I return in the early evening from a day out with Jono, to find Saffron sitting in the kitchen with her head in her hands.

'What's the matter? What's happened?' I ask.

She shakes her head. Tears stream down her face. 'It's the Social Care Department from the local authority. They've been here to talk to the children about abuse.'

'About abuse?' I repeat, frowning as I ask, hoping I look sufficiently shocked.

'Yes. A complaint from someone outside the family, apparently. I just feel so upset. So sick. How could anyone think we would harm our children?'

'I just can't imagine,' I reply, voice stretched with pain as I remember my walk into Esher.

To the phone box on the corner by the pub. The one Jono had told me was still in use. I stepped inside. The acidic stench of urine attacked my nostrils, compounded by the stale malignancy of regurgitated stomach contents. My shoes stuck to the floor every time I tried to lift my foot. It was obvious they don't clean phone boxes in the UK anymore.

I fumbled in my purse to find a pound coin, pushed it into the slot and dialled. Much to my surprise the phone actually worked. I heard it ringing out. A cheery male voice answered. 'Social Care. Can I help?'

I took a deep breath and swallowed. 'I want to report a possible case of child abuse.'

'Please can I have your name and address?'

'No. I want to remain anonymous. I'm a neighbour, advising you to look into the health of Ben and Harry Jackson, Wellbeck House, Lexington Drive, Esher.'

Oh guilt, you burrowing worm.

99

Saffron

I wait in the doctor's surgery, watching the receptionists answering the phone and listening to the kindly tone of their voices. Harry and Ben, one on either side of me, are reading. Harry is engrossed in *Redwall* by Brian Jacques. Ben's head is stuck in *Fantastic Mr Fox* by Roald Dahl. I'm sweating. Stomach churning. How has my life come to this?

'Ben and Harry Jackson,' the tannoy screeches like a crusty-voiced Dalek. 'Doctor Pennington, room 3.'

I stand up. 'Come along, boys.'

We walk along the corridor, towards the doctor who has looked after them since they were babies.

Dr Pennington is an angular man, with the lean body of a runner. He swivels his chair away from his desk, and faces us.

'How can I help?' he asks, with his quirky lopsided smile.

'I explained to the receptionist on the phone. We need an independent assessment of the boys' physical condition, for . . . for . . .' I pause and swallow. I can't say it in front of the children. 'Please could you just look at the notes,' I almost whisper.

Dr Pennington taps his computer keys, pulls up the boys' files, and reads.

'OK, I need to see them one at a time. Ben first. Would you and Harry wait on the chairs outside?' he asks.

'Of course,' I reply.

Harry and I step back into the corridor, and sit on the plastic office chairs outside. Harry puts his nose straight back into his book. My world has stopped. My body is not a body, but a conduit of suppressed panic. After fifteen minutes that feel like fifteen hours, the door opens. Dr Pennington's head appears around it and Ben emerges.

'Do come in, Harry,' Dr Pennington says, smiling reassuringly as if this is routine.

My stomach churns. Harry disappears into the consulting room as Ben sits down next to me.

'What was the examination like?' I ask.

'He made me take off my clothes and looked at my bruises.' Alarm pulsates through me. 'Bruises? What bruises?'

'I've got a few, from days ago.'

'How did you get them?'

'I don't know.' He shrugs. 'We mess around so much in the playground at school. Could have been anything. Why is the doctor examining us, Mummy?'

'It's just a routine inspection. They do it to all children from time to time, to keep the world safe. It's nothing to worry about,' I lie, with a wide stretched smile.

Dr Pennington steps out of the surgery. Harry dashes towards me and hugs me.

'Boys, please could you wait for your mother in the main waiting room. I just need a quick word with her. The receptionist will keep an eye on them.'

Harry unpeels his body from mine and the boys skip down the corridor. Dr Pennington holds his consulting room door open for me to enter. I step inside.

I sit in his patient's chair as I have so many times before, with a boy on my knee. When they had chest infections. Chicken pox. Conjunctivitis. Tonsillitis. He sits at his desk, slender legs crossed, displaying trainers and sports socks, despite his formal shirt and Gant chinos.

He looks at me and his eyes soften. 'This must have been

214

very stressful for you.' He pauses. 'As I expected, with a patient I have known and trusted for so long, I found no indication of physical abuse.' He smiles. 'And from questioning the boys, no indication of any mental cruelty. On the contrary, they speak of their parents with respect and love.' He shrugs. 'The boys have a few faded bruises consistent with the playground rough and tumble they described. After my medical report I can assure you there'll be no way this complaint will be pursued.'

100

Hayley

You have returned from your conference bereft, because you were not here for Saffron when she took the boys to the doctor. You are making up for your absence by cooking a vegan curry for supper tonight. Bent over the chopping board, preparing onions, ginger and chilli. Your musky aftershave permeates the room.

I step towards the kettle. You turn around and try to smile. But it turns into a twist of your lips, compounded by mournful eyes that are sadder than sad. 'How could anyone know so little about us to make up lies and complain?' you ask.

I would like to take you in my arms and comfort you. Hold you against my breasts.

I shake my head. 'Could it be someone who is envious of everything you do? Everything you have?'

Caprice

You are knocking on the door of my boudoir, shouting, 'Caprice, Caprice, there's a visitor for you.'

I open the bedroom door and step out onto the landing to find you looking particularly scruffy today in an oversized man's shirt and bright yellow leggings. Yellow doesn't suit you. Why do you wear it so often?

'What's the matter?' I ask as I watch you run your fingers through your hair, which needs combing.

'Sonia Watson from Social Care is downstairs, asking to see you,' you reply.

'Why does she want to see me?' I ask. 'I thought it would be *you* she was after.'

You narrow your eyes. 'I don't know why she should be after any of us,' you reply. 'But it's you she has asked to speak to. She's waiting in the drawing room. I've made her a cup of tea.'

'I'll be down in a minute,' I snap as I step back into my room.

I freshen my make-up and douse myself in Opium by YSL. Check myself in the mirror. So long as I don't smile and crease my face with wrinkles, I still look good for my age. As I walk downstairs it comes to me – Sonia Watson must be here to suggest I take a greater role in looking after the children, because you are so unsuitable.

I enter the drawing room. Sonia Watson is sitting in the

armchair by the fireplace. Lank hair. She needs to go to a good stylist. Wearing a calf-length A-line skirt. Not a good cut.

'Caprice Jackson,' I introduce myself. 'I gather you want to see me.'

'Do sit down,' she suggests as if this is her house, not mine.

'How very kind,' I reply, trying to keep the edge out of my voice.

I sit on the sofa and cross my legs.

'As you probably know from Saffron, we recently had an anonymous report of child abuse at this house. We have thoroughly investigated, and there is no reason to believe there is any truth in the allegation. But in conversation with the children it seems that the only adult in this house they are wary of is you.' She pauses. 'It's not a problem at the moment. But I thought I'd let you know, so that you would have an opportunity to adapt your behaviour and become less confrontational with them.'

We're at our favourite restaurant on the high street, Pincho. A high-end tapas bar. Exotic curved ironwork decorating the bar and the windows. Polished wooden floor and shiny polished tables. Subtle lighting. Mood music. You sit opposite me, frail and sad. Thin shoulders rounded, face almost buried in your wine glass. I lean across the table and top up your Rioja.

'The social worker's visit has shocked you to the core, hasn't it?'

You grimace and shake your head slowly. 'I can't see how anyone could have complained about us.' You shrug your tiny shoulders. 'I mean, our lives revolve around our children.' Your eyes pool with tears. 'It's making me paranoid. Worried someone is out to destroy our family.'

I reach for your hand and squeeze it. 'No one is ever going to do that.'

Your plaintive eyes burn into mine. 'I think someone is trying to.'

I take a deep breath. 'Lots of parents have a brush with Social Care at some point.'

You bite your lip. 'Not like this. A family like ours. A report and an inspection. It's outrageous, and disproportionate.' You pause. 'I've spoken to friends who have rushed to casualty after an accident and been asked rather a lot of questions about how their son or daughter broke their arm. But all they did was explain to the doctor or nurse and that was the end of it. And Ben and Harry haven't even had an accident.'

'But this is the end of it. Our GP said the children are fine.'

'It's the end of it for now. But . . . but . . .' you splutter. 'Whoever has complained for no reason, may complain again.' You stab at your vegan tapas. 'I think it has something to do with your mother.'

My stomach tightens and I take a deep breath to calm myself. 'Look, Saffron, I know she can be difficult, but she wouldn't do anything as awful as that.'

'Then who the hell was it?' you ask.

103

Saffron

I look across the polished wood table. Across the wine glasses, the half-empty bottle of Rioja. The scented candle. Listening to my husband denying the possibility that you could cause trouble with the Social Care Services Department. I am opened-mouthed, full of wonder at his trust in you. His gullible innocence.

And I am back, standing on our landing, telling you that Sonia Watson is downstairs, asking to talk to you. You are wearing your silk housecoat, elegant hair sleek and shiny, pulled back from your face.

'Why does she want to see me?' you ask. 'I thought it would be you she was after.'

Why did you think that? It was you wasn't it, Caprice? You reported us. I can't prove it. But I know.

Every day, you tell me you hate me. With the twist of your head. The twitch of your mouth. And eyes that turn to stone whenever they meet mine. I hate you back, Caprice. You'll have to go. Soon.

104

Caprice

It's a sunny March day. Cold, but bright. I'm sitting in the garden, beneath the weeping willow tree, trying to calm down. Breathe. Breathe. But the audacity of that frumpy woman, Sonia Watson, obsesses me. She doesn't know how to dress. She doesn't know how to think.

The only adult in this house the children are wary of is you.

I clench my fist and bang it on my teak bench. How dare she speak to me like that? I'm the backbone of this family. I do so much to help. Covering on Hayley's day off. Babysitting whenever they all go out. Trying to introduce the children to good manners. Sonia Watson is irresponsible. Bad at her job. Social workers are very badly paid. No wonder the profession attracts people of such poor quality. No wonder they make so many mistakes. All you ever read about them in the papers is their catalogue of catastrophes. Well congratulations to Sonia Watson – she really triumphed yesterday. Standing in front of me wearing washable polyester telling me to *adapt my behaviour. Become less confrontational.*

Someone needs to be confrontational in this family. Someone needs to make sure the children understand boundaries. Saffron, you are too soft with them. To make up for the time you don't spend with them, you let them do whatever they want when you are with them. They watch unsuitable films and cartoons. Play bloodthirsty games on the Xbox. You ply them with unsuitable vegan food. Don't you know that our bodies were designed to eat meat and dairy? They will become anaemic because of you. The social worker is a real idiot not to have caught you out.

How could the doctor have dismissed the children's bruises? You seem to have put a spell on both my sons. Did you put a spell on the doctor too?

Breathe. Breathe.

I look across at the daffodils. They bloomed early this year. Once so dazzling and proud, they are dying already, their leathery yellow trumpets withering at the edges, heads bowed and bent. I look at them and feel tired. So very tired.

My iPhone tells me it's 11 a.m. The day stretches in front of me, pointless and empty. My back is throbbing and painful. I pull myself up and hobble across the lawn. I've got no energy. I'm going to take some ibuprofen and go back to bed. What do the young people call it? A duvet day. That's all I'm capable of. Or maybe, just maybe, if I lie down in the warmth I'll be able to incubate another plan. Even if I'm too tired to action it yet.

105

Saffron

Monday morning. Ted's friend Stan is in my office, again. He is tall and thin, with a long nose and a long face. Bald on top with a greasy, hairy monk's ring. His belly is so large he looks as if he's pregnant. Sitting next to me, smelling of cigarettes and alcohol. Glancing across at me with narrowed eyes. As usual, for a second I fear that Ted has told him what I said I wanted to buy on the darknet. But I push that thought away. Ted, my trustworthy, long-standing friend, wouldn't do that.

'We've nearly finished our training. If you concentrate really hard, after a few more serious sessions you'll be able to manage on your own. Get hold of anything you want. Watch me carefully,' Stan barks.

I lean towards him and bury myself in his alternative, evil world.

106

Caprice

I feel tired all the time. So tired that I have to fight against my body to keep going. I am so low, so depressed. Whatever I do to try to harm you backfires. Until now I've always been in control, powerful. The matriarch. The head of this family. But my power seems to be ebbing away.

There is, however, a small glimmer of brightness in my future. I have had another idea about how to damage you, Saffron. No one can set up their own multi-million-pound business without the occasional slip-up. You must have done something incorrect since you set up Belgravia Private Clients. Most solicitors don't have the wherewithal to set up their own firms.

I went on your website and saw that someone had left an arsey message about the way you handled one of your cases. I bigged up the point and wrote a letter of complaint to the Law Society. I've read their procedures online and know which buttons to press. They will inspect you, no doubt, very soon. And with a stroke of luck they will discover you've made a mistake, and strike you off as a solicitor. When you don't have your career to hide behind, Miles will find out your true worth.

107

Saffron

I'm turning over a new leaf, Caprice. I'm going to treat you better. I'm going to take a considerable interest in cooking, for as long as you live with us. I'm going to make all your favourite things. Healthy soups and meaty casseroles. I will even use the Kenwood mixer you gave me for Christmas. Put it to good use. I will make lemon meringue pie. Macaroons. Chocolate brownies. Taking control of your diet, for your and my greater good.

108

Hayley

I watch Saffron playing Monopoly with her children and sigh inside with relief that my complaint to Social Care fell on deaf ears. To be bruised like that the boys must have had a fight when no one was looking. Saffron would never hurt them. Saffron would never hurt anyone. She is kindness itself.

The Monopoly game is coming to an end. Harry seems to own a raft of hotels at the expensive end of the board. Ben looks glum. He is already bankrupt. Saffron lands on Mayfair.

'OK. You win,' she says, throwing the last of her money across to Harry. Harry jumps up and down, smiling and gloating.

Saffron stands up. 'Hayley, do you have time to come and help me check the food for tonight?'

'Of course.'

We step through the shiny kitchen into the shiny back utility room, paved in thousands of pounds' worth of granite and travertine. She opens the larder fridge and pulls out a large plastic container and a smaller one, marked *Caprice*.

'This is the coq au vin that I made last night. The large one is for all of you. The small one is for Caprice. Make sure you give it to her. I'm cooking separately for her right now because I think she is gluten sensitive. Her portion isn't thickened with flour. She doesn't like talking about it but I think she's having digestive issues.'

'That's fine. Where are you going tonight?'

'I've got to go and schmooze with a prospective new client. He's a media mogul.'

'On another superyacht?'

'No such luck. It's a plastic hotel at Chelsea Harbour. You know the sort of thing: glass and mirrors and air conditioning. Pallid tasteful colours and superficial artwork.'

I don't know the sort of thing. I wish I did. I expect it's beautiful. That's the problem with money: when you have a lot of it, you don't realise how lucky you are. What is special to other people becomes mundane.

She disappears upstairs to change, and reappears when we've tidied up the Monopoly, wearing a punky dress and dangly earrings, surrounded by a waft of vanilla scent. Looking seriously delicious. She leaves with a fanfare of hugs and kisses from her boys.

'Look after Caprice for me,' she shouts as she leaves.

Miles, you are late. So we eat without you, as instructed. Coq au vin from two separate dishes. Caprice is tired. She picks at her food and doesn't eat much. She snaps at the children about their table manners. She stares into the air in front of her.

'Did you listen to *Gardeners' Question Time* this week?' I try.

She bites her lip and shakes her head. After supper she goes straight upstairs to bed. When you arrive home the children and I are sitting in front of a film. You look stunning in your tight jeans and a toffee-coloured shirt that matches your eyes. The shirt clings perfectly to your hard torso. I try not to look at you. I try not to think about what a dish you are. You sit down next to me. Just being near you is making it hard to catch my breath.

Your brown eyes meet mine and engulf me. I would be happy if my life ended here. 'Are you going out with Jono tonight?' you ask.

'No,' I reply, deciding to cancel. Jono and I were going to go to the pub on the corner to do shots. He's always available. I can do that anytime. All he talks about is repairing cars. Another diatribe on brake pads will doubtless just make me yawn.

'Well in that case, do you fancy a glass of wine and another movie when the boys are in bed?'

I can't tell you what I fancy – it would make you blush – so I simply say 'Yes.'

109

Saffron

I sashay down the corridor of the Harbour Hotel. Leaning across a glass dining table, I shake hands and smile at Jenny Bletchley. Media mogul. Prospective client. I am so hopeful of attracting her business that a draft contract is neatly folded in an envelope in my briefcase. She is a smooth-looking woman. Hair cut in a stylish bob. Small neat features. Small neat smile.

'I'm drinking mineral water. Would you like anything stronger?' she asks.

'Mineral water's fine,' I reply.

She pours me a glass and looks at her watch. 'Let's order quickly. I have to leave by nine.'

She waves her hand at a passing waiter, who immediately changes direction to hover by our table. We start to look at the menu. From the sea. Fish. From the land. Meat. Not even a vegetarian option, let alone vegan. I order a side salad. Jenny Bletchley goes for chicken and honey-roasted carrots. The waiter taps the order through to the kitchen on his iPhone, and disappears.

My dinner companion puts her elbows on the table and leans forwards. 'How would you handle this?' she asks. 'I've made a lot of money after investing in a disused oil well in Kazakhstan. Unexpectedly we discovered more oil. I've made another five million sterling. I want to bring the money back to the UK without paying tax on it.'

I take a sip of mineral water and shake my head. 'You can't. If you want to avoid paying tax on money earnt abroad that's fine. But you need to live abroad. Switzerland is a good option.'

'Don't be ridiculous,' she snaps. 'I can't live in Switzerland. My family and my business are here.'

'I know the rules. You can reside in Switzerland without becoming a Swiss citizen, and still enter the UK for a substantial number of weeks a year. Different Swiss cantons have different rules. But in some the tax breaks are phenomenal. After all, now, with modern technology you can work from anywhere in the world.'

She narrows her eyes. 'I've just told you that I don't want to live anywhere in the world. I want to live here.'

I sigh inside. 'Well then, we're going to have to look at schemes to create artificial losses to whitewash the profits you bring into the country. I don't particularly like them but let me look at it and get back to you. If you become my client, I would have a proposal for you within one week, even if I have to work day and night. I told you I provide a 24/7 service.'

'Well, hang fire for now. I want to sleep on it over the weekend.'

Our food arrives. I don't feel like eating the limp salad. It's Friday night. I wanted her to commit. I poke at my food and resent being left in limbo. I just want to go home and watch TV with Miles.

110

Caprice

My son is in my boudoir walking towards me with a cup of tea, and a plate containing a Kit-Kat and some lemon drizzle cake. So handsome. Such a credit to me. Only a fine-looking woman could have given birth to an Adonis like him. He places the tea and carbohydrate on my bedside table.

'Thank you, dear.'

'Are you OK, Mum? You've been so tired lately. You're not eating very much. I've brought you a few treats to fatten you up.'

I smile at his concern. His kindness. So empathetic.

I shake my head. 'I'm fine. It's nothing to worry about. It's my age. I'm sixty-eight. Pushing towards seventy. An age where people need more rest.'

'So nothing's upsetting you? Worrying you?'

I take a deep breath. 'There is the small matter of my relationship with Saffron.'

Miles stiffens as if I have poked him with a cattle prod. Shoulders wide. Back straight.

He frowns. 'But you haven't been arguing lately, have you? If you have, I haven't caught you at it.'

'We're hardly talking. We're not communicating properly.'

He sits on the edge of my bed and takes my hand in his. 'What do you think we can do about it?' he asks.

'She's underconfident. Not secure enough in her relationship

232

with you. That is why she takes it out on me. And on the children. She needs to go and see a psychiatrist.'

He raises his eyebrows. 'A psychiatrist?'

'Yes. I mean she's not coping, is she? Why do you think Social Care paid us a visit?'

'Because . . . because . . .' he splutters, 'because someone vindictive wanted to cause us trouble.'

'Maybe this person was concerned rather than vindictive. You should always think of things from both sides, Miles.' I give him my best smile.

111

Miles

'Mother, I'm a philosopher. I don't just think of things from both sides. I think of them from every angle. That is my speciality. But what I think right now is that you are living on a different planet to me.' I pause and lean towards her. 'Are you seriously implying that Saffron isn't capable of looking after our children properly?'

My breath is quickening. My stomach tightening. Saffron, maybe you are right. Maybe Mother did contact Social Care to cause trouble between us. 'How do you expect to get on with my wife when you have such a low opinion of her?'

'I don't have a low opinion of her. She's a brilliant woman. I'm saying this because I'm concerned.'

'Thank you for your concern,' I reply, voice clipped.

I nod my head cordially at my mother and leave. I find you in the kitchen, Saffron, making fudge brownies.

'I've been talking to Mother,' I say as I put my arm around your shoulders. Your body stiffens. 'She thinks you are under-confident in your relationship with me. And that is why you are antagonistic towards her.'

112

Saffron

'Antagonistic towards your mother?' I say, wide-eyed and aston-
ished, as I adjust the ingredients of the special fudge brownie
mix I am baking for her tonight. 'Miles, I can't think what she
means. We've been getting on splendidly recently.'

113

Saffron

Into the office after a tiring weekend at home. Busy with Ben and Harry. Taking them rollerblading in the park. Worrying the whole time in case they fall and hurt themselves and Social Care visit again. You, Caprice, moaning to Miles about how difficult I am. Telling him I need to see a psychiatrist. I think it is you who needs help. But then even psychiatrists can't do much with evil psychopaths. So, basically, I've come into the office for a rest.

I boot up my computer and clamp my earphones to my head. I turn up the classical music. Brahms. A bit of Brahms always helps me to relax. I close my eyes and imagine I am dancing to the music. Spinning and pirouetting on points across fields. Leaping over hedgerows. Racing through beautiful countryside. Someone taps me on the shoulder. I open my eyes. Ted is standing in front of me, perspiring in his heavy wool suit. I switch off my earphones and pull them from my head.

'Ted. To what do I owe this pleasure?'

'I need to talk to you.'

'Sit down. Fire away.'

He leans forwards, eyes burning into mine. 'Our loan will run out in six months. Jenny Bletchley didn't bite, did she?'

I shake my head. 'No. I just couldn't relate to her. She was selfish and unreasonable. You can't win them all.'

'Well we need to win some more business soon.' He sighs and pats me on the shoulder.

'Don't worry. Six months is a reasonable length of time, and I'm hoping to raise some money from home, before too long,' I reply with a smile.

114

Caprice

I press speed dial on my phone.

'The Law Society. Can I help you?' a crisp, sharp female voice answers.

'I sent a letter of complaint to you about the solicitors Belgravia Private Clients of Ebury Street, two weeks ago. I haven't received an acknowledgement yet.'

The owner of the crisp sharp voice takes a breath. 'Did you fill in the online complaint form?' she asks.

'No. I sent a letter.'

'Snail mail is no good anymore. You need to follow the Law Society's complaints procedure and fill in an online form.' My stomach knots. Online forms are not my forte. 'You'll find the link on our website.'

'Thank you,' I reply as crisply as I can.

Sitting at the kitchen table, I sigh inside as I boot up my computer. I take a deep breath as I download the form. It sprawls across the computer screen in front of me, print so small it makes my head ache. They want detail. So much detail. How can I proceed with this?

115

Hayley

Saturday morning. I'm in the kitchen giving a cookery demonstration to my three favourite men. Making kiwi pie, a New Zealand favourite. Ben, Harry and Miles are sitting in a row at the breakfast bar, watching me. If it comes out well, the boys want to take a photograph and send it to the *Blue Peter* cooking club. *Blue Peter*, that British phenomenon. The longest running children's TV programme in the world. I intend to take a photograph and write a section in my diary. Teaching Pommies to make kiwi pie. Hopefully Mum will find it amusing.

'We need to start with the biscuit base,' I announce. 'We use Graham crackers back home, but we can't get them over here. So we'll have to make do with digestives.'

I measure out the ingredients for the base. Macadamia nuts, sugar and biscuits. I zap them together in the food processor.

'Watch me now. I'm going to melt the butter, which will bind the base together. Who would like to help?'

Ben, Harry and Miles all put their hands in the air.

'Harry, I pick you to help first.'

He beams and slips off his chair to join me. I hold him up to the gas ring so that he can stir the butter as we melt it gently. He mixes it into the biscuit base with a wooden spoon.

'Your turn now, Ben – you can help me line the pie dish with the biscuit base.'

My helpers change places. Ben and I together prepare the

first part of the pie. I put it into the oven and set the timer on my watch for five minutes.

'Now for the tricky bit. The fruity filling. Shall we let Daddy do that? I expect Daddy is good with fruity fillings.'

Ben and Harry nod their heads. Miles comes and stands next to me. So close I can taste his aftershave of musk and sandalwood. So close that yet again my breath quickens. He follows the recipe and combines condensed milk with egg yolks and lime juice and zest. I take the pie dish out of the oven and he pours the filling in. His leg presses against mine, behind the kitchen counter. His touch pulses against me like electricity. Does he know what he is doing to me?

Miles puts the pie back in the oven.

'It'll need fifteen minutes in the oven to bake. Do you boys want to go and play in the garden for a bit, while Daddy and I clear up? I'll call you in when I need you to help.'

'Yes please, Hayley.'

I open the back door and they dash past me to gallivant in the early spring sunshine. Arguing as they go about whether to play catch or football.

As soon as we are alone Miles smiles at me. 'I didn't know you liked cooking.'

'There are lots of things you don't know about me. I've always loved cooking. But it can be so time-consuming. I just thought it would be a bit of fun to keep them amused today; as Saffron is away.'

'Saffron never lets the children anywhere near her cooking. So this is a treat for them.'

'Has Saffron always enjoyed cooking?'

'No. It's a very recent interest. She's doing it to relax. I think she's distracted at the moment. There's something on her mind that she isn't telling me.'

Is he trying to tell me that there is a chink in the armour of their relationship? Will there be room for me, one day?

116

Caprice

Despite my permanent exhaustion I manage to book a taxi to Esher Railway Station and board a train to Waterloo. My mission is to meet my new acquaintance, Andrew Cunningham, at the Skylon Restaurant, on the Southbank.

I sit at a table by the window, waiting for him to arrive, muscles aching with fatigue. The Thames slides by, grey and wide. A flowing stream of steel. People meander past. Wide-eyed tourists drinking up the atmosphere of the big city. Youths loitering. Businesspeople on a mission, marching towards a lunchtime tête-à-tête, or the office. To pass the time I peruse the menu. But I'm not hungry. Despite all your efforts to fatten me up, Saffron, I'm not interested in food at the moment.

'Wotcher.' I look up. A large bear of a man with floppy brown hair and tree-trunk legs is grinning down at me. 'Cunningham, Andrew, at your service. What can I do to help?' His already wide grin widens and splits his chunky face in half.

'Hello. Thanks for coming to meet me. Do sit down.' He joins me at the table, so tall he dwarfs it. He rests his hands in front of him. Even his fingers are oversized, like a row of fish fingers. 'Shall we order first and then I'll explain why I wanted to see you.'

'Good with me. Thanks for inviting me to lunch. It'll cost you. I have to warn you. I've got a big appetite.'

I smile a tight smile. 'I can imagine.'

'Imagine all you like. You'll soon find out.'

We sit looking at the menu. The more I look at it the more I don't fancy anything to eat. The waitress saunters over. She is a very pretty girl, like Scarlett Johansson, pink-lipped and delicious.

'What can I get you?' she asks.

'A green salad, and a bottle of sparkling mineral water,' I reply.

'Burger and chips and a double whisky will do for starters,' Mr Cunningham quips.

Scarlett Johansson melts away. 'So, what did you want to see me about?' he asks.

'It's about your comment on the Belgravia Private Clients website.'

He taps his substantial fingers on the table and frowns. 'Well, that was a while ago. So much changes in business all the time. I'll have to rack my brains to remember.'

Our drinks arrive. Mr Cunningham slugs back his whisky and gesticulates to the waitress. 'Another double please.'

'You said Belgravia Private Clients were slow releasing money for the deal you were negotiating.'

'Ah, now that does ring a bell.' His frown re-emerges and deepens. 'I nearly lost the deal because of it. I was surprised because until then they'd worked hard. Arranged a good deal for me.'

'It sounds serious.' I pause. 'You should report it to the Law Society.'

His drink arrives. He takes a sip. 'Do you think so?'

'Yes. Maybe Belgravia Private Clients was using the money in your client account for their own purposes and that was what caused the delay. If so, they deserve to be struck off. People need to be protected from dishonesty.'

He takes another slug of his whisky. 'It doesn't seem likely. I was friendly with Saffron. She seemed like a good egg. Why are you worried about what happened to *me*?'

I lean forwards. 'It's my daughter-in-law's company. I think she is dishonest. People need protecting from her.'

He inhales sharply, and leans back in his chair. 'People? I'm surprised. Has she caused other problems?'

'She may well have. But she's good at covering her tracks. She needs stopping.' I put my head in my hands and pretend to cry. 'She's swindled me out of money.'

'That's a serious accusation. What has she done?'

I take a handkerchief from my pocket, sniff and wipe my eyes. 'I lent her and my son a lot of money, to help them buy their house. To make sure my investment was protected it was agreed I should have a charge against the property. Just lately, I've started to need the money so I went to see my solicitor to discuss it. He checked the document. It was null and void. Incorrectly drafted. What a fool I was to accept her kind offer to do the legals.'

'You poor thing. But do you think she did it deliberately?'

'Oh yes. She's a nasty piece of work. When I explained to Saffron and my son what had happened, he initially agreed to pay the money back. But then she threatened to leave him if he facilitated me in any way. She is the mother of his children. He went along with her. Told me the house was legally theirs and there was nothing I could do about it. I am heartbroken, short of cash. Bereft. My daughter-in-law needs stopping before she does something worse. Damages a client's life, like she has damaged mine.'

I put my hand on his arm. 'Please, Andrew, report your complaint to the Law Society. Protect the world from a dishonest solicitor.'

117

Hayley

I'm sitting in the kitchen drinking a cup of coffee, watching Saffron gathering together the ingredients for her next cooking marathon. Her chin juts out a little as she lays out onions, shallots, mushrooms, chuck steak, red wine, garlic and bouquet garni. Even though she is vegan she cooks a lot of meaty dishes for the house these days. Mozart's *Horn Concertos* blast from the Sonos. Whistling along to the melody as she works. Distracted, Miles said. Determined, more like.

118

Saffron

Sitting in my office, I google *The Times* Rich List, considering who to approach next. Despite all the encouragement from Julie and Ted, despite all my efforts, I still need a new client. A knock on the office door. It opens and Julie appears. She is wearing Margaret Thatcher blue today, so bright it hurts my eyes. Julie is a lovely woman. She has forgiven me for my dreadful possessive behaviour, and treats me with kindness, just as she always has. But I haven't forgiven myself, every time I think about my hissy fit, I feel ashamed. She walks across the room and hands me a letter.

'It's first class, from the Law Society. I thought you'd better open it straight away.'

'Thanks.'

I do as she suggests. She stands watching me as I read. They've received a serious complaint about BPC. The words on the page push into my mind like daggers.

119

Caprice

Saffron is home from work early. I hear her car pull into the drive. The front door slams. She stomps up the stairs like an angry teenager. I open my bedroom door and step onto the landing. She looks awful. No make-up. Hair that needs combing.

'Is everything all right, dear?' I ask.

She glowers at me with blazing eyes. 'If it wasn't, you'd be the last person I'd talk to about it.'

120

Hayley

I'm lying in bed thinking of you. Always thinking of you. How many ways do you please me? Your brown eyes melt into mine like honey. Your body is taut. Hard. Muscular. You keep strong by working hard in the swimming pool. I watch your chest rising from the water as you glide up and down, practising butterfly stroke. You have a flurry of downy hair on your pecs. When you get out of the water I admire your thighs. Neat, not over-muscled, but powerful. Masculine but not macho. A perfect balance.

It feels like a teenage crush, but it isn't. It's not all about oestrogen and testosterone. You are thoughtful and intelligent. You make me laugh. You make me think. You gave me a second chance to stay with your family; didn't turn Saffron against me. You make me smile. You are considerate. Good with children. You adore opera.

I don't care about the twenty-year age difference. I value your life experience, your maturity. If we had a relationship it would be made in heaven.

121

Miles

You're standing in front of me, in our bedroom. Wearing a short silk dressing gown, and kitten heel slippers. In tears, on this sweltering summer evening. The window is open and the scent of climbing jasmine mingles with your perfume. Heady and sweet.

'What if we *have* made a mistake?' you ask, biting your lip to suppress your sobbing.

You dry your face with your handkerchief, and sniff.

'You won't have.'

You shake your head, slowly. 'Keeping money for too long in a client account, when the client has asked for it back, is a serious accusation. The worst kind of serious for a solicitor.'

'There'll be a reason for it. Please don't worry.'

You blow your nose, swallow and take a deep breath. Your azure eyes are icy with fear.

'What if there's not?'

'I can't bear to see you like this. I wish this would just go away.'

'What if your mother's been into the office and stitched me up? Infiltrated the computer? Made it look as if we did something wrong?' you continue.

I shake my head. 'Now you're being paranoid. She wouldn't do anything like that.'

'Wouldn't she? I think she's responsible for every trouble in my life.'

'She was responsible for making me,' I point out. 'Do you think I'm trouble?'

You almost smile. 'You know I don't. You know I love you, Miles.' You walk across the room and sit down on the edge of the bed. 'It's just I'm frightened. Very frightened.'

I sit down beside you and put my arm around you. You turn and cling to me, body trembling.

122

Hayley

A month has passed since my kiwi pie cooking extravaganza with Miles and the boys. Saturday morning, again. Aiden at the house, again. He doesn't seem to spend much time in his bachelor pad in Chelsea. He has shown me some photographs of it on his iPhone. It looks simple and stylish – glass, metal and mirrors. Nothing out of place. No clutter. No photographs. Almost into Knightsbridge, quite near Harrods. But I know why he spends so much time here. He can't take his eyes off Saffron.

I gather from the way he talks about her that he has been obsessed with her for years. He knows her dress size, her shoe size. Favourite colour. Favourite flowers. Every mark she obtained in her Cambridge finals. How long she spent in labour with both boys. How many stitches she needed. What she chose for pain relief. Every country she has ever visited. The make of her favourite lipstick. It's too intense. It's weird.

When he arrived today his face fell, because Saffron wasn't here. She had already left for the office to tidy up her files. And Miles had gone with her to give her moral support. Even his mother wasn't around. Caprice is resting. Despite the love of his life's absence, Aiden is helping me with the children. He often helps with Ben and Harry and they love him. We are sitting in the shade on garden furniture that would enhance most people's sitting rooms, listening to him laughing and giggling through *The Twits* by Roald Dahl. When the story is over, the children chorus, 'Read us another one. Please, please, Uncle Aiden.'

'No.' I stand up. 'Come on, it's a lovely day. I've packed a picnic. Let's go to the park. Will you join us, Aiden?'

'Please, please, Uncle Aiden.'

He drives us to Windsor Great Park in his brand-new Maserati. Shiny midnight blue metal work. Seats of white calf's leather. Surround sound sharp as an orchestra. It purrs along so smoothly I wonder whether its wheels are even touching the ground. Admiring glances at traffic lights. Admiring glances as we park the car.

We walk towards the lake to find a scenic spot to eat, Ben and Harry running off ahead, Aiden carrying the picnic for me.

'How's Saffron been this week?' he asks.

'Miles thinks she's distracted at the moment.'

He turns to me, eyes sharp with concern. 'I wonder why? Is she worried about something?'

I shrug. 'I don't know. I'm just repeating what he said.'

And suddenly I decide to make trouble. My love for you is growing, Miles. It's out of control. I want you so much. If only you could step away from Saffron and notice me, I could make you want me back. You worry about Aiden and Saffron, don't you? It must be hard having a wealthy brother who is madly in love with your wife. I am going to push it, really push it, one last time.

I take a deep breath. 'But I do sometimes wonder whether she's got the hots for you and she's trying to suppress it.' I finish off with an encouraging smile. Head on one side. Young and pert and pretty, biting my lip.

'The hots for me?'

'Yes.'

123

Aiden

Hayley's words are like nectar.

And, Saffron, you have been so kind to me lately. You have forgiven me for plying you with drink and kissing you. Your face lights up every time I call at the house. When I tell a joke you laugh with me. Last week you sat on the bed next to me, while I read a goodnight story to the boys. The boys stayed awake, but you drifted off, head on my shoulder. Just lately, my beautiful Saffron, you have been so relaxed with me. Relaxed and loving towards me. Are we on the road to love?

124

Saffron

I knew this would happen. I knew the Law Society would send an investigating team to check our books. As I feared, a lawyer and an accountant arrived unannounced at 10.30 this morning.

The accountant, Tony Waterford, is sitting at Ted's desk, frowning at Ted's computer screen, Ted hovering nervously behind him. Tony Waterford is a solid man, with a bald head and round eyes. His suit is too tight and too shiny. His shoes look as if he has been up all night polishing them. He taps his fingers on the computer keys. Neck stretched, he leans forwards and his frown tightens. I cannot bear to watch him any longer. I worry because even I couldn't explain how Ted keeps his accounts. I pull my eyes away and stand up to close my office door so that I cannot see him.

But just as I am about to shut the door, Siobhan McConnaughey, the Law Society's solicitor, appears in front of me. A woman of a certain age, with bushy hair and a curvy figure. A faded soft blonde who I suspect once had flaming red hair. She smiles at me. I try to smile back, but my lips don't move.

'Can I help you?' I ask.

'Yes. I need access to your email account. I'll sit at your desk and use your computer if that's OK?'

But I know she's not really asking my permission. It's what she's going to do whether I agree or not. I have no choice. The letter of intended investigation they handed to me as they entered the premises made that abundantly clear.

I nod my head limply. 'Yes. Do you want me to log in for you?'

'No thanks. Just give me your email addresses, all of them, and your passwords. I will log in and run certain interrogatory checks on the system.'

She sits at my desk looking crisp and cool in her navy floral-print dress. My hand trembles as I write my email address and password on a Post-it sticker and hand it to her. I take a deep breath and bite my lip, in an attempt to calm myself.

'Is this the only email address you have?'

'It's my office email. I have a private one.'

'I need access to that as well.'

I sigh inside. That seems rather intrusive. Why should she look at the loving messages I send to Miles? But if I make a fuss it will look as if I'm covering something up. So I duly scribble down the details of that one too, and force myself to give her a wide stretched smile.

'Should we go and have a coffee in the café over the road? Get out of your hair?' I ask.

'No. We need you all here in case we want to ask you any questions.'

'Fine. But can you give us any idea of how long you will be?'

'As long as it takes. Sometimes we are in offices for days. With private client companies we sometimes find all sorts of money laundering issues.'

Days. Money laundering. Panic rises inside me. I am not sure I can cope with this. 'I'll just pop to the bathroom,' I mutter.

Keeping my eyes to the floor so I don't have to look at Tony attacking Ted's computer, or suffer the gaze of Julie's worried eyes, I slip into our tiny cloakroom. Hardly a cloakroom, more a broom cupboard with a toilet and handbasin in it. I put the toilet lid down and sit on it, head in my hands. I close my eyes. I feel sick, as if I am about to vomit. Faint. Even though I am sitting down. I wish I was anywhere but here. Anywhere? Not quite anywhere. I'd pass on a desert island with Caprice. My stomach tightens. Caprice. Is she behind this? No. Miles is right. Her influence couldn't stretch this far. Even she could not make the Law Society do her bidding.

I lower my head to between my knees. I begin to feel stronger. Slowly, slowly I pull myself to standing, splash my face with cold water from the basin and brace myself to step back into the office. Reminding myself that I am the founder and owner of BPC, not a criminal who has done something wrong. I am a businesswoman who has always worked hard and with integrity. *Don't let the bastards grind you down. Grind them down instead.*

I walk back into the office to find Ted still standing at Tony's shoulder, watching Tony flick through our bank statements now. Julie is hiding behind a large arrangement of roses, fiddling with her iPhone. But despite my best intentions I don't know where to put myself. I can't get on with any work. There is nowhere to sit. I stand looking at the flowers. They rotate in front of me. They fade into grey and white dots, and my world turns black.

I wake up to find Ted and Julie leaning over me. Julie is fanning my face with a magazine.

'Don't worry. You'll be fine. We've called an ambulance.'

So much for grinding the bastards down. 'I only fainted. I don't need an ambulance,' I bleat.

'You need checking on. We can't be sure why you fainted,' Julie says.

I sit up. 'It's nothing to worry about. It used to happen to me all the time when I was a child.' I pause. 'Cancel it please,' I hiss.

Julie and Ted exchange glances. Ted shrugs. 'OK then. If you insist.'

He steps away from us and begins to tap on his mobile.

'Where are the inspectors?' I ask.

'They've gone.'

'Did you get any information out of them?'

255

Julie's eyes darken. 'Tony Waterford said he was concerned about how little capital we have. He says we aren't going to survive much longer unless we get a huge cash injection. He's obviously wondering whether that was the reason for delaying the release of the client's funds.'

My heart races. 'Did he say that?'

'Not exactly, but he implied it.'

'When will we hear?'

'He said investigations don't run to a timetable. They just take as long as they take.'

Blood rushes from my head. If I stand up, I fear I will faint again.

125

Aiden

Oh, Saffron, I trust Hayley's judgement. Deep inside, I have known for years that you have a secret yearning for me. We have always been friends, haven't we? From the first time you came to our house for lunch and Mum kept calling you Julie. You find me far more attractive than you admit. Sometimes desire can be buried very deep. It isn't surprising really. After all, I have a much bolder personality than Miles. He was a stooge to our parents. You are an exceptionally bright woman, and I am an independent-thinking man.

Miles only managed to get into Cambridge because he was a rote learning swot, studying every hour that God sent. He didn't have raw ability. His academic achievements involved studying day and night. Whereas it takes a special type of native ability to build up your own business. You need a naturally enquiring mind, and an empathy with people, to do that.

Saffron, if you leave Miles and come and live with me, you will never want for anything. I will always be able to look after you financially. Soon I'm adding an enormous Sunseeker motorboat to my portfolio. Gone will be the days when you have to cosy up to obnoxious clients to be on a floating palace. With me, it would be yours.

I'm at your house, waiting for you. It's 7 p.m. You're half an hour late. You are usually home early on Friday. I can't contain myself any longer. I dial your mobile and you pick up.

'Saffron Jackson here. How can I help?'

'It's Aiden. You're late – I just wanted to check whether you were all right. I'm at your house, waiting for you to come home.'

'Of course I'm all right,' you reply. 'Why are you at our house? Are you all right? Is everything OK at home?' Your voice is strained. Cross.

'I just fancied a bit of company this evening.'

126

Saffron

I press red on my iPhone to silence Aiden. Waiting at home to see me, after the worst day I've ever had at work, in my whole life. The ambulance arrived after I had fainted, even though we had done our best to cancel it. I felt so guilty wasting the paramedics' time. But they were patient and kind. Two young women, both less than thirty, I guess. When I apologised and said I was sure I was all right, they just replied, 'We're here to check. Every call is a priority to us.' So they took my blood pressure, my heart rate, and even an ECG. Obviously looking for a stroke or a heart attack. Fortunately everything was normal, and they left to go to their next call. Ted and Julie finally released me from the prison of my office, allowing me to take an Uber home. I couldn't face tube and train today.

But now I'm stuck in the taxi, gridlocked by traffic, and Aiden is lying in wait for me at Wellbeck House. The driver is listening to my favourite radio station, Classic FM. John Brunning's melodious voice soothes me. He plays some Holst and the music wraps me in the comfort of beauty. The scream begins to die inside me.

When I arrive at the house it's strangely silent. Aiden steps into the hallway to greet me, a grin enveloping his cheeky face.

'Where is everyone? Hayley? The children? Caprice?' I snap. 'I know Miles is stuck in a staff meeting. He texted me half an hour ago.'

'I encouraged them to go out because I wanted to talk to you, alone.'

He steps towards me and puts his arms around me. My body stiffens. I push my elbows into his ribs so hard he jumps away.

'Get out. Go away. Leave me alone.'

And the scream that has been bursting inside me, trying to explode for hours, rises. It reaches the air and blasts into the hallway.

127

Aiden

You pushed me out of your front door on Friday evening, after screaming and screaming. It gave me such a shock when you had been so nice to me lately. And now I am sitting at the ritual family Sunday lunch, watching you. You look depleted. You haven't spoken to anyone since I arrived. Not even to your children, or to Miles.

I am sitting here feeling guilty for upsetting you so much. Hayley may have thought you are secretly in love with me but she was wrong. I shouldn't have believed her. I believed her because I so wanted it to be true. She is young and lacks life experience. Maybe she is fantasising about magazine romance for other people because she is with that prick Jono and she doesn't have enough of it in her life. I have been admiring you from a distance for so long, Saffron, I am used to it. I will just have to continue doing that. At least I can stay close enough to be your friend. To share your life as a brother-in-law, an uncle to your children.

Lunch is the usual. Two different meals. A roast dinner with all the traditional accompaniments, and a vegan casserole that looks like vomit mellowing in dishwater. Everyone except my mother is eating. Mother isn't touching her food. She is just sipping a glass of tap water, and looking tired. So tired. Waif-thin, with bags under her eyes. Even her colour is wrong; her pale skin brushed with a glint of lime.

After lunch I volunteer to help you wash up and clear the table. My best chance to speak to you, as it's your turn on the rota. We load the dishwasher and our fingers accidentally meet. The touch of your skin against mine sends a pulse of electricity through me. I look into your eyes.

'Saffron, I'm really sorry about Friday. I truly promise it will never happen again.'

'Thank you, Aiden, because as you noticed, I can't cope with it. I love Miles. My life would fall apart if our marriage didn't work. Your attention has caused enough trouble already. I can't cope with any more.'

I take your hand in mine and squeeze it. 'I absolutely promise. And this time I mean it, I can assure you. I apologise for the damage I have caused already. I want what is best for you, nothing more. I just hoped . . . and I thought maybe . . . and I'm sorry. I will respect your wishes and leave you alone.'

Your scream resonates in my head. It will haunt me forever. A scream of anguish. Not the scream of a woman in love.

128

Miles

I pop my head around the kitchen door. Aiden and Saffron are holding hands, eyes locked.

129

Saffron

Aiden is leaving at last. I sigh inside with relief, as I escort him through the hallway towards the front door. As I watch him pull away from the driveway in his dark blue Maserati; his shiny new look-at-me car. Today he has behaved as if he finally believes that the only man I want is Miles. So that is an improvement. A breakthrough, I hope.

Siobhan McConnaughey, the Law Society's solicitor's words sear through my head.

With private client companies we often find all sorts of money laundering issues.

They will find something, won't they? Something Ted and I have done wrong without even noticing? What about my time sheets? Have I filled some in incorrectly? Have I charged too much VAT? Not enough? What about Felman Holdings? My heart sinks. They were overseas customers with UK directors. Was I wrong not to charge them VAT? The more I think about it, the more I know I was wrong. My business is over. I'm falling off a precipice.

I pop my head around the drawing room door. My family are watching Disney cartoons, snuggled on the sofa, in a line, eating popcorn.

'I'm exhausted. I'm going to lie down,' I tell them.

Their eyes do not move from the TV screen. 'Can You Feel the Love Tonight' belts from the surround-sound. Engrossed in

The Lion King. They are obsessed with it, watching it time and time again, even though they have already seen it at the theatre, on that dreadful outing with Caprice. The time when she was so rude about the restaurant I chose. The time she lost her temper with me during the interval.

I pad upstairs, limbs like lead. I step into our bedroom, collapse onto our bed, and cry. Softly to begin with, but the more I think about my life, the way it is imploding, the more my sobbing increases. Panic throbs through me like a simmering toothache.

The door bursts open. Miles stares down at me, looking handsome in his weekend casuals. Lips tight. Face like stone. He pushes his golden hair back from his forehead.

'What's the matter with you?' he asks, voice sharp.

I sit up and wipe my eyes. 'I'm just so worried about the inspection.'

He shakes his head slowly. 'It isn't that.' He pauses. 'I know there's something going on between you and Aiden.'

His words stab into me. 'What? No. Don't be ridiculous, Miles,' I reply.

He shrugs. He bites his lip. 'I saw you together, holding hands in the kitchen.'

I stiffen. 'It isn't what you think.'

He walks towards the door to leave. He turns. 'Isn't it?' he almost spits.

I don't reply. I just look at his ashen face and wither inside. The last thing I wanted to do was to upset my husband again.

'At least you weren't kissing him this time.'

His voice pounds against my eardrums like a hammer. My head begins to ache.

130

Miles

'At least you weren't kissing him this time,' I shout so loudly that my jaw vibrates.

I want to storm out of the bedroom and slam the door. I want to go and see Aiden and smash his face. What is happening to me? I used to be a pacifist. I have only ever hit anyone once in my whole life: my brother, when he kissed you. And now I am imagining the sound of his nose cracking. The stench of his blood. I push my violent desire away, take a deep breath to calm myself, and stand watching you.

'I can't deal with this. I can't deal with anything right now.' You roll over in bed, put your head in the pillow and weep. 'You don't understand,' you whimper between sobs.

'What is there to understand?' I ask.

You pull your head from the bed, sit up and glare at me. 'Just how much Aiden comes on to me. Just how often I have to push him away.'

My stomach tightens. Anger builds inside me again. 'So you push him away by holding his hand?'

'I was begging him to stop.'

'Funny way of doing that.'

You get off the bed and walk towards me. 'I was begging him to stop and I'm begging you to believe me.'

You push your eyes into mine. Sadder than sad. I soften inside. You stand in front of me, with your perfect tear-stained face. I pull you towards me and put my arms around you. Your body melts into mine. You smell of rose and vanilla. Our lips meet. I believe you. I have to believe you. I have no choice. I don't ever want to lose you. I believe you and forgive you once again.

131

Caprice

I feel discord in the house. It rises from your bedroom into the eaves. It floats on the airwaves and makes me feel happy.

You and Miles are both shouting. Saffron, you deserve my son's animosity. You never had the perfect relationship, did you? Not like Rupert and me. Rupert, with his strong, wavy copper hair and cheeky smile. He had kindness in his soul, and kindness in his eyes. I was his shining star, his muse, his angel. We kissed every night before we went to sleep. Every morning he told me he loved me. We never had a cross word. Ever.

After one of your tirades, I mentioned this to you, Saffron. You put your head back and laughed. With your sharp pointy nose and razor-blade cheekbones, you looked like a hyena.

'You need arguments in a relationship. It's an important part of standing your ground, listening to each other and communicating. If you never have a cross word it must be because you don't care about each other enough.'

Oh, Saffron, what you said was so wrong. I cared very much. What is wrong with companionable silence, peace and laughter? Your relationships are a complex mixture of anger, and anger management. I overheard Miles accusing you of infidelity again. What or whom have you been doing now? Is it Aiden? Ted? Aristos? Or someone I've never heard of, let alone met? A toy boy? A sugar daddy? For a stick insect who wears thick horn-rimmed glasses, you do seem to attract a lot of sexual attention.

So, your relationship is hanging on by a thread. How are you going to manage when your firm goes under? Even though I am tired, so tired, I smile inside as I contemplate your ruin. Will you be arrested for fraud? For money laundering? Will you go to prison? Will you have a mental breakdown? You've been showing the signs. Even more irascible than usual. Fretting about the smallest thing. Neglecting the children, even though Social Care wouldn't believe me.

I rub my back. It's killing me. The pain is so intense, I stumble out of bed and hobble to the bathroom to fetch my painkillers. I'll ring the doctor tomorrow. Despite all the pills he's given me, my symptoms are getting worse.

132

Hayley

I'm up early because I couldn't sleep. Sitting in the kitchen drinking coffee waiting for the sun to come up. You and Saffron have had another argument. Last night, when I returned from my night out with Jono, I heard you shouting as I walked up the stairs. Maybe Caprice is right. Maybe you will soon be looking for a way out with an attentive younger woman.

Drinking coffee, comparing the men in my life.

Jono.

Twenty-eight years old. Smokes like a trooper. Thin as a rake. Always wears his signature outfit, an out-of-date punk look. Purple, orange, pink or green hair, depending on the latest rinse. Skinny black jeans with rips in. T-shirt. Tight black blazer covered in studs and badges. An eclectic range of badges: armed forces, punk bands, heavy metal, poppies, butterflies, CND, *Blue Peter*. When I asked him how he got his *Blue Peter* badge, he said he stole it from his brother. Fingers stained with engine oil. His hair, pink at the moment, is scraped back from his face in hedgehog prickles. He has a weird accent. Studs in his ears and in his nose. And somewhere else. But only girls he sleeps with know about that one.

You, Miles Jackson.

Dreamboat. Thirty-nine years old. Voice resonant. Accent educated. You don't drink too much (usually). Don't smoke. You smell of musk and sandalwood. You swim and work out regularly. Figure toned. Intellectual job. Good with children.

There really is no comparison between who I am dating and who I dream of having a relationship with one day. As I sit in the kitchen of this modern mansion I can't believe I live in, I take a sip of mild Italian coffee, Caprice's favourite, and think what it would be like to live in this place not just as a nanny but as an equal partner. I imagine yet again what it would be like to sleep with you. We stand eyes locked. You are wearing pale toffee-coloured chinos, Tod shoes, and a white Gant shirt. I lean towards you. You take me in your arms and kiss me.

I am interrupted by the kitchen door opening. You're standing there in your old towelling dressing gown. The Gant-clad Adonis disappears. The real Adonis is in front of me, even more attractive than in my imagination, running your fingers through tousled hair, blinking in the early morning sunlight. You nod your head.

'Good morning,' you mutter.

'I've made fresh coffee if you'd like some. Caprice's Italian.'

'Sounds good.'

'Sit down. I'll pour it.'

You flop into a chair at the kitchen table and sigh. You have bags under your eyes, as if you haven't slept. Your argument with Saffron must have really got to you. I pour coffee into your favourite mug, carefully adding the right amount of milk, so that it is the perfect strength for you, the strength you always have. I place it gently in front of you, leaning down to expose as much of my breasts as I can manage from my low-cut top. I see you glance. A quick subtle glance. Nothing lecherous. I want to pull you towards me and hold you against them. Desire rises in my stomach.

'You're up early, what's up?' I ask.

You shake your head. 'Nothing, I just couldn't sleep.'

'Any particular reason?'

You shrug. 'It just happens sometimes.'

I smile inside. Arguments with Saffron are what happen some-

271

times. Arguments about Aiden. This is it. Soon I will have an opportunity with you. It was too early last time. But your kindness towards me has continued. You have even implied you would pay for me to do a gardening course at Wisley next year, if I stay working for the family. Why would you want to do that? I watch you sipping your coffee and looking out of the window. A cloudless August day, piercing blue sky. Too hot already, even with the back door open. If only I could take a cold shower with you. You could soap my sweat away, and then we could make love. An idea comes to me.

'What about a swim? That'll blow the cobwebs away. I challenge you to a race.' I pause and smile my best smile. The one that Jono says he likes. 'Dump the coffee. Go and change. I'll meet you by the pool in five minutes.'

I stand by the pool in my new designer swimming costume with an under-strung push-up bra. The one I blew £150 on in Harrods last week, and it sent me into overdraft. Hugo Boss. My first designer purchase. It makes me feel invincible. You are standing next to me, in your orange swimming shorts. Your trunk and legs are softly tanned and golden. You push your hair back from your eyes and frown into the sun.

You turn and grin at me. 'You're the challenger. Your call. How many lengths?'

'I always do twenty, every time I swim.'

You nod your head. 'OK then.' You pause and put on your goggles. 'And let's agree on stroke.'

'Well I can't do butterfly, so that's out.'

'Let's alternate. One length of crawl, one length of breaststroke. Beginning with crawl first. Get it wrong and you're disqualified,' you say and chuckle. 'You count to three and let's do it.'

'Three, two, one, go.'

I dive in. My racing dive. The one I perfected at Queenstown Swimming Club many moons ago. I flip into the water. It slurps past my face, and the world becomes silent and strange and blurred. When I come up for air and breathe deeply in relief, you are already halfway down the pool, arms slicing through the water like a machine. Why am I doing this? The last time I took part in a swimming race was when I was eight. But then I think about your syrupy eyes, take another deep breath and launch my right arm into the water like a missile, as hard as I can manage.

Twenty lengths later, puffing and panting, I drag my exhausted body out of the water. You're standing by the pool, waiting for me to finish.

'I won,' you say with a grin.

'Surprise, surprise. As you are quite the athlete.' I shrug my shoulders. 'I'm not very competitive. I only wanted a race to distract you. You seemed so sad.'

'Yes, well, you distracting me has cheered me up.'

I stand in my best position. The position I have perfected for selfies. Right leg slightly in front of my body. Head up. Stomach pulled in. I put my hands on my hips and turn my head a little to the left.

'I'll distract you any time you like.'

133

Miles

A woman of nineteen with an hourglass figure and perfect creamy skin is flirting with me. Not just any woman, but our nanny Hayley. She has tried it on before and apologised. Now she's laying it on thick again. She's pretty in a healthy, energetic, outdoorsy sort of way. Not quirky, unusually flowerlike, and beautiful like my wife. I suppose if I was a promiscuous man, interested in casual sex, I would have already had my way with her. But that is not the sort of man I am.

Saffron says there are two species of men. Shits and saints. Saints treat women with respect. Shits do not. Saints are very much more like women than shits. They understand how women think. They live with their wives all their lives and love them, comfortable in their company. They do not crave a younger woman's body, because their body couldn't cope with it; their body is ageing too. Their wife is more than a lover. She is a friend, a companion. Shits really only want sexual relief. Shits, in Saffron's opinion, are a lower species of male – more animal than human. Not the sort of men she would deign to mix with.

So sorry, Hayley. I'm not interested in you. You are gorgeous. You are kind. You are sexy. But I am a saint, who loves his wife. Not an animalistic shit.

134

Saffron

Depressed, mind and body heavy as lead, I force myself into the office. At least Miles and I have made up. If I don't have Miles on my side I can't cope. The heatwave continues. As I sit at my desk, air presses against my skin, so hot it feels solid. The window is open but it makes no difference; there is no breeze.

Julie steps in, bearing a letter. Fingers trembling, the letter shakes as she hands it to me. Ted enters the office, face ashen, and stands watching us. I open it. The words on the page contort in front of me. Somehow I manage to tighten my mind and decipher them.

The complaint against BPC has been dismissed. No evidence of financial or accounting impropriety was found.

135

Caprice

The complaint against BPC has been dismissed.
The Law Society is even more incompetent than Social Care. Next time, Saffron. My next plan will bury you.

136

Saffron

When the euphoria of relief dies down, I don't know why, but the heaviness inside me rises again. Something is wrong. Very wrong.

'Let's get back to work,' I announce.

'We haven't got much,' Ted replies.

'Small detail. Off you go. Onwards and upwards. "*Per ardua ad astra*," as the RAF would say.'

Ted and Julie sidle out of my office. I close the door and scrutinise the report. It concluded that the delay in releasing the funds was caused by the client. He thought he had sent an email to us to release the funds but it had bounced back. The email was nowhere in our system, not even in spam. So why did he bother to complain to the Law Society three years later, when his deal had come in anyway? He had posted on our website feedback form about the delay in funds being released, and I had left it up because if all our comments were too five-star and shiny they wouldn't look real. But as it was such a minor incident I never worried about it. I need to get to the bottom of this. I need to talk to Andrew to understand why three years later he lodges a complaint that risks ruining my life.

I pick up the phone and dial his number. He answers.

'Cunningham, Andrew.' Voice is as brusque as ever. Resonant and clipped.

'It's Saffron Jackson here. If you've got time I'd love to meet up. Find out a bit about why you complained to the Law Society. We like our clients to feel satisfied. I wouldn't like to disappoint a client like you again. I'd be most grateful for your time if you could spare me half an hour?'

'Yes, Saffron. That's fine. I guess I owe you an apology.' He pauses. 'I'm coming to a meeting near your offices this afternoon. Why don't we meet up for a quick coffee and a sandwich.'

Tom Tom's coffee bar. Andrew Cunningham is approaching. He hasn't changed. He is about the same age as me, but I like to think he looks much older. He is wearing a pinstripe suit, with a pink shirt and red tie. Red and pink clash with his bold chestnut hair. His mouth gapes a little at the sides, as if he is perpetually about to speak or smile. I stand up and shake hands with him.

He shakes my hand with his bear of a handshake. 'Good to see you again.' He guffaws and then sits down opposite me.

I return his smile, tight-lipped.

We order. Falafel, salad and herbal tea for me. Bacon, lettuce and tomato sandwich and chips, and black coffee, for my companion.

He leans forwards. 'Come on, Saffron, what is it you want to know?'

I stir in my chair. 'I want to know why you made a complaint about us to the Law Society, so many years after we acted for you.' I pause and take a deep breath. 'Why didn't you just ring me to discuss it? I was hurt. I thought we got on rather well.'

'It was Caprice Jackson who encouraged me. She put me up to it. She said you had to be stopped.'

I gasp. It *was* you, Caprice. A shock. And yet . . . and yet . . . deep down inside it is what I suspected. It is so awful, I did not want to be right.

'Not a word in advance. Not a request for an explanation. Just a complaint that could have ruined my firm, my career, and me. That isn't the Andrew Cunningham I used to know.

You realise, I am sure, now, that you forgot to send the email to release the funds at the right time. It was your fault, not ours.'

Andrew shakes his head slowly. 'I'm sorry, Saffron. Caprice Jackson sounded so convincing. I shouldn't have let her make me suspicious of you. I should have trusted my own judgement.'

'Did you know she was my mother-in-law?'

He nods his head, as he takes a bite of his BLT sandwich. Mayonnaise squidges from the side of his wide lips. 'She did mention it.'

'How did she manipulate you?' I ask.

He wipes his mouth. 'She said you swindled her out of money.'

I frown, caught off guard. 'Do tell me how?'

'By making sure the charge she had against your house was incorrectly drafted.'

'But . . . but . . .' I splutter. Then I laugh. 'I had nothing to do with it. Her solicitor drafted it. As far as I know it is of full force and effect. She hasn't even tried to action it yet. And if she wanted her money out, my husband and I would give it back immediately. She has never asked. It was a lot of money way back then, but the house has gone up so much in value, we could easily borrow more money against it and pay her back any time now. She lives with us. She has never mentioned the fact that she wants to move out.'

'She lives with you?'

I nod my head.

'So why is she causing trouble for your business?'

I take a sip of my camomile tea and look him in the eye. 'To be perfectly honest, she's the mother-in-law from hell.'

He laughs, a loud belting laugh that sounds like a helicopter. 'She said you were a nasty piece of work and needed stopping before you caused any more trouble.'

'And you believed her?'

'She seemed like a sweet, vulnerable old woman.'

'That's the trouble with the elderly, because they seem vulnerable we always have to give them the benefit of the doubt. They can get away with anything.'

He shakes his head and sighs. 'I was gullible. I'm sorry. And I feel even worse because the delay was all my fault.' He pauses. 'What if I make it up to you and send some business your way.'

I lean across and put my hand on his arm. 'That would be wonderful, Andrew, thanks.'

137

Hayley

Sunday lunch again. How life rolls on. Roast beef again. Today served with Mediterranean vegetables, carrots and asparagus. Aiden is here as usual. Eyes resting too long, and too often on Saffron. She looks as quirky as ever, in a denim miniskirt, a tie-dye T-shirt and her Doc Martens. You are sitting opposite me, making my heart beat faster. I am trying not to look at you.

Saffron leans across the table and offers a plate of gluten-free Yorkshire puddings to Caprice. Caprice takes one and pours gravy all over it.

'Could I try one, please?' I ask.

'I want one, Mummy,' Ben demands.

'Me, too,' Harry insists.

Saffron frowns at us all. 'There aren't enough. I made them specially for Caprice.'

'Come on,' Miles interrupts. 'There are plenty. Mum will never eat four more puddings.'

Caprice looks up from her meal. 'Of course I won't. Everyone help yourself.' Saffron moves the plate towards me, but her hand slips. The Yorkshires slide onto the carpet.

'Oh goodness, I'm sorry,' she mutters.

She gathers them up and disappears into the kitchen. She returns a few minutes later.

'I've put them down the waste disposal. I'll make some more next week.'

138

Caprice

The heavy lunch has made me feel sick. Overcooked beef with Bovril gravy. Yorkshire puddings with a touch of cement powder. You have never been a good cook, Saffron. Everything you create for your family is too stodgy. I notice you don't eat it yourself. Everything you cook for yourself is even worse, and looks and tastes like vomit. That's how you stay so slim. No wonder you have a bird-like appetite. But Miles is here, so I have to pretend I admire your culinary talent.

'Thank you for cooking lunch, Saffron, my dear,' I manage.

'It's a pleasure.' You beam, flicking your tangled hair from your eyes.

'If you'll excuse me, I think I'll just go to bed and rest.'

'That's fine,' you reply, voice and lips tight.

'Are you all right, Caprice?' Hayley asks. I sometimes think she's the only one who cares about me.

'Don't you worry about me, I'm just a bit past my sell-by date.'

I lumber upstairs, feeling light-headed. As if I am about to vomit. My legs are no longer legs, but stone pillars. Try as I might, I can hardly move them. Every step a mountain, I eventually climb onto the landing and hobble towards my favourite landscape painting. The one Rupert bought me on our honeymoon. I stop in front of it and close my eyes. For a second I am back on the beach with him holding hands, sun and sea spray in my eyes. He tells a joke. We stand looking at the sea, laughing. Sand between my toes. The lacy edge of a wave tickling my feet. The water feels warm. The water is soothing me. My dizziness is increasing. My body is swaying. I continue to stagger along the landing.

I sigh with relief as I enter the comfort of my bedroom. Pink, and pretty, and frilly. The floral patterns wrap themselves around me, and their familiarity lifts me. I sink into my bed. The mattress is soft. It caresses and engulfs me. My eyelids are heavy like my legs. Someone has put weights at the base of my eyelashes. I cannot keep my eyes open a second longer. I close them. I am no longer in my bedroom, but walking along that beach at Mawgan Porth with Rupert again. The first day of our honeymoon. Rupert young again. Rupert and I in the first throes of our love.

Then blackness descends.

139

Hayley

You and Saffron left early for work. I took the boys to school and returned home. I've put the washing in, tidied the kitchen, and there is still no sign of Caprice. She was so tired last night. I will make her favourite breakfast and take it to her bedroom with the newspaper. Breakfast in bed for a treat.

I boil two eggs for six minutes, just the way she likes them. I toast two slices of her favourite ciabatta bread. I pop into the garden, pick a red rose and place it on the tray with her food, coffee and carefully folded *Daily Telegraph*. Pleased with my efforts, I race upstairs, looking forward to giving her a special surprise.

I knock on the door. No reply. I knock again. Still no reply.

'Caprice,' I shout.

Silence.

I hold the tray carefully pressed into my stomach, turn the door handle and push the door open with my shoulder. Caprice, but not Caprice, is lying on her back. Instantaneously, without knowing why, I know she is dead. Even though I have never seen a dead person before. The difference between life and death so obvious yet so indefinable. A slight almost imperceptible stiffness.

The tray falls from my hands and crashes to the floor. The eggs crack across the carpet, coffee falls in a torrent and the red rose tumbles to the floor, followed by the vase.

My friend. My mentor. I walk across the room towards her, body trembling. I lean across the bed and kiss her on the forehead.

'Rest in peace,' I whisper.

140

Miles

I'm in my office, reading. My mobile rings. Hayley. I pick up.

'Miles, I have terrible news.' Silence for a minute. A minute that seems like forever. 'Your mother is dead,' Hayley continues, voice like lead.

'How . . . ?' I splutter. 'Where . . . ? What . . . ?'

'She didn't come down for breakfast this morning. So I took a tray up for her. And when I went into her room, she was lying on her back in bed. Dead.'

This must be a dream. It can't be real. My mother is part of me. I always felt she would live forever. I want to hold her. I want to touch her. Tell her that I will always love her.

'Dial 999, immediately,' I manage.

'I already have.'

141

Saffron

Mother-in-law, you are dead, but it doesn't feel as good as I thought it would. For years I have longed for you to be gone, but now it has actually happened, I feel nothing, not even remorse. There is just an empty space in my head.

142

Miles

The ambulance has been and gone, because Mother could not be resuscitated. Two police officers are in our house. A male, DS Stephen Badminton, who has grey hair and a grey face. He doesn't look well. And a young female PC, Jenifer Tomlinson, with shiny black hair glued to her head like a helmet and eyes like a little beetle. They're sitting in our drawing room sipping tea that Hayley made, dripping with authority and sympathy. Saffron and I are sitting on the sofa by the window holding hands. Hayley is sitting in the middle of the room opposite the police. Thank goodness the boys are at school.

'So what did she look like when you found her?' Jenifer Tomlinson asks.

'Her eyes were open, staring at the ceiling.'

Hayley bursts into tears. PC Tomlinson looks across at Saffron and me.

'Someone needs to ring her surgery. Get a doctor to come out, inspect her body and sign the certificate. Would you like me to do that for you, Mr Jackson?'

'Yes please. It's Broadbent Surgery, Esher.'

I look up the number on my phone and give it to her. She dials through.

'PC Jenifer Tomlinson, from the Surrey Police here,' she barks at the receptionist. 'I need a home visit from Caprice Jackson's GP, to confirm her death and sign the death certificate.'

Black beetle eyes blink as she waits, holding the phone patiently to her right ear. If she is married she has decided not to wear jewellery. Her nails are short and practical, like her hair.

She nods. 'Yes, that is the right address, Wellbeck House, Lexington Drive, Esher. Thank you,' she says crisply and ends the call. She stands up and walks towards us. 'A doctor will be here in about half an hour to examine the body.'

Your hand trembles in mine. The doorbell rings. Feeling surreal, as if I am moving inside a plastic bubble, I move away from you and step to answer it. I open the door. Aiden stands on the doorstep, in front of me. His familiarity confronts me and brings the reality of Mother's death a step closer. We have spent so much time together with her. As soon as I see him I burst into tears. He puts his arms around me and holds me.

'Where is she?' he asks.

'Upstairs. Still in her bedroom,' I reply.

'Let's go and say goodbye to her together,' he says. His voice is bombastic. It sounds more like a command than a suggestion.

I step away from him, shaking my head. 'I'm not sure I can bear to.'

'It's the best thing. It means you will have closure.'

'I don't want closure. I want her to be alive.'

'Brother, we all know that isn't possible.' He holds my hand and starts to lead me through the house, as if I am a child. 'It's not what you want; it's what you need.'

I brace myself to comply. My legs are like lead as I force myself to climb the stairs, as I force myself to step into her bedroom, behind my younger brother. I have never hidden behind him in my life before. We step around the tray debris that Hayley couldn't face entering the bedroom again to clear up. We hold hands and stand looking at Mother. Mother but not Mother, a strange stiff contortion of what our mother once was. Lying on her back, staring at the ceiling, eyes open. Feet together. Arms by her sides. A sarcophagus of skin and clothing covering what was once our mother's warm body. I can't bear to look anymore. I release Aiden's hand and walk away. Back downstairs.

Not half an hour, as promised, but hours later, my mother's GP Dr Pettyfour arrives.

'Sorry for your loss. Your mother was a special woman. And I'm sorry I've been so long. I was busy with an emergency.'

I cannot bear to look at the strange stiffness that was once my mother yet again, so I allow PC Jenifer Tomlinson to lead him up to her bedroom. I sit in the drawing room alone. DS Stephen Badminton and Aiden have left. The DS has more important matters to attend to than the death of an elderly woman. Aiden spent ages in the bedroom with Mother's body, but now has gone back to his flat in Chelsea. He said spending time with her had helped with closure. But he wanted to go home to cope with his grief alone. I'm not ready for closure. Not yet. I am still in the first throes of shock.

The boys are still at school, and are off to stay at a friend's house tonight. So at least they are spared any angst for now. You and Hayley are pottering about in the kitchen. Saffron, you did not want to see my mother's body, as you felt too squeamish about it. I hear the periodic clatter of dishes as the dishwasher is unloaded.

Time stops. I sit in the drawing room, back in my mother's arms as a child. Snuggled in her arms, head leaning on the cushion of her breasts.

'I love you, Miles. I'll love you forever.'

That is what she always used to say to me, every day when I was young. Tears roll down my cheeks as I realise I will never hear her say that again. Never hear her voice again. Never watch her ready smile light up her face.

After what seems like hours, but when I look at my watch I realise is fifteen minutes, Dr Pettyfour reappears with Jenifer Tomlinson. He stands running his fingers through his floppy hair in the middle of our drawing room, shoulders wide, legs slightly apart. You have appeared and are standing in the doorway, Saffron.

'I cannot ascertain the cause of death. I'll have to refer this to the coroner's office,' Dr Pettyfour announces.

You turn paler than pale.

143

Saffron

Keep calm. Breathe. Breathe. I was expecting this.

144

Miles

'The coroner's office? What does that entail?' I ask.

'They'll send a coroner's officer to examine your mother's body. I'm very sorry, but I expect they will need to perform an autopsy.'

'An autopsy?' I stammer.

'Yes. It is a requirement when death is unexplained.'

It feels as if a knife is stabbing me repeatedly in the chest. The thought of my mother's body being desecrated is giving me a panic attack. Saffron puts her arms around me and I cling to her like ivy.

145

Saffron

We're talking to the funeral directors today, even though we're not sure when your body will be released. At the moment it is too early to set a date.

Miles and Aiden are devastated of course. And, much to my surprise, Hayley is too. She is skulking about the house, head down, red-eyed and sniffing. And the children? They seem to be taking it in their stride, using the opportunity of us all being distracted to watch *Harry Potter* videos, endlessly.

I always imagined how I would feel when you passed. I thought I would feel free as a bird, with a soaring sense of happiness. But now, even after your body has been taken away, I just feel empty.

146

Miles

I am standing in Mother's bedroom, looking out of the window, at the tennis court and the swimming pool, thinking about her life; all she gave to me. How she cared for me. How much she loved me. How she minimised Aiden, and treated me as if I was the only one. How much I came to rely on her love; to take it for granted. My body aches for her. I feel physical as well as mental pain; as if she has been cut away from me with a knife.

But our love is so strong it must transcend death. Her energy and love will live inside me forever. I must take comfort in that. And if at the end of my life, I am alone, dying slowly in an inescapable corner, at least I will always know I had the warmth of my mother's love.

147

Saffron

Miles is upstairs in your bedroom. He spends a lot of time up there at the moment, now that your body has been removed. Gentle sunlight pours in through the kitchen window, as I sit drinking a cup of tea. I need to try and distract Miles from his grief. I'll try and coax him to come for a walk in Windsor Great Park later, for old time's sake. We haven't managed to go for ages. We might as well do something. We've both taken time off work, and we have been so directionless we haven't even chosen the hymns for the funeral service yet.

The post thumps through the letter box. I step into the hallway and pick it up. A letter addressed to me, franked by your solicitor. Strange it isn't addressed to Miles as well. Curious, I rip it open.

Dear Saffron,

If you are reading this letter, I will already be dead. I pre-arranged for my solicitor to send this letter to you posthumously.

I know you murdered me. So do the police.

Did you really think you had fooled me? By the time you receive this letter I hope the police will be on their way to arrest you. They have received a letter too. A letter to help them carry out their duty.

I will be looking down from heaven with a bird's-eye view of your suffering. My son won't tolerate being married to the woman who murdered his mother. Mothers are always more important to sons than wives. Did you never understand that? Your life as you knew it is over, Saffron. Ever since you met me you have fought against me.

You thought you had won, didn't you? But I am free of pain and it is I who will now rule from beyond the grave. It is you who will now suffer. I have won the war in the end.

With all the love you deserve, always,
Caprice

The letter slips from my trembling hands and falls to the floor.

148

Miles

Early morning. Hayley has just left to take the boys to school. I look out of the window on the landing. A police car with flashing lights is pulling into our drive. I watch PC Jenifer Tomlinson and DS Stephen Badminton step out and walk towards our door. Stephen Badminton has unsightly grey hair sprouting from his cheeks. I thought policemen were supposed to look smart and shave, at least.

The doorbell buzzes. I pad downstairs to answer it. But by the time I reach the hallway, you are opening the door. The DS and PC step inside.

'Saffron Jackson, I'm arresting you for the murder of Caprice Jackson.' My heart stops. My brain does not comprehend. 'You do not have to say anything, but it may harm your defence if you do not mention when questioned something which you later rely on in court.' He pauses. 'Anything you say may be given in evidence,' DS Badminton continues. PC Jenifer Tomlinson forces your arms behind your back and handcuffs you.

'Are you out of your mind?' you spit. 'As if I would murder my husband's mother.'

Thin. Pale. No colour in your face. You struggle against Jenifer Tomlinson as she manhandles you through our hallway and bundles you into the back of the police car. Just before your head disappears beneath her arm and you are pushed through the car doorway, you fix your eyes on me and mouth *I love you.*

'You need to leave the property immediately. I need to watch you pack your bag. Your house is now a crime scene,' DS Badminton informs me.

149

Saffron

I'm sitting in the police car, with handcuffs burning my wrists. DS Stephen Badminton is driving. PC Jenifer Tomlinson is sitting next to me, dark eyes watching my every movement. I shake my head. I can't believe this.

'What on earth am I supposed to have done?' I ask.

'Poisoned your mother-in-law with arsenic,' Jenifer Tomlinson replies, her voice high-pitched and watery.

I shake my head and laugh. 'But that's ridiculous – how could I have done that?'

A condescending smile. 'We'll interview you formally at the custody suite. You can comment on the toxicology report then. There's no point in having an argument in the car.'

'I'm entitled to a solicitor. I want you to telephone John Thornton of Thornton Associates, at once.'

She doesn't reply. The black holes that she has instead of eyes harden.

Inside the custody suite they remove my jewellery and my iPhone, and place them in brown paper evidence bags.

Photograph. Blinking in front of a computerised camera.

Fingerprints. Fingertips splayed on a machine like those I've seen only once before at Miami Airport.

DNA. PC Jenifer Tomlinson takes a swab by scraping my cheek with a cotton bud. She leans over me and forces me to taste her stale breath. She frogmarches me to a cell and locks me in.

The cell is worse than my worst imaginings, worse than my deepest fears. It is a hard white plastic bubble, with a shelf-like indentation in the wall for a bed. No windows. High ceiling. It looks like a hole inside a beehive made of slippery plastic. It contains a small metal toilet, with no toilet paper. That disgusts me. And a hole in the wall that sprays water. To drink. To wash my hands. So basically if I need to do a number two, I cannot wipe my bottom or wash my hands hygienically. I'm so upset and stressed that I am already trying to suppress diarrhoea. I look up. Cameras are pointing down at me. So this is the game the police play. No dignity. No privacy. I lie on the hard plastic slice in the wall and cry inside. I cannot think. I cannot sleep.

At last the window in the door of my cell is opened. PC Jenifer Tomlinson's head appears. 'I'm coming into the cell to take you to the interview room,' she warns me. 'Sit up and don't try anything on. You are being watched.'

My solicitor, John Thornton, is waiting for me in the interview room. A room padded with plastic. Plastic table and chairs. Cameras watching. Recording. The sight of him comforts me a little. Kind eyes. Neat face. Rolls-Royce brain.

'You can have ten minutes alone,' Jenifer Tomlinson announces as she presses a button in the control panel. 'I've turned the recording off so that you can talk in private.' There is a pause. 'Just ten minutes,' she repeats as she leaves.

'No time for small talk. I know you've been arrested for the murder of your mother-in-law.' John Thornton stares at me. 'What do you know about her death?'

'Nothing,' I snap. 'They told me in the car that they think I poisoned her with arsenic. That is just ridiculous. Where on earth would I get it from?'

'They will assume you bought it on the darknet. In all likelihood they will have already confiscated your home computer and be checking it. They will be examining all your computers at work. But that is more complicated because of solicitor–client privilege. Privacy protection is so important in your profession, so it's likely your computer will be hard to crack.'

'Well, I didn't buy arsenic from anywhere. So that's all right. They won't find anything.'

John Thornton leans back in his chair. 'Good. Good. Well, they can't nail something on you that you haven't done. Sounds like you've nothing to worry about.'

'I wish I had your confidence. I can see why people call the police pigs.'

DS Badminton and DI Sarah Jones burst into the room. DI Sarah Jones is a big-boned woman with pale blonde shoulder-length hair and broad shoulders. DS Badminton looks perpetually worried.

They sit down opposite us. DS Badminton presses a switch to begin the recording.

'Let's begin. DS Badminton and . . .' he stares across at DI Jones.

'. . . DI Jones,' she announces clear as a bell. 'Present.'

'Also,' he points at me, 'Saffron Jackson.'

He points at John. 'John Thornton.'

Then he re-arrests me. The words pierce into me again. Panic rises inside me.

'Where did you get the arsenic?' Sarah Jones asks, leaning forwards across the plastic table, face hard. Arms folded.

'I didn't,' I reply.

Her broad lips curl. 'We know you're lying.' There is a pause. A long deliberate pause, designed to intimidate. 'Where did you get the arsenic?' she repeats.

I shake my head. 'I didn't get any arsenic. I don't know what you're talking about.'

Her eyes harden. 'You'll get a lower sentence if you co-operate and tell the truth as soon as possible.'

I smile a short, clipped smile. 'Check my computer. Check my house. Check anything you like. I'm clean. Whiter than white.'

John Thornton coughs. 'Please explain to my client why you are treating her like this. She denies the charge vehemently.'

DS Badminton and DI Jones exchange glances. A buzzing sound trills in Jones' earpiece. She frowns as she listens to whoever is speaking to her through the earpiece. She nods her head.

'OK then. We found arsenic in a glass bottle beneath your kitchen sink. Your fingerprints and no one else's on the bottle,' she announces. She leans back and folds her arms. A flicker of a smile. Raised shoulders. 'And we found traces of arsenic in your mother-in-law's blood. Pretty conclusive if you ask me.'

Anger explodes like a volcano inside me.

'She hated me. She sent you a letter, didn't she? She set me up. I think you had better look into this case properly. I think you had better do your job.'

'I think you should be wary about being rude to a police officer.' DI Jones scolds me with her eyes, and I know I need to calm down. 'Tell me about your relationship with your mother-in-law,' she pushes. 'You just said she hated you? Did you hate her back?'

I take a deep breath. 'I didn't find her easy, but I worked at it. I thought things were improving between us. That's why I am so shocked and upset by what has happened.'

DI Sarah Jones sits watching me, face like stone. I hear a buzz in her earpiece.

'Interview terminated at 20.00 hours,' she says in a steely voice.

'You don't look shocked and upset. We'll continue this in a few hours. We'll be interviewing you on and off all night. You've got plenty of time to confess.'

150

Miles

We are driving to Aiden's flat.

'Where's our mummy?' Harry asks.

'Why can't we go home? I want to go home,' Ben whinges.

'The police are just asking Mummy a few questions,' I reply as I pull up at the lights. 'Trying to find out why Granny died. And just checking there's nothing dangerous at our house. We'll only have one night at Uncle Aiden's.'

'Are they stupid?' Ben asks. 'Granny died because she's old.'

'The police always check what has happened when someone dies. It's one of their jobs.'

'How can they?' he asks, putting his head on one side. 'The world population is 7.8 billion. So the police must be very busy.'

When did my older son became so full of facts and opinions? I should be pleased about this as I am a philosopher, but today, upset and jaded, it's too much for me.

'The UK police don't have to patrol the whole world,' I reply, sighing inside as I park the car.

'What's Hayley doing at Jono's? Why didn't she come here with us?' Harry starts.

'He's her boyfriend. I expect she just wanted to see him.'

'He looks like a drip,' Ben announces.

'Yes he does,' Harry chirrups.

'It isn't very nice to call someone a drip. Have you met him?' I ask.

'We've seen him through the window. He's very thin and wears a lot of jewellery. His hair is purple and sticks out. He has a nose piercing.'

I think about Hayley. So wholesome and appealing, she should star in a cereal advert. And yet her boyfriend is a punk. The memory of her flirting with me by the swimming pool pushes into me. Surely if she likes edgy and interesting, a middle-aged philosophy professor is not her type. And even if I was her type, she isn't mine. Saffron, you are mine. My heart rotates.

Saffron.

The love of my life, who could not, in a million years, have committed this crime. Or could you? Did I never really know you? I tremble inside.

Hands shaking, I park the car behind Harrods, and drag our suitcase out of the boot. I breathe deeply to calm myself as we walk around the corner to the entrance of Aiden's block of flats. Red-brick sophistication in this famous part of London. I admire the curved doorways and elaborate floral designs carved into the brick. It's hard to imagine, when he lives in such city centre splendour, why he spends so much time out with us in the sticks. But then my stomach tightens. I know exactly why he does.

Aiden has given me the codes to his luxury life. I press buttons, the door opens and we step inside the marble-floored building. We call the lift. It whips us up to the third floor in seconds. Aiden, dressed in his silk housecoat and pointy slippers, is waiting for us at the door of his flat.

'Welcome,' he says.

We step into his bachelor pad. Cold white stone. Mirrors. Glass. An apartment designed to look at, not live in. Another reason why he spends so much time at ours?

'Come with me, boys. I've set up the computer,' Aiden says taking their hands and leading them through the living area, towards the bedrooms and his study. 'What do you fancy to play?' He pauses. 'Cuphead? Minecraft? Super Mario?' he suggests.

Relieved to be free of my responsibility for a while, I sink into Aiden's low-backed designer sofa and close my eyes. Trying to behave normally in front of the children when I'm dying inside, means every hour is a battle. Everything is exhausting. I feel as if I am wading through lead. Living life in slow motion.

Aiden is back. 'Would you like a whisky?' he asks.

I open my eyes, and look at my watch.

'It's eleven in the morning,' I reply.

'I didn't ask the time. I asked whether you wanted a whisky.'

'Hell, yes.'

He pours us both a stiff one, with ice. He sits down next to me.

'How is she?' he asks.

I put my head in my hands and cry.

151

Hayley

Jono's squat is a bit of a dump. I don't know why he's so proud of it.

'What's not to like about my comfortable home?' he asks as he catches me wrinkling my nose as I enter.

I don't know where to start, so I don't reply.

'You know I like it because it's rent-free,' he continues. 'I've told you before just how sought-after this area is. But I suppose because you're a Kiwi you're not impressed to live near a shed-load of Chelsea footballers. Esher is where they have their training ground. How cool is that? I saw Frank Lampard in Waitrose last week.'

'You are seriously weird, living in a squat and shopping at Waitrose. Posh boy gone wrong.'

He grins. 'Posh boy gone wrong. I like that. And I can afford to shop at Waitrose because I live in a squat.'

I sit on one of two deck chairs, in the middle of his uncarpeted concrete-floored lounge. Even though it's a sunny day, I shiver. The dampness of the flat presses against me and makes me feel cold.

'Let's go and sit in the garden. It's warmer outside,' I suggest.

'No. We can't let the neighbours see us. They would report it to the police and I'd have to move out, pronto.'

I sigh. 'That would be a pity, wouldn't it. Can we watch telly or something?'

He shakes his head and shrugs. 'The electricity has been turned off now.'

'So you can't even eat food from your toastie maker, or the microwave anymore?' I ask.

'No. I've started buying sandwiches and salads, and chip shop treats.'

'Fabulous. Sounds delicious. And how do you charge your phone?'

'I do it in the day at work, numbskull.'

'You're the fucking numbskull, living in a dump like this,' I say keeping my voice light and jokey.

'Thanks for that, Hayley. Charming as ever. Let's hope you don't ever need somewhere to doss after tonight. Remember your nob of a boss is in prison – that's why you're here right now. Don't look down your nose at me. My home hasn't been cordoned off for the police to investigate.'

152

Miles

I am sitting opposite you at a plastic table, visiting you in prison. We are not allowed to touch. You are thinner than ever, black-eyed and tired. I long to push the world away, take you in my arms and hold you.

You hated my mother, didn't you? But did you kill her? I can't make my suspicion go away. If I ask you outright, you'll never forgive me for not believing in you. If I don't ask you, I'm in denial, not willing to search for the truth.

'I know you must be feeling very confused right now, but I need you to believe me. I didn't do this,' you say.

'I can't believe you would.'

You shake your head. 'That's not good enough. You need to understand utterly and completely, I didn't do it.'

'Then who did?' I ask.

Your eyes fill with tears. 'Asking that is one way of telling me you don't believe me. Let me explain. Your mother must have set me up.'

I shrug. 'From beyond the grave?' I ask.

'And long before that, too. She must have planned this ages ago, so that if she died I would suffer. It wasn't me. So it must have been someone else. Who do you think it was, if your mother had nothing to do with it?'

'What about Hayley . . . or Aiden?' I stutter.

'My bet is on your mother. She was always making trouble for me.'

Your words stab into me like daggers.

'Setting someone up for murder is so serious,' I protest, 'much more so than trying to make out someone is playing away. She loved me so much, it's hard to believe she would harm the person I love most in such an extreme way.'

'Loving you so much, too much, is precisely why she would. Maybe as a man you can't understand. She wanted to be the woman you loved best. The only woman.'

I look across at your delicate face, contorted with despair. I reach for your hand beneath the table and wrap my fingers around yours.

153

Saffron

He doesn't reply. He wraps his fingers around mine, and frightened of losing him, I tremble inside.

154

Hayley

I'm sitting in the garden, laptop on my knee, drinking iced lemonade, 'organising' the household for the week. Meal plan first. Then Ocado delivery. I zap into the online calendar, just to check the boys' activities for the week. To make sure they fit in with Miles and me. To check they meet with my approval. I'm enjoying this. Enjoying being in charge of the household. Admin done, I snap my laptop shut. Time for my swim.

I walk through the garden. The gardeners are busy. A young boy of about sixteen with a pudgy face and a pudgy hairstyle is mowing the lawn. A young woman in her twenties with a slim figure and tousled honey blonde hair is dead-heading the roses. Their boss, I think he is their father actually, is trimming the high hedge, with a machine that looks like a strimmer, but has a long, jagged saw on the end of it. I stand behind him, until he senses I'm there. He turns the saw off and stops. He pulls his ear protectors off, to talk to me, and smiles.

'Is everything OK?' he asks, addressing me as if I am the boss. The owner. I like that.

'Thank you, that looks lovely, but you've missed some on the top to the left.'

'I'm about to do it, but I have to get the higher stepladder for that.'

He is always 'about to do' whatever I ask. I have to keep an eye on him. Sometimes he's a bit too hasty. A bit too Jack the

Lad. I understand he has a bit of a local reputation as a woman-iser. He's someone young women have to be wary of. Caprice told me that.

I stand at the edge of the swimming pool and press the button to remove the cover. The motor whirs, as the grey plastic pool guard pulls back slowly. I slip off my wraparound dress, kick off my sandals, and stand at the deep end of the pool in my swimming costume.

I dive in. The water slips past my body, amniotic fluid, comforting me. My head emerges from the blurred world beneath, and the bright August day pushes into my eyes and makes me blink. I begin my swim. Twenty lengths of breaststroke. I do this every day. My body has never been more toned.

I push through the water, stretching every limb, every muscle, every cell. From the tips of my fingers to the edges of my toes. Push. Push. Breathe. Breathe. Go. Go. Go. After ten lengths I hold on to the edge of the pool, panting. And then I go again. Sliding my body back through the water. Pushing, pulling my limbs through the water. Projecting my torso. So fast I'm pushing through pain. Twenty lengths over, I step out of the pool, and check the time on my waterproof watch. Twenty lengths in thirteen minutes. Not bad. I'm improving.

I grab a towel from the basket by the pool and wrap it around my shoulders. I look at my watch again. I'd better hurry up or I'll be late for yoga. My iPhone buzzes. A text.

Jono.

See you tonight?

Sorry. Busy.

I'm not in the mood for Jono right now, I think as I step into the kitchen to fetch the keys to Saffron's Merc. I grab a bottle of San Pellegrino from the fridge to drink as I drive to the RAC Club. Saffron's membership has temporarily been assigned to me.

155

Miles

PC Jenifer Tomlinson is sitting in the drawing room opposite me; back straight, hands neatly on her lap. Every time I see her, there is something beetle-like about her: scurrying, shiny, neat.

'We've received the full autopsy report. Your mother had cancer.'

My heart stops.

I shake my head. 'I didn't know.'

Jenifer Tomlinson's mouth grimaces slightly, but not enough to spoil the shape of her pert little lips. She shakes her head, sadly. 'It had metastasised throughout her whole body.'

'But . . . but . . . what sort of cancer?' I splutter.

She frowns. 'They think the primary site was her breasts.'

I want to scream. I want to cry. Why didn't she tell us? Her own mother died of breast cancer. Maybe it was hereditary.

Jenifer Tomlinson crosses her legs and adjusts the angle of her back in the antique chair she is sitting in. 'Do you think your mother knew she was ill?'

I raise my palms to the ceiling. 'Who knows. She was tired, lacking in energy. Whenever we expressed concern, she blamed her age. We should have guessed. Sent her for a check-up. She was only sixty-eight. That's not old in the scheme of things.'

Jenifer Tomlinson's dark eyes soften. 'No, it isn't, and I am very sorry for your loss.'

She pauses. 'We need to find out as much as we can about

her medical condition and her mental state around the time of her death. Are you willing to come to the police station to make another statement?'

'I'll do anything to help find out what happened,' I reply, sighing inside. Last time the statement took seven hours to make. Seven hours on eggshells, not wanting to mislead in any way. Another day of torture, but how can I refuse to help?

'Two p.m. tomorrow?'

'Fine.'

Jenifer Tomlinson stands up. 'Did your mother have a laptop?' she asks.

I stand up and hover by the drawing room door. 'Yes, but she only used it occasionally.'

'Have you still got it?'

My stomach tightens. I have been too upset to touch her things. I know I need to sort them out, but it's still too soon. Too painful.

I nod. 'Yes. All her possessions are still in her bedroom and in the annexe. The laptop will be in her bedroom. She kept it on her bedside table.'

'We would like to have a look at it. It might clarify a few details about her illness.'

'Do you want me to get it?'

'No. We don't want anyone touching the objects in her bedroom. I'll go and put it into an evidence bag. We need to check your mother's possessions forensically again. I'm going to cordon her room off with police tape. No one must go in.'

A crime scene again. Will this nightmare I am living in ever end?

156

Hayley

Low lights. Mood music. Silk underwear. No. No. No. It'll frighten you if I come on too strong again. Should I just try and snog you by the swimming pool? By the dishwasher? Slide too close to you on the sofa when we're watching a film?

Or should I wait until the middle of the night and burst into your bedroom? I know Caprice was right. I've seen you looking at me with glimmering eyes. Glimmering more brightly now Saffron is out of the way. It really turns me on when your gaze meets mine.

Late at night I step into the kitchen. You are sitting at the table, drinking red wine.

'Are you all right?' I ask.

You hadn't realised I was in the room. You turn towards me, startled, and shake your head, slowly, sadly.

'I don't think I'll ever be all right again. Did you know my mother had cancer?'

I step towards you, and shake my head. 'No.' I pause and think about it. 'But it makes sense actually,' I continue. 'I was worried about her because she was often really tired. She had a lot of back pain. And back pain can be caused by cancer secondaries.'

Your face stiffens. 'Why didn't you say something?' you ask, voice sharp. 'We let her soldier on. We didn't take her to the doctor. I can't stop blaming myself. You were the only one who ever asked her how she was feeling.'

You sit in front of me, shoulders rounded, cheeks wet with tears. I step towards you and put my arms around you. You cling on to me, body trembling. A platonic bear hug. Nothing more for now. One step at a time.

157

Aiden

I ring the doorbell of Wellbeck House, and Hayley answers, hair coiffed, make-up lathered exuberantly across her usually natural face. Strangely artificial. Eyelashes like spider's legs. Slugs for eyebrows.

'You don't usually wear a dress,' I comment on her pale blue chemise. 'It's the first time I've seen your legs. Wasn't sure you had any.'

'Legs or dresses?'

'Both.'

'Ha, ha. Thought I'd make an effort. What are you doing here? What are you after?'

I grimace. 'After? Is that your opinion of me, that every time I come here, I have to be *after* something?'

She smiles, her warm wide smile. 'Everyone's after something in life.'

I raise my eyebrows. 'And what exactly are *you* after, Hayley?'

She laughs. 'Right now all I'm after is a coffee to perk me up. Would you like one?'

'Yes.'

We move into the kitchen. A large arrangement of lilies and orchids bristles from the central station. The family photographs have been rearranged. Less of Saffron. More of Mother. Miles must be adding them because of his grief. My favourite one of Mother takes centre stage. It was taken at her sixtieth birthday party. A sideways view of her sitting in a chair reading a book. Miles' idea. He said if she wasn't staring straight into the camera it would be more natural.

'Where's Miles?' I ask. 'I was hoping to see him.'

She moves towards the coffee machine. 'He's gone to the police station to make another witness statement. Didn't he let you know?' Hayley bustles about pressing buttons on the coffee machine. 'They want to speak to us all again, now they know Caprice was ill.'

I sit down and tap my fingers on the pine table. 'No. He just rang me distraught because he hadn't been able to take her to a doctor. I didn't realise he was having to give more evidence.'

The coffee machine spits and hisses.

Hayley raises her voice above it. 'I expect he'll phone you about it later. It sounds as if we'll all have to.'

Not again, I groan inside. Giving a statement to the police when Saffron was arrested was a long-winded and painful process, far more long-winded and painful than I had imagined.

I notice a pink leather diary on the counter, with a biro next to it. 'Are you keeping a diary?' I ask.

Her face lights up. 'Yes. I promised my mum I would do while I was on my trip. She so wants to read all about the UK when I get back. She said if I didn't write down the details of what I've seen I would forget.'

I envy Hayley her closeness to her mother. I feel empty inside. Caprice believed in Miles but not in me. If I could turn the clock back, what could I have done that would have impressed my mother more?

Hayley places a large Americano in front of me and a miniature jug of hot milk. And a plate of homemade cookies. She sits opposite me.

'Thanks. Are you playing domestic goddess?'

'Well, I could have been a barista or a baker, in another life,' she says with a smile. 'Even a barrister.'

'And I could have been less of a disappointment to my mother.'

She leans across the table and puts her hand on my arm. 'Don't speak like that Aiden. We've all got to stay positive after the loss of your mother. Your mother loved you very much. She was very proud of your success.'

'She loved Miles more. She was always in awe of his academics.'

She frowns. 'A mother's love is not a competition. And neither is life. We need to enjoy it as much as we can. Envy and resentment won't help.'

I bite my lip to stop myself from crying. I sip my coffee.

'Go on, have a cookie,' she insists, handing me the plate.

'Thanks.'

I help myself to a crumbling mass of soft biscuit and white chocolate. I take a bite. It is buttery and delicious. When I have finished eating I wipe the crumbs from my mouth with my hankie.

'Have you been to see Saffron? Do you know how she is?' I ask hesitantly.

She shakes her head. 'No. Only Miles is visiting.'

I take a deep breath. 'What does he say about her?' I ask.

Her face stiffens. 'Very little. He is very tight. Very closed in right now.'

'He must be so worried about her. I don't know how he's coping.'

I feel empty inside. I don't know how I'm coping. I'm worried too. But there is no point in telling Hayley that. All she ever does is think about Miles.

'They both must be going through hell.'

'Saffron being in prison is hell for all of us,' I say. 'We've been friends most of my adult life.'

We sit in silence. After a while I cut through it. 'I'm a bit stressed that Saffron won't let me visit her.'

Hayley shrugs. 'I expect she just wants to see Miles.'

Miles. Miles. Miles. Everyone's favourite. Fucking Miles. My stomach coagulates with envy.

320

'What about the children? Haven't they been to see her?' I ask, voice bristling.

'No. She misses them like mad, but she doesn't want them to see her in there. Maybe she feels the same about you. She would find it upsetting for you to see her in such a degrading environment.'

She leans across and puts her hand on my arm. 'I've told you before, I am sure she has feelings for you.'

My heart pulses with anger at the trouble she has caused me. I know she is wrong this time. 'Every time I've approached her she's pushed me away,' I insist in a stony voice.

She smiles condescendingly. It annoys me. 'Watch a few romantic films on Netflix. The heroine always pushes her lover away to begin with. It's part of the game.' She pauses. 'Trust me.'

Trust her? How can I?

Her mobile phone rings. She picks up and listens, head on one side. 'OK, OK, I'll come and have a look right away.'

She ends the call and stands up. 'I've just got to go and speak to the gardener. He's worried about the crab apple tree. He thinks it has a fungal disease.'

'Hayley Smith, mistress of the house.'

'One day, perhaps.' She smiles. 'I won't be long with the gardener. Make yourself at home, while I make sure he does everything I want. He's a good worker as long as I keep an eye on him.'

One day perhaps? What does she mean? Is she making progress with Miles? Is that what trying to stitch me up with Saffron is all about? To make Miles mistrust Saffron again? To give her more of a chance?

She steps through the back door. I stand up and watch her through the kitchen window, marching down the pathway past the tennis court and the swimming pool. Towards my mother's beloved back garden, which I know will be at its best this time of year. Mother was more interested in her garden than she was in me. Now she has gone I know it's over. I will never be able to please her, to impress her. I feel angry. I feel disappointed. I always imagined we would be closer by the time she passed.

I turn my head. My eyes rest on Hayley's diary. I pick it up and flick through it. She has written about me and I do not like what I read.

158

Saffron

I sit alone in the prison canteen at lunchtime. The women in this prison are not too keen on Oxbridge-educated solicitors, and they seem to think the name Saffron is a laugh a minute. So I try to keep my head down. Fortunately, so far, I have been considered too green to have to put up with a cell-mate.

Loneliness is better than emotional cruelty or physical injury. So here I am, sitting solo at the edge of a table, picking at my food, ignoring everyone, eyes down. Pushing a hotdog, shiny with grease, to the side of my plate. I contemplate the vegetables. Frozen peas and broccoli, so overcooked they look like early-stage compost. Khaki, with a hint of brown. They smell of sulphur. A scent that floats on the edge of the wind if you live near a sewage works.

I look up. A prison officer is approaching me, face flushed with determination. A middle-aged woman with grey hair and large round glasses. Her hair falls around her face in grizzled curls. She leans towards me across the plastic dining table.

'Are you Saffron Jackson?' she asks.

'Yes,' I say. 'Or at least I used to be, in another life.'

She pushes her face closer. 'I need you to come with me. Do you want your food taken to your cell to finish later?'

I look down at the greasy sausage, that looks like a turd on my plate, and the vegetable compost. 'I reckon I can manage without it.'

Eyes slide towards us as we leave the canteen. I tremble inside. What is coming now? Has my trial date been moved forwards? Are Ben and Harry OK? Does Miles want a divorce? Miles. He seems so distant at the moment. Hardly says anything when he visits.

I breathe deeply, in an attempt to calm myself, as the prison officer leads me, not towards a meeting room, but back towards my cell. Winding along white corridors, door after door locking behind us. No one else is moving about the prison right now. We arrive.

'Get inside please.'

In my cell, the aroma of damp air cuts into my nose. What a hovel. A shower with no curtain that sprays water across the plastic flooring. A toilet and a hand basin. But better by far than the custody suite. At least I have soap, paper towels and toilet paper now. I stand by my plank of a bed. She steps inside and pulls the door behind her. But she doesn't lock it.

She smiles. The lines around her eyes crinkle. 'The charges against you have been dropped. You are free to go.'

The words hang in the air between us and don't seem real. 'What . . . ? How . . . ?' I splutter.

She shakes her head. 'Don't sound surprised. It makes you seem guilty.'

Guilty. That jars me into action. 'I didn't murder my mother-in-law. That isn't the issue,' I reply, voice clipped. 'The case against me was rather entrenched,' I continue. 'I'm surprised it's over so abruptly, and I'm simply curious to know what happened.'

She doesn't reply. 'Pack your things. I'll escort you to the exit.'

'I want to see my lawyer. I want to know what's happened before I leave.'

'Are you implying you don't want to leave?'

'Goddammit. I'm implying I want to see my solicitor, John Thornton,' I bark.

★ ★ ★

324

Hours later, after collecting my confiscated possessions, and signing a barrage of forms, I am finally shown into the meeting room where John Thornton is waiting for me, dressed in his city suit. He stands up and hugs me, smelling of citrus and musk.

Brown eyes twinkle into mine. 'I'm so pleased for you. I knew you'd be OK. But I'm thrilled your ordeal is over.'

'Not as thrilled as I am.'

He smiles, his cheeky, dimple-assisted smile. 'Maybe not, but nevertheless, I'm thrilled, believe me.'

'Thank you, John.'

We sit down opposite one another. I take a deep breath. 'I want to be armed with the details of why I have been released, before I go home to talk to Miles. He has been so suspicious of me, which has been heart-breaking.' I pause. 'I know it has been hard for him, still grieving his mother.'

'OK. First things first. As you suspected, the police found no dirt on your computer.'

I nod my head. 'I told you.'

He leans across the table and puts his hand on my arm. 'Never mind Miles, this has been very hard on you too.'

I swallow. 'Yes. Losing such a close family member has been very painful in itself, never mind being accused of her murder.'

He takes my hand and squeezes it. 'As you know, the autopsy discovered that Caprice had cancer.'

'Yes. Poor, poor, Caprice. Miles was so upset she hadn't told us.'

Slowly, slowly, he shakes his head. 'It is really sad. The police confiscated her computer and ran a check on it. They discovered she was ordering the arsenic from the darknet herself, in order to speed up her end. The police now believe she did indeed set you up – as you told them in the first place.'

I smile inside. Ted's nerdy friend, Stan, has really come up with the goods. Stan, the chubby man with a pregnant stomach and a hairstyle like a cartoon monk. He has been expensive, but discreet. You were so angry when you couldn't find your computer, the weekend I removed it and deposited it at Stan's flat on the Archway Road in Highgate. Your grey eyes turned metallic. Your chin jutted out like a strange, contorted gargoyle. You turned on Harry and Ben. Blamed my children. A week later I returned it to your shed in the garden. You believed you had left it there, and apologised. You took the boys to McDonald's for a treat. I did this to protect myself. As backup. I never realised you had cancer and that your actions would be so perfectly believable.

I look across at John Thornton. I widen my eyes in sadness. 'Poor, poor Caprice.'

159

Miles

You are about to be released. I'm waiting in the prison car park, on a grey, drizzly day, feeling numb and confused. I don't think you would deliberately poison my mother. Yet I don't think my mother would poison herself. Then again, I never thought my mother would be riddled with cancer, and not tell her family. Despite being a philosopher, I don't know what to think. Aristotle and Plato don't seem to have provided any answers here. My mother's death has blown our lives apart.

You step out of prison wearing the clothes they arrested you in. Your black Armani suit, razor-blade heels and Hugo Boss blouse; the one that tumbles with lace and frills. Your long blonde hair streams behind your head in the breeze as you walk towards the car. Your face lights up as soon as you see me. I step out of the car and take you in my arms. You smell of desire. Of warmth. Of love. I hold you against me, guilt-ridden for doubting you.

And I know, the only philosophy I need to understand right now, is that I am part of you, and you are part of me. We will always belong together.

160

Saffron

I'm sitting in the car, as Miles drives me home. Nestling into the soft leather of his Range Rover. Driving me away from my nightmare. Someone pressed a button and my life had stopped.

I look out of the car window and my life begins again. The world moves towards me fresh and colourful. Trees. Fields. Homes. Real homes containing real people. Not just passive objects who are locked behind closed doors, and fed food that tastes like the smell from the garbage dump. We drive past people walking along with a purpose. Friends to meet. Stuff to do. Their bodies not laden with the idle procrastination of those who are incarcerated. Zombies whose lives have stopped.

I can't wait to get home. I can't wait to see the children. Hold them against me, skin on skin. My body ached for them, every hour of every day, last month.

We turn into Lexington Drive. Past the James' house. Past the Naracotts'. The Taylors' and the Carrington-Smiths'. People we only see at dinner parties. The handmade iron gate, full of swirls and crevices, swings open as we pull into the drive of Wellbeck House. What a difference it makes to control the iron enclosures. After so long in prison, Wellbeck House looks like a palace. Portland stone porch. Ornate stone mantels. High ceilings. High windows. I step inside feeling like a princess. Princess Saffron of the Lexingtons. This is my jewelled kingdom. And now that you are gone, I am about to be crowned Queen.

'She's here,' Miles yells, stepping in beside me.

The boys come bounding into the hallway. Even though I have only been away a month, it has seemed like forever. They have grown. Ben looks slimmer than I remember. Eight years old now, nearly nine. Losing his baby fat. Lean and leggy. He has lost another tooth and the gap at the front of his mouth is bigger. Did Miles remember to ask him to leave it under his pillow, remove it, and put a pound coin in its place? So much to ask. So much catching up. He runs towards me and I hold him against me. I want to stay like this and press my love into him forever.

Harry is here, snuggling up between my arm and Ben's head like a pushy puppy dog. My heart sings with love.

I look across towards the kitchen. Hayley is standing by the doorway. Slimmer. Elegant and sophisticated in a clinging soft jersey dress. High heels showing the curves of her calves and the thrust of her pelvis. Made up as if she's about to go to a wedding or appear on a TV advert. She folds her arms, puts her head on one side and gives me a look. For a second I think she looks sanctimonious. But then her lips twitch, and burst into her usual broad smile.

'Welcome home, Saffron,' she barks in her New Zealand twang.

161

Hayley

'Welcome home, Saffron,' I manage through gritted teeth.

She looks so beautiful, like a delicate butterfly. I know I shouldn't resent her, but I was so happy when she was away. Handing back the keys is going to be really, really difficult.

162

Saffron

The children are in bed. Hayley is upstairs relaxing in her room. Miles is cracking open a bottle of champagne in the drawing room. He pours the celebratory drink carefully down the side of our crystal goblets and hands me a glass. We clink our bubbles together.

'To your freedom,' Miles says.

We sit in antique chairs, on each side of our white marble fireplace.

Miles takes a sip and wriggles uncomfortably in his chair. 'Do you know what, I'd rather have flat.'

Given the circumstances does he find Moët and Chandon too celebratory? He places his champagne on the mantelpiece and walks to the wine fridge behind the curved mock Georgian cupboard in the corner. He rummages about until he finds a bottle of Viognier. He pours a third of a bottle into an extra-large glass.

'Cheers.'

He takes two large gulps of Viognier and necks half his glass. I have never seen him drinking like this. His eyes are empty. His face is red.

'So,' he says. 'Why would Mum poison herself, and not tell us she was ill and needed support and help?'

I shake my head. I do not know what to say.

'Why would she do something as dreadful as killing herself

and setting you up for it? I am so shocked, my mind can hardly focus. It is as if the ground I walk on has been pulled from under me and I don't know how to move forwards anymore.'

'Miles, don't make me say it.'

He turns his empty eyes towards me. 'Don't make you say what?'

'I told you so.'

His body bends. He winces as if I have punched him in the stomach.

'I know you did.' He bangs his wine glass onto the coffee table, stands up and walks towards me. He stands in front of me, bereft. Devastated. 'Hold me, Saffron.'

I stand up and step towards him. He pulls me against him. We cling to one another like ivy around a tree trunk, clasping, burrowing, digging for comfort. I feel the vibration of sobs building in the back of his throat.

'I'm sorry, Saffron, for not believing you.'

These words, so long in coming, fill me with warmth. They contort to jubilation, which I suppress. Jubilation is too much. All I want is peace. Peace to live my life with the man I love; without your interference, Caprice.

'It was hard for you. She was your mother. You loved her.'

His body trembles against mine. 'What has happened is impossible to accept. It has shattered all my perceptions of my family life. Made my past a lie. I will never be able to come to terms with it.'

'You will, Miles. Together we will come through this. Together we can come through anything.'

163

Hayley

Over a hundred people are at Caprice's funeral. The ancient church is swathed in a moving mass of people dressed in black. School gate mums. Bridge club. BPC. Your university friends. Aiden's business associates. Saffron's colleagues, Ted and Julie. School friends. Past neighbours. Even some people from the 'look-at-me' houses down the road have turned up to pay their respects. The turnout comes as a surprise, but I wonder how genuine their feelings are. I suspect most people have come to support you, Saffron and Aiden.

I'm sitting right at the front in the cheap clingy dress I bought at Primark. Part of the family; responsible for looking after the children. No longer mistress of the household. You and Aiden look smart, in dark suits and ties, flanking Saffron, who is sitting to our right. Saffron looks as funky as ever. She is wearing a black and white block dress, and a tiny black hat with an enormous feather, which curves halfway down her back. My charges are sitting next to me, backs stiff, smart in children's suits we found in John Lewis; mouths tightly shut, eyes glued to the altar at the front. No wriggling. No giggling. Little angels today, please.

The only person who is lightening the colour of the occasion is the vicar, a young woman with a sweet sing-song lilt. She is wearing layers of white, which represent the righteousness of Christ. Ben told me that. He seems to know so much these days. A purple stole around her neck. We sing Caprice's favourite hymn: 'Now Thank We All Our God'. We kneel to pray. The vicar stands up. Time for the eulogy.

'We are here, not to mourn for our beloved Caprice, but to celebrate her life. She was a devoted wife to her adored Rupert, a devoted and much-loved mother and grandmother. A giver, not a taker. Everyone who met her loved her.'

164

Saffron

Not everyone who met you loved you. Not everyone, I shout in my head. Some of us hated you. Some of us wanted you dead. Then a mystical sensation wraps itself around me. I have been in this situation before, listening to the eulogy at your funeral. I look around. Everything is the same as my dreams, except the church is larger and there is no beach. The same silver cross stands in front of me, moving towards me, growing larger in my memory, in my mind. My body jolts as if I am about to wake up, but nothing happens. This time, my nemesis, you are dead. I will never have to put up with you again. Long may you rest in peace.

165

Hayley

Memories flood towards me. I see Caprice standing in front of me, wearing cream silk, and magnificent waterfall earrings of sterling silver. Kitten-heel sandals in matching cream. Always so smooth. So elegant. Always doused in her favourite perfume, Opium by YSL. She looked a little bit like Audrey Hepburn but paler.

I am back walking around the garden of Wellbeck House, arm in arm with her. Admiring the clematis and catmint, the salvia, the geraniums, the laburnum. Sitting beneath the weeping willow tree, the day she told me you had feelings for me, and my life opened out. I look across at your handsome face, today engulfed by pain and grief. My heart aches with love for you. I wish I could hold you against me and comfort you. Saffron is sitting so close to you, her arm draped across your back. Your shoulders are shaking. You are sobbing silently. Aiden is calmer. Head up high facing the front. I tear my eyes away from Caprice's sons and step back into my memories.

My birthday. The look on her face, eyes soft with kindness, as she handed me my card and a bunch of roses at breakfast time. She had made me American pancakes, and she served them to me with Canadian syrup and strawberries. Just a dash of icing sugar, sprinkled across the pancakes like snowflakes. The scent of the roses she had placed in a vase in the middle of the pine kitchen table wafting around the room.

And the necklace she bought me. She took me to London to choose it the day after my birthday. At her favourite jewellers, the Silver Mouse Trap, behind The Royal Courts of Justice, on the Strand. I lift my hand to my neck to check my treasured piece of jewellery is still there. My fingers press down against the firmness of the gold chain I wear every day, and more memories come flooding back.

Cups of coffee drunk at leisure together in the morning after I'd taken the boys to school. Italian Lavazza, her favourite. Listening to music with her. Unusual for her age, she liked Radio 1 as well as Radio 4.

The way she made me laugh repeating gossip from the school gate mums.

'The chap in our office who checks the computers is sleeping with the head of Marketing, and they're both married. Don't tell anyone will you,' she told me Penny Langton yelled into her iPhone in the playground. Everyone in the playground heard and giggled. Caprice's stories sometimes made me laugh so much my eyes watered and my mascara ran. So black-eyed from mascara, I looked like a panda after some of our chats.

The day she took me to Wisley, the Royal Horticultural Society. Giving me such inspiration for the gardening course I hope to study when I return home. Too early for the summer borders to have reached their full magnificence. Caprice and I had a competition to see who could recognise the most plants. Caprice won. I close my eyes and try and remember what was there. Roses, allium, lavender, red thunder, silver ghost, echinacea, achillea coronation gold. Dahlias. We walked to Battleston Hill, flanked by a sea of lilies and hydrangeas. Purple, pink, and powder blue.

Lunch in the café. Eating steak pie and chips, drinking red wine. The exotic garden. Fronds and palms from all around the world. Bold vibrant tropical flowers. The gentle tranquillity of the woodland gardens. The sweet, homely prettiness of the cottage gardens. The lake, the trees, the pinetum. The waterlilies. The rockery and its tumbling waterfalls. Caprice bought a trolleyful of plants from the garden centre.

'Next year,' Caprice said, as I drove her home, 'we'll come later in the season to catch the summer borders in their full glory.'

For Caprice, next year will never come. Tears well up inside me. I bite my lip to try and push them away. But they are volcanic.

166

Saffron

Hayley's sobs and moans echo around the church, like a stuck pig's. Miles and I exchange glances. She's attracting too much attention. Overegging her importance within the family.

167

Aiden

Sitting in a conference room at Mann and Mann Solicitors with my brother. Floor-to-ceiling windows, looking out onto a low-maintenance leafy shrubbery. Board meeting table. High-backed leather chairs. Stiff central flower arrangement of orchids and lilies. White lilies, a favourite of Mother's. The flowers we chose for her casket. Mr Mann, our mother's solicitor, is dressed in black as if we are still at her funeral. His grey hair is wispier than ever. He has aged since we were sorting out Father's estate. The fat has gone from his face, and he is painfully thin and frail. He coughs a little, to clear his throat.

'This is the last will and testament of Caprice Jackson.' A long severe pause. 'I bequeath my estate in equal parts to my sons, Aiden Jackson and Miles Jackson. Aiden is to receive his share immediately. Miles' share is conditional. He will receive £100,000 immediately, but the remainder only if six months after my death, his wife Saffron is still alive. If Saffron should die within the first six months of my death, the rest of his share shall pass to Hayley Manville Smith.'

Mother had always said it would be clear-cut. Fifty–fifty. What has happened? What is this? I look across at Miles. His eyes are dark and thunderous. He is ashen.

'What has happened? What has Mother done?' Miles asks.

Miles

The wording of my mother's will burns me, like acid.

'What has happened? What has Mother done? We always thought the money would be split fairly between Aiden and I?'

Mr Mann leans back in his chair. 'This is how your mother wanted it to be. It was her money. She was very definite in her instructions, which I faithfully recorded in her will.'

'But what's all this about Saffron dying?' My body is rigid with fear. 'When did she add that? Why does she think Saffron might die?'

Mr Mann widens his shoulders and folds his arms. 'She rewrote her will a month before she died. I don't think she meant to imply Saffron might die. It's just a condition of her will that she decided to impose on Miles' inheritance.'

'Was she compos mentis?'

His eyes harden. 'That is tantamount to accusing me of malpractice.' He pauses. 'Of course she was. As a solicitor I wouldn't have allowed her to change her will, if she wasn't.' His voice is tight and clipped. 'I knew your mother for fifty years. I was always very aware of the clarity of her mind.'

I stand up, put my hands on the conference table and lean towards him. 'You don't need to get heavy with me. I have no intention of contesting my mother's will. Or accusing you of anything. But I'm sure you must understand, as a lot of money is involved, I am now most concerned for the safety of my wife.'

Aiden

We step out of Mann and Mann Solicitors, and stand on the pavement outside. I am shocked and surprised. Worried about Miles. Worried about you, Saffron. What was Mother up to? Why Hayley? She hardly knew her. She had been your nanny for less than a year. Hayley being mentioned in the will is a lightning bolt.

I look across at Miles. He has an expression on his face that I have never seen before, despite all that we have been through over the years, including our childhood fights, the death of our father, our mother. Even when he punched me after he caught me kissing you.

It's a dull August day. A gritty sky. Pan-scrub clouds blocking the sun. But despite the cloud the background temperature is high. Solid heat presses against my body. I wipe the sweat from my brow with my hankie, and undo my tie.

'Come on, mate, let me take you for a drink,' I say. 'Let's go to The Bear for a quick one.'

Miles' face softens a little. 'Yep. I think I need more than one before I go home.'

We walk to The Bear in silence. We step inside. Tuesday night. Not many customers. A group of scantily dressed young women in the corner. Bras showing. Lycra sliding from their shoulders. Two elderly men, heads together over a pint, and us.

'What can I get you?' I ask.

'A double whisky.'

'All right, you sit down. I'll go to the bar.'

As I set up a tab and order the drinks, I look across the room to Miles, to check he is all right. He has chosen a table near the fireplace and is sitting, body stiff, with his head in his hands.

I place his whisky in front of him and sit down next to him.

He looks up. 'Thanks,' he mutters, lifting the glass to his lips and knocking it straight back.

I put my hand on his arm. 'We're in this together. What are we going to do about it?' I ask.

'First, I am not going to tell Saffron.' He pauses. 'And I don't want you to either. She'll freak out, start to panic that someone is going to kill her. You need to help me protect her for the six months. We need to watch where she goes, everything she does.'

'Protecting Saffron will be my pleasure.'

The look I have never seen before intensifies. 'If you touch her, I'll kill you.'

'I can assure you, your wife doesn't want me to touch her. And after so much rejection, I don't want to touch her anymore.'

He stands up. 'Just getting another drink. What would you like?'

I look down at my pint. I've hardly touched it. 'I'm fine thanks.'

I watch him walk to the bar, body a little looser after his double whisky. He returns with another large one, bangs the glass on the table and sits down again.

'You asked me what we are going to do about this situation. I'll tell you what we are going to do. I want you to pretend that we are both only getting £100,000 to begin with, so that Saffron won't be worried. Can you help me on that?'

'That's fine with me.'

We sit in silence. I finish my pint.

'And we'll be getting rid of Hayley, of course.'

I smile. 'Absolutely. Come for lunch at mine at the weekend. I can help sow the seeds for that.'

170

Miles

Feeling blurred around the edges, after drinking so much alcohol, I stagger through our hallway. Our modern art swims towards me. I weave my way through it.

'Saffron,' I shout. 'I'm home.'

Fingers to your lips, 'Shush,' you whisper as you tiptoe through the hallway, dressed in your silk negligee. 'I need a little peace. I've just put the boys to bed.'

You take me in your arms, the scent of your favourite perfume, Juliette Has A Gun, engulfing us. Your body feels warm and comforting. You kiss me, and make me feel like a teenager again. You pull away.

'How did the trip to the solicitors go?' you ask.

'Let's get a bottle of wine, and I'll tell you.'

Sitting in the drawing room, I sip white wine with my arm around you. 'Well, was the will what you expected?' you push.

'No.' I pause. 'Well almost.'

You look at me quizzically. 'Come on. Tell me. Explain.'

'Aiden and I only get the first £100,000 to begin with. We have to wait six months for the rest.'

'Why?'

I shrug my shoulders, and force a smile. 'No idea. Bizarre isn't it?' I try to speak slowly, and clip the end of my words. I have had so much to drink that I might be sounding slurred. 'But

'£100,000 is more than enough to tide us over. To invest some money in BPC if you want?'

171

Saffron

Miles is right: £100,000 is enough to tide us over. And six months to wait for the rest is nothing in the scheme of things. What a weird stipulation. Why? And at least the probate is simple. Nothing in trust. Mainly cash not shares.

I have nothing to worry about. You have done all the damage you possibly can from beyond the grave, Caprice. You are finished. Over. Kaput. As Miles said, we have more than enough to begin to invest in BPC if I want. Oh yes, I want. Of course I want. Yes please. I want my business to succeed. Thank you, Caprice, for dying at the right time and rescuing me. I will hide my desire for my business to succeed, and try not to make my benefits from your demise too obvious. I will wear my smile inside.

172

Aiden

Sunday lunch, at mine for a change. I have sweated over a Nigel Slater vegetable curry to please you, Saffron. And I'm serving it with an Ottolenghi salad, containing too many ingredients, including a herb that I can't get at Waitrose, but grows in a friend's garden. I had to drive to Putney to collect it. Burgundy wine. San Pellegrino, your favourite mineral water. You are fussy about that.

Your black net dress shows your red lacy bra. I like your red ankle boots and perfectly toning lipstick. Your Deborah Harry in her heyday look. Punky and delicious.

Miles is his usual self. Complacent and charming, wearing chinos and slip-on mules. I really can't understand why he was always Mother's favourite. There is so much more bite about me. I was more rebellious at school. That's why I wasn't a prefect. He was a prefect because he was such a yes-man. Didn't Richard Branson say you should ditch education if you want to be successful? Or was it Bill Gates? Anyway, Miles is too embroiled in intellectual activity to ever be truly top of the pile.

We finish the main course and I clear the plates. I put the homemade vegan meringues, made with chickpea water, into the oven, and step back into my dining room. I sit down, place my elbows on the table, hands together and lean across toward my indolent brother and his feisty wife.

'Now the funeral's over, there's something I need to discuss with you both.'

You put your wine glass down and look at me wide-eyed. Miles necks the end of his glass, and tops it up. He leans back in his chair. 'Fire away.'

'It's slightly sensitive.' I pause. 'It's about Hayley.' I look straight at Miles. He nods for me to continue. I turn my head towards you, Saffron. 'One day, when you were in prison, Saffron, I popped to the house hoping to see Miles. But he was out giving a police statement. Anyway, Hayley invited me in for coffee and we got chatting.' I pause. 'Did you know she writes a diary?'

'No,' you reply.

'Yes,' Miles replies almost in unison.

'Well,' I continue, 'Hayley got distracted, having to check on the gardeners. They had a problem with one of your trees. So she inadvertently left me alone with it and I had a quick peek.'

'Voyeuristic,' Miles says.

I shrug my shoulders. 'I'm glad I did. That young woman is a troublemaker. And she seriously has the hots for you, Miles. She would go to extreme lengths to snare you. You both need to be very wary of her.'

You exchange glances with Miles. A frown furrows your brow.

'Let me show you. I took some pictures of the text on my iPhone.'

I press my phone, and pass it across the table to them. They sit heads together and read. After a while they look up.

'See what I mean? She's seriously into Miles, so much so that she lied to me. She told me she thought Saffron had feelings for me. Leading me to hope. Leading me to behave inappropriately, when in fact all she wanted was to cause trouble between you both, so that she could attempt to bag Miles. I'm furious. I feel played.' I stop for breath. 'And I'm sorry for behaving so badly. I want to apologise.'

Miles takes a large sip of wine, puts his head on one side and smiles.

'Well you've always been a pain, so I'm used to it, mate.' He pauses. 'And you have always been over-interested in my wife, you bastard, so you deserve to be played.'

His eyes shine into mine the way they always do when he is teasing me. I know he loves me. He needs my help. He has forgiven me.

'And you saw the way Hayley behaved at the funeral,' I continue.

'It was appalling,' you bristle. 'Totally over the top and inappropriate. And she was supposed to be looking after the boys.'

'But it was useful. I think it showed she was far closer than we realised to our mother. Look, I couldn't photograph the whole diary, but it's a no-brainer. She wants Miles as her partner. She was in cahoots with Mother. Mother set Saffron up. Hayley may well have helped. She's in love with Miles. What else might she be about to do to cause trouble for Saffron? And Saffron has been through enough. It's simple. You need to let Hayley go. If I were you, I'd get a new nanny as soon as possible. I suggest you contact the agency immediately.'

173

Saffron

We leave Aiden's. The Uber driver blasts through Fulham and Wimbledon. He screeches towards the car in front of us at the traffic lights before we get onto the A4.

'Slow down,' I scream. 'Or stop the car so we can get out.'

The driver doesn't reply. But he tames his driving the rest of the way home.

As soon as we step through our front door, 'Come on,' I say to Miles, 'let's have some lemon and ginger tea, and sit down to talk about Hayley.'

'I'd rather have some more wine.'

My heart sinks. I am worried he needs to drink to tolerate what has happened. I take a deep breath. I need to confront him. 'No, Miles, you're drinking too much since I came out of prison. Is it because having me home is difficult?'

He shakes his head. 'No. I'm so pleased you're home. I love you, Saffron. But I have felt low since Mother died. I do feel better when I drink.'

'Alcohol's a depressant. It makes you feel better for a few hours in the evening, but by the next morning it will be lowering your metabolism and your spirits. Come on, lemon and ginger tea, and a chat about Hayley. You'll feel better in the morning if you don't have any more wine.'

He sighs. 'OK.'

He makes the tea. I go and check on the boys. I kiss them

gently without waking them, on my favourite spot on their foreheads, just below the hairline. My boys, who I am sure you tried to separate me from, Caprice.

I pad downstairs. Miles is waiting for me, sitting obediently at the kitchen table, with two mugs of tea. I join him and take a sip. Then I place my cup on the table, take a deep breath, and start.

'Hayley will have to go.' I lean back and twist my palms to the ceiling. 'It's a pity because she has looked after the children well. They've been happy with her. She's a good nanny. And it's always such a drag finding someone else.'

Miles reaches across, takes my hand in his and squeezes it. 'But Aiden's right. You can't be exposed to any more trouble.' He shakes his head sadly.

'I think I'll take some time off work. I'll look after Ben and Harry and the home for now.'

Miles stiffens in surprise. 'But . . . but . . . what about BPC?'

'Well, I'm putting the business on the back burner at the moment.'

'What do you mean?'

'Well, we've only got two clients at the moment and Aristos is very quiet these days, so the small amount of work I'm doing, I can do from home.'

'That's a surprise. Why didn't you tell me?' He raises his shoulders and his palms.

'Because you've had so much on what with losing your mother. I didn't want to worry you about my business.'

He frowns. 'But what about Ted and Julie?'

'Ted's freelancing doing a few tax returns, sorting out another friend's business accounts. Julie's helping her new partner set up a business. So they are coping.' I pause and sigh. 'They'll be OK for a while, I suppose.'

Miles' golden brown eyes darken. He squeezes my hand again. 'We'll soon get that money from my mother's estate and then

351

you'll easily be able to use it to build BPC up again. Is that what you need, some more capital when the loan runs out?'

'In a word, yes.'

'Well I can't think of a better use to put my inheritance to.' I lean across the table and kiss him. 'Thank you so very much.'

'That's fine. It's a no-brainer isn't it, wanting to help my wife?' He pauses. 'Are you sure you're happy to stay home and look after the boys for a while? I don't want you bored and unhappy at home. You could apply to work for someone else in the meantime. We can get a nanny again anytime you want.'

'After everything that's happened I think a short break from a guest in the house will do us all good. And we can use me staying at home as the excuse for letting Hayley go. But yes. As soon as Caprice's money comes in I'd love to pump it into BPC and go back to work.' I pause, and sip my tea. 'So who's going to tell Hayley?'

'I'll tell her,' Miles says. 'She's closer to me.'

174

Miles

Sacking Hayley is a no-brainer this time. The sooner I do it the better. The solicitor has made it quite clear he will inform Hayley about the will any day now. As soon as she knows the situation she'll be a danger. I do not want her anywhere near our family. So I'm looking for any opportunity to catch her alone. And I do not want Ben and Harry listening to the conversation. They really like her, so they will kick up. And I am not venturing into her bedroom area. She's so flirty with me, she'll take that as a come-on.

Every time I have tried to approach her it has been impossible. The boys were glued to her side all weekend. Saturday night and Sunday night she disappeared out with her on-off boyfriend, freaky Jono. His hair is green at the moment. I saw him skulking at the end of the drive smoking a roll-up that emitted a spicy scent. Wearing weird trousers a bit like Ronald McDonald. Monday, she took the boys to school and then went out shopping all day. She returned laden with bags from Primark and Top Shop, the boys again attached to her side. As soon as she had put them to bed she vanished straight into the no-go zone. The red-hot heat of her bedroom.

I am determined to fire her. Whatever happens. Today is the day. I will catch her somewhere. By the swimming pool. Late at night when she returns from Jono's. I'll even get in the car with her if she goes shopping again.

Early evening, I look out of the kitchen window. She is walking towards the garden, notepad in hand. I hear the theme tune from *X-Men* blasting from the playroom. The boys must be watching a film. I bound out of the back door. Out of breath and panting, I tap her on the shoulder. She turns around and her face lights up.

'Miles!' she exclaims. She puts her head on one side and treats me to one of her broad, teeth-flashing smiles. Sexy, but contrived.

For a second I feel guilty for what I am about to do. Then I remember why I have to do it, and my guilt is overtaken by resolve.

'I need to talk to you, Hayley.' My voice sounds heavy, thunderous.

Her smile sticks to her lips and freezes. 'Let's go and sit on the bench in the garden,' I continue.

'Is everything all right?' she almost whispers.

'Come with me and I'll explain.'

We walk across the lawn, past the west-facing flowerbed, rich with geraniums, phlox, roses, campanula, jasmine. Past Caprice's favourite tree, the crab apple that my father, Rupert, gave to her on their silver wedding anniversary. She treasured that tree. A tree is worth a million pieces of jewellery, she said when he gave it to her. After he died she always told us that this tree symbolised their life together. Her favourite book was *Birds Without Wings* by Louis de Bernières. She always quoted what he said, likening a couple's love to tree roots growing together.

'That's how I felt about Rupert,' she often announced after quoting Louis de Bernières' haunting words.

Words that moved me. My insides tighten as I think about it. She loved Rupert like I love Saffron. And yet she deemed it all right to cause so much pain and trouble for me.

Hayley and I sit together on the bench beneath the weeping willow. Her eyes simmer into mine. Surely after the harsh tone I used when I asked to speak to her, she doesn't think I'm

354

about to make a love declaration? My stomach is heavy. I take a deep breath.

'Hayley, Saffron is leaving BPC for a while. She wants to stay at home and look after Ben and Harry herself.'

Eyes and mouth shape into circles of surprise. She doesn't look like Hayley Smith for a second, but a cartoon character from *South Park*. She soon sharpens up.

'That's a turn-up for the books. What's brought that on? Is her business failing?'

Is that why Hayley and Caprice got on? Are they riddled with the same kind of bitchiness?

'No. She just wants to enjoy some free time with her family. Alone.' I pause. 'So, we don't need you, from tomorrow.'

Hayley gasps. 'That's not much notice.'

'We will pay you a month's salary. It's just that we would like you to leave immediately.'

She looks crestfallen. Eyes brimming with tears. 'Will you give me a reference?'

'You've done a great job. Of course we will, Hayley.'

175

Hayley

I'm packing, so sad to be going. Living here has been like moving through a beautiful dream. I stuff my expensive swimming costume, my designer clothing I bought to beguile you, and my Christian Dior make-up into my scruffy rucksack, grey with dust from my travels. I won't need any of this in the squat with Jono. It will be jumpers, jeans and trainers. Eating crappy left-overs from the local market, and drinking cider that tastes like methylated spirits. As I leave I steal three photographs from the album Caprice used to show me in her bedroom. No one will notice they are missing. One of you. One of Caprice. One of Ben and Harry cuddling each other in the armchair by the white marble fireplace. I know which male I'll miss most and he isn't a child.

Saffron

I've just taken Ben and Harry to school, returned home and cleared up the breakfast dishes. I'm sitting drinking Lavazza coffee at the kitchen table. It's so peaceful in Wellbeck House, without your stabbing grey eyes. Without your sulky lips mispronouncing *dear*. I do not miss your bitchy ways. Your bitchy comments. And as for Miles, who was my biggest worry, he seems to be getting over your death. His drinking has returned to its normal level. And he has returned to being full-on in bed. A friend of mine, who is a relationship counsellor, once told me that when a man feels in control in the bedroom he feels in control of his life. So maybe our antics between the sheets have helped improve Miles' perspective.

Aiden is keeping away. I guess he has finally accepted I'm not interested. That has taken another weight off my shoulders. The way he doted on me never pleased me, it just made me feel uncomfortable. Both his presence, and you, my mother-in-law's, were like a cloud hanging over me.

And Hayley? I miss her in a strange sort of way. She was helpful and kind. Calming and sensible. It just bugged me the way she used to look at Miles.

Miles

I didn't enjoy your comments about my drinking, Saffron. So I'm sitting in the drawing room, drinking my new tipple, elderflower pressé. Looking out of the window, thinking about my mother. She was a beautiful woman. Doe-eyed. Sleek. Elegant. I was nurtured in the hothouse of her love. But why has she caused all this trouble?

Now I have been made aware of the contents of her will, I know you have always been right. My mother was dangerous; and so is her legacy. I won't let anyone harm you, my beautiful Saffron. I am so relieved Hayley moved out without making too much fuss. For the next six months I'll be watching out for you like a hawk.

178

Hayley

Living in the squat with Jono is worse than camping. I'm in despair. I won't be able to tolerate this level of discomfort much longer. If I don't get a job soon I'll ask Mum for the money to fly home. But I'm not sure she can afford it. She has a job at the Four Square supermarket in Queenstown. She works long hours but doesn't have much to show for it. It's a good thing my dad and my brother Sam bring in a bit of cash from strapping up bungee jumpers. But every penny they bring in gets spent on food and rent.

You promised me a good reference, but you can't have kept your word. The agency haven't offered me a single interview. The nights are drawing in. It's October now. The squat is cold. We have no electricity. We go to the pub every evening to keep warm. And charge our phones. We make a pint of cider and a plate of chips each last all evening. When we return, we go straight to bed. Except it isn't a bed. It's a saggy mattress that Jono acquired from a friend who works at the tip. We dive into our sleeping bags fully dressed.

Tonight has been no different. I'm shivering as I pull my sleeping bag over my head. My mobile beeps. A text. I press the screen and it lights up so that I can see it. Mann and Mann Solicitors, 25 Newport Street, Esher. *Hayley Manville Smith. Please visit our premises with proof of I.D. We have possession of a legal document we need to inform you of.*

My heart races. What is this about? Am I about to be accused of something? Is it a class-action scam? I can't guess. And I can't sleep. The night is torture. The bare windows offer no protection from darkness or light. Moonlight burns into my eyes and spills across my face. An owl hoots. Jono is lying on his back snoring. I thought he was too young to snore. The cold drills through the sleeping bag and permeates my bones. And then somehow, despite all the discomfort, my eyes open and Jono is rousing from his sleeping bag, rubbing his eyes and groaning. I must have dropped off, in the end. Sleep came as suddenly and terminally as I imagine death. The miracle is that from such sudden nothingness, I am now awake.

'Oh God, what time is it?' Jono is asking.

I scowl and look at my watch. 'Nine o'clock,' I reply.

'Shit. I promised Barry I'd be there at 7.30 a.m. We've got a big job to finish from yesterday.'

He pulls himself out of his sleeping bag, still wearing his Kid Rock T-shirt, and his black oil-stained jeans. I watch my unsavoury boyfriend and tell myself for the hundredth time, I must be mad to live here with him.

'See you later, Hayley,' he shouts as he leaves.

I don't reply. The roar of his motorbike vibrates into the distance.

We do not have running water in this derelict cottage, but I managed to travel to Euston station yesterday and have a shower. This morning I wash myself with facewipes and apply copious amounts of perfume and deodorant. I dress myself in clean clothes. I manage to apply some make-up using the cracked mirror in the bathroom.

As I stride through Esher, the sting of the crisp, cold autumn day, pushes the damp smell that permeates the flat from my nose. From my head. And even though I am worried about what Mann and Mann are going to say, it's good to be out. Along Esher High Street. Past the Good Earth Chinese restaurant. Past the Giggling Squid, Red Peppers and the post office.

I stand in front of Mann and Mann Solicitors. Floor-to-ceiling tinted windows. Grey canopy. Gold lettering. I step inside. The reception area boasts wide grey leather sofas either side of the path to a young woman in a sharply tailored suit, who is beaming at me from behind a welcome desk. I look around. The dusky peach walls are adorned with well-lit modern art. Coloured brushstrokes. Sunsets that tone perfectly with the sofas and walls. Seascapes. Mountains. You can only tell what they are by their names. The air is thick with silence.

I move towards the receptionist. She looks so manicured. I look down to check that I don't look too much of a sight. At least my jeans, T-shirt, and ankle boots are clean. That's all I can say about my drab outfit.

'Can I help you?' she asks.

'I'm Hayley Smith. I was asked to come here to see Mr Mann.'

She nods her head. 'I'll let him know you're here. Please sit down. Can I get you a coffee?'

'That would be lovely. Yes please.'

Lovely indeed. Since I moved in with Jono I only have hot drinks when I'm out. I sink into the sofa and sigh with pleasure at the feel of a comfortable seat. I've hardly sat down when the receptionist places coffee and a biscotti, a miniature jug of milk on the side, on the glass table in front of me.

'Thank you,' I simper.

I sit drinking, relishing every sip.

After the sumptuous reception area, Mr Mann's office is a pigeon-hole. Small and stark. Neat. Cream walls, cream carpet. Pale ash desk with a laptop attached to two large viewing screens. He sits behind his desk. I sit in the chair in front of it, stupefied as to what's coming. I cannot even begin to guess.

I sit, eyes fixed on Mr Mann. He is elderly, thin on top, but with lank grey hair flanking his ears and framing the sides of his face. Small, sharp pinprick eyes and a slender, pointed nose.

'I'm acting on behalf of the estate of Caprice Jackson. You

are a beneficiary, but it's complicated. If her daughter-in-law, Saffron, dies within six months of Caprice's own death, half of her estate, minus the first £100,000, which Miles has been awarded, will go to you, rather than him.'

This can't be real. I must be dreaming. But I pinch myself and it hurts. 'Why would Caprice leave me anything, under any conditions? This is really, really strange.'

Mr Mann smiles. The wrinkles around his eyes tighten. His skin looks like walnut shells. 'She had a very high opinion of you.'

'But even so . . .' I pause. 'Does Saffron know about this?'

He shakes his head. 'No. I informed both of Caprice's sons – Miles and Aiden. As she isn't a beneficiary, I'm not obliged to tell Saffron. And Miles and Aiden do not want her to know.' Mr Mann hands me two envelopes. 'This is your copy of the will. Any questions, don't hesitate to contact me. And a private letter to you from my client. Her personal goodbye.'

I feel choked. 'Thank you,' I mutter, then pause. 'How much would my stake in the will be worth, if it came to fruition?'

'It's hard to say exactly until her affairs have been verified by her accountant. But I guess it will be somewhere in the region of four million pounds.'

Even though I'm sitting down, I have to put my head between my legs to stop myself from fainting.

179

Hayley

Envelopes trembling in my hand, I walk back to the squat. The world moves past me in a blur of colour. So distracted, I find my way like an automaton. I open the door that is falling off its hinges and move into the hallway. The cold dank air assaults my nostrils and makes me sneeze. I throw myself onto the saggy mattress. It is still daylight so I can see to read. I wrap my sleeping bag around me like a blanket and digest every page of Caprice Jackson's will. Then, hands trembling, I open my personal goodbye.

Dear Hayley,

I left money to you because I know in the event of Saffron's death, you will be able to make Miles fall in love with you, and marry you. This way Miles ends up with the wife he deserves to spend his inheritance with. All you need to do is deal with Saffron, and my world is your oyster. I know you love him. Go get him. Please destroy this letter.

With all my love and respect,

Caprice

I cannot believe this. Was she mad? How could she expect this of me? I'm not a cold-blooded murderer. I couldn't kill anyone, let alone a woman who has always been kind to me. 'Deal with Saffron' as a beneficiary of the will and immediately get banged up. The cancer must have affected her brain. Made her irrational. I crumple up the letter and put it in the sink.

And yet . . . and yet . . . Mum telephoned me yesterday in tears because she might lose her job. The supermarket she works for are relocating and getting serve-yourself tills. They don't need as many staff. Four million pounds. Four million pounds. My family could have a new life with this.

I get the matches for Jono's smokes and set fire to the letter. Yellow and orange flames engulf it and it is destroyed. If Saffron *did* meet with a random, fatal accident, how would anyone know what I had to do with it? Surely it would be possible to cover my tracks?

180

Saffron

After my brief sojourn at home I'm feeling well. Recovering from the trauma of my time in prison. And the way you tried to stitch me up, you bitch. The first tranche of your money has come in and so we're opening BPC up again. Miles and I decided we couldn't face sharing our house with another person yet. So he's working from home for a while to look after the children.

It's a cold November morning, and I scrape ice off the car before I can drive to the office. Breath congeals into mist in front of my face as I walk from the car to the office. I step inside. The familiarity of our compact office space wraps itself around me. I flick on the lights and turn the heating on full blast. The cleaners have been in, and it smells of bleach and polish. I'll soon rectify that. At lunchtime I'll go and buy some flowers with a heady scent. A pile of post is stacked neatly on the reception desk. I take off my coat and begin to flick through it. Most of it is junk mail. Nevertheless, I feel alive and energised.

Ted arrives, dressed more appropriately than he used to. A suit without a waistcoat. A single-cuffed shirt instead of a double. I hold him against me and hug him. 'So good to see you.'

And now Julie is here, wearing a pink woollen dress with matching lipstick, brightening up our ivory office. She hugs me too and surrounds me with the scent of gardenias.

'It's so good to be back, Saffron. I have missed all this so much.' She steps back.

'How's Miles?' she asks.

'Still pretty cut up about his mother.'

'And what about Aiden? He didn't even talk to me at the funeral.'

'He's more philosophical about his mother's death. But I think he's still finding it difficult.'

'You'd think it would be the other way around,' Ted quips, 'since Miles is the philosophy professor.'

Julie raises her eyes to the ceiling. 'That's enough, Ted. Save your jokes for our trip out to celebrate, tonight.' She pauses. 'Let's get down to business. What are your plans for the day, Saffron?' she asks.

'Well, this afternoon I've a marketing agency coming in to pitch. And at 4 p.m. Aristos is popping in. He's getting divorced again,' I tell them with glee. 'Every cloud has a silver lining, sometimes even gold. Surely our business can only go from strength to strength now?'

181

Hayley

You texted. You want to meet me for lunch. I feel like dancing on the ceiling, or walking on sunshine; any cliché you can think of.

182

Miles

You are having your first day back in the office. You were so excited about it; like a child at Christmas. I am working from home. Husband. Nanny. I have dropped Ben and Harry off for their first day at school of the new term. Being polite to the school gate mums was a struggle. One of them was boasting about her son's IQ. Another asked me whether I wanted to be on the PTA Committee and seemed most perturbed when I refused. Then I spent two hours at home working on my research project. *Modus tollens* again. My brain is aching thinking about P and Q.

And now I'm in The Bear waiting for Hayley to join me for lunch, a year after she first started with us, sitting at a small table pushed against the wall, in the corner. I'm nervous. I don't want anyone I know to see us. Saffron, what will you say if you find out I'm having lunch with Hayley? We will have one of our terrible arguments. I will end up sleeping in the spare room, because I won't be able to tell you the truth. It would make you worry too much. That is why I have chosen this uncomfortable table, with no leg room, right in the corner. So we are tucked away, out of sight of prying eyes.

Hayley is here, walking towards me looking as wholesome as ever, wearing a short dog-toothed shirt and clinging white jumper caressing the curves of her generous breasts. Pantomime boots that reach to her thighs. She sits down opposite me, and crosses her legs. Our knees touch.

'Thanks for coming.'

'Why do you want to see me?' she asks, brown eyes holding mine.

I pull my eyes from her gaze and hand her a menu. 'First things first. What do you want? We can order on my app.'

She puts the menu down on the table in front of her. 'I know the menu here off by heart. Jono and I come here most nights.'

'So it's not much of a treat for you.'

Her eyes sparkle into mine. 'Is it supposed to be a treat?'

I don't reply.

'I know what I want,' she continues. 'Prawn cocktail, steak and chips, and a large glass of Merlot.'

I tap the order into my phone.

'What are you having?' she asks.

'Pie and chips.'

She folds her arms and her chest protrudes across the compact table. 'So come on, what did you want to see me about?'

'I just wanted to know you were OK.'

'I'm fine,' she replies, lips in a line.

'Where are you living?'

She stirs uncomfortably. 'With Jono, here in Esher.'

'That's nice.'

She laughs. 'Not really.'

I frown. 'Do you mean the boyfriend or the place?'

'Both. But the place is a dump. It makes Rik Mayall's flat in the *Young Ones* seem like a palace.'

'You're joking aren't you?'

She shakes her head sadly. 'I wish I was.'

'And where are you working now?'

Her jaw stiffens. Her eyes harden. 'I'm not.'

'That surprises me. Any interviews coming up?'

'No.'

'I've given you a good reference, really first class, so it shouldn't be long before the tide changes.'

Her prawn cocktail and wine arrive. She falls on the prawn cocktail and soft brown bread on the side, as if she hasn't eaten proper food for weeks. I sit sipping Diet Coke. She takes large gulps of the Merlot, as we plough through an awkward silence. She finishes her prawn cocktail and wipes her mouth with her serviette.

She looks straight at me. 'You sacked me because Saffron had decided to stay at home, and look after the children. But I know she's back at BPC full-time now.'

My insides tighten. 'How did you find that out?'

She smiles. A small flat smile. 'I happened to be walking past and I saw her wearing work clothes, unlocking the door to her office and stepping inside. It wasn't a difficult guess.'

Happened to be walking past your office, fifteen miles away? She must be spying on you, Saffron. Panic rises inside me. 'Well I'm taking care of the children now,' I inform her, voice flat.

She leans across the table and puts her hand on my arm. 'But . . . but . . . what about *your* job, Miles?'

'I'm working from home for a while.'

'Well if you need me, I'd come back anytime.' She pushes her knees closer to mine. I wriggle away.

'Actually, working from home at the moment is fine with me.'

Fortunately our conversation is interrupted by the main courses arriving. I eat my chicken and mushroom pie, which tastes like frozen pastry and tinned meat. Nothing special. She demolishes her steak. We lean back in our chairs, replete.

'That was delicious,' she says. Her cheeks are red. Drinking at lunchtime has made her flushed. 'I need to pop to the loo,' she announces.

She shimmies away, swinging her behind provocatively. I look down. She has left her iPhone on the table. This is it. This is my opportunity. This is why I wanted to meet her.

As soon as she has walked around the corner, I grab her iPhone. I know her passcode. I had to borrow her phone once and she gave it to me; a contortion of her birthday – easy to remember. Hands trembling, stomach tight, worried she will return too quickly and catch me, I manage to put the iPhone tracker on her phone, and synch it with mine. I sigh inside with relief. Now I will know where she is at all times. If she goes anywhere near you, Saffron, I'll be there to protect my you, my love. Hayley will not get away with anything. As soon as she makes a move, I will jump.

183
Hayley

Miles, lunch was rather stilted, a bit awkward at times. You are stringing me along, arranging to meet me, without making a proper move yet. But you wouldn't have arranged to meet me if you weren't interested. You wouldn't take the risk. What if Saffron finds out?

You asked me how I knew about Saffron being back at work full-time. I smile inside. I have my secrets. No need to divulge too much information yet. You sounded scared. Overprotective. Don't worry, Miles. When she's dead I'll make you happy. Grief is just a process. You'll get through it in the end.

184

Saffron

Julie has just shown in my new client, Crispin Montague. He first made money in the mining industry in South Africa. When he moved to the UK he bought a string of nightclubs, restaurants and high-end fashion retail outlets. He is beginning to acquire stately homes, which he turns into luxury hotels: Grantley Hall, Ripon, the Castle Leslie estate, County Monaghan, Ireland, and Leeds Castle in Kent.

He is settling into the leather armchair in front of my desk.

'Can I get you a tea or coffee?' Julie asks.

'Skinny vanilla latte,' he requests.

And I know Julie will have to dash to Starbucks around the corner, because we do not have a machine that makes fancy drinks. She disappears. He crosses his legs and smiles at me. He is white-blond, so pale that I can't see his eyebrows or lashes. Skin like Caribbean sand. His eyes are a piercing cornflower blue. His pale suit complements his eyes. Extravagant cream leather boots with triangular toes, painted-on flowers, like curvy embroidery. A supercool combination of masculine and feminine.

'Thank you for coming in. What can I do to help?' I ask.

185

Hayley

I am lying in bed at the dump of a squat, watching Saffron sitting in her office. She looks quirky with her hair in a bird's nest bun, and she's wearing heavier eyeshadow than usual to go with her quirky hairstyle. But it suits her.

She doesn't know I'm watching her, does she? I don't suppose she'll ever find out. Ages ago Caprice paid someone to come to Wellbeck House and insert software to control the camera in Saffron's laptop. She told me it was there, and I should use it if I needed to. At the time I wasn't sure why, or what she was talking about. But then, when I received her last missive, I remembered. And I soon learnt from the internet how to switch it on remotely.

'Please go to Marazion House tomorrow to check the tenancy agreements; some of them are tricky apparently,' Crispin Montague is saying. His voice booms into the squat, loud and clear. 'If you think it's all OK, I'll go ahead and make an offer.'

'That's fine,' Saffron replies. 'When should I arrive?'

'Travel down in the morning, so that you can start as soon as possible. We're in a contract race with another bidder. Time is of the essence. I need you there by 9 a.m.'

186

Miles

You are home from work. You dump your briefcase in the hallway and walk towards me. You look so fragile in your black silk dress decorated with Chinese embroidery. A kimono look but tighter, more fashionable. I like your bird's-nest, chopstick-enhanced sweeping hairstyle. My heart sinks when you tell me you have to go to Cornwall tomorrow morning. I want you to stay at home near me so that I can look after you.

'How long for?' I ask.

'Not sure.' You shrug. 'Four days at the most, I guess.'

'It's a long way to drive,' I say trying to suppress my panic.

You smile. 'Why are you fussing about my driving? You never used to.'

I shake my head. 'I guess I'm just getting a bit neurotic about things as I get older.'

You entwine your legs and arms around me like ivy and kiss me. 'Neurotic or not, I love you.'

187

Hayley

Tonight's the night to set Jono and his friends up as my alibis. We are holding a get-together in his dead-end squat. Frosty Jack's, mixed with a touch of vodka. Devil's punch, I call it. My special recipe. Served in paper cups. I am drinking lemonade, which I had decanted into an empty bottle of Frosty Jack's. His motorbike gang are here. Jumbo, Tod and Kelly. I don't know why Jumbo is called Jumbo. He is handsome and he isn't fat. No peculiar features such as outsized ears. Tod is long and lean with white-blond hair. Kelly wears an earring and is heavily bearded. I am tossing back the lemonade and slurring my words.

'Iss verrry late. I fink I neeed to go to ssleeppp.'

'Are you all right, Hayley?' Jono asks.

'Nooo. I fink I need to go to bed. I'm pisssedd.'

Before I stagger to our bedroom I fix Jono one last cocktail of vodka and Jack's. I hand it to him with a smudgy, slurred smile. I know he won't be long out of bed. He's up at six tomorrow.

In the bedroom I splay across the damp mattress and pretend to be asleep. Jono tumbles into the room about ten minutes later using the torch from his iPhone. He collapses on the bed beside me. As soon as the depth of Jono's breathing indicates that he is asleep beside me, I slip out of bed, making sure my iPhone is beneath my pillow. I mustn't take it with me.

His snoring increases until he is grunting like a truffle-hunting pig. I pull a dark tracksuit over my jeans and T-shirt. I slip out of the squat, slowly, quietly. The motorcycle gang have left, thinking I am fast asleep in bed. Jono is comatose, out for the count, thinking I am lying next to him. I set off at half past midnight, skulking in the darkness at the edge of the pavement, not wanting to be seen. Or, if seen in passing, wanting to be too uninteresting to notice.

Past Waitrose, into the centre of Esher, along the High Street. Past The Bear. Past the post office. Turning right into Lexington Drive. Past all the 'look-at-me' houses, every one of which I have dreamt of owning.

I stand outside Wellbeck House, and press the gate code. Thank goodness they haven't thought to change it. Slowly, slowly, it creaks open. I wait in the shadows praying silently that Miles and Saffron don't hear. I have bought a gadget that I point towards the house and press. It will clone Saffron's car keys. I hear a strange clicking sound. I press it and, sure enough, I hear the thunk of Saffron's car door unlocking. I slip inside her Mercedes into the soft comfort, and intoxicating smell, of fine leather. I fumble in my pockets to find the cheap torch I bought at Asda. Small and neat with a powerful beam. I switch on the engine and press a symbol that I know will open the boot. It begins to rise. I step outside the car.

Not long ago, I initiated a game with Jono. Asking him the worst problems he had encountered. The most confusing. The most difficult to check.

I fumble to the left-hand side of the boot to find the fuse box. It is exactly where Jono told me, when I was pretending to be interested. I need to find the green and red striped wire that triggers the brake alarm, and pull it out. I climb into the boot, pull the top off, and lie flat, squinting down at the wires, torch pointing towards them. I push my face closer and crane my neck to get the best angle. I make a grab at the green and red. It comes away easily.

Nearly there. Time to do the real damage now. I lie beneath the car and fumble behind the front passenger side tyre to find the hydraulic line. I need to find it, and pierce it with the special pliers I have borrowed from Jono without his knowledge. I will return them as soon as I get back to the squat. He will never know they were missing. Now I need to repeat the damage to the other three wheels. The hydraulic lines will leak slowly. At first she won't realise she has a problem. But some time into her journey, her brakes will fail. Probably when she's on the motorway. Hands trembling, I pull the pliers from my pocket. This will be the end of Saffron Jackson. This is it. This is my opportunity for wealth and happiness.

188

Miles

You are sleeping like an angel. Lying next to me in your pale blue silk chemise, cherubic mouth slightly open. I can't sleep. All I can do is think about what my mother has done, giving someone our family hardly knows a motive to kill my wife – the centre of my universe. I am neurotic. Terrified. I do not feel relaxed at any time of day, morning, noon, or night. Whenever you aren't with me, I have dark thoughts. Strong imaginings of what could be happening to you. Thoughts that make me tremble inside.

Restless, tossing and turning in bed. I hear a slamming in the distance. My body jumps. This is it. Hayley coming to kidnap you. I jump out of bed and pull on my dressing gown, and ram my feet into my slippers. I grab my torch from my bedside table. For the first time in my life I wish I had a gun. What has happened to me? When I was a teenager I was a pacifist. I think the noise is coming from the back. So I unlock the door, and step into our garden. The security lights snap on and dazzle me. I blink and the tennis court and the swimming pool come into focus. My heart is thumping. I cannot hear or see anyone.

I walk along the passageway to the garden. Darkness and silence press against me. I snap my torch on and walk around the garden pointing its beam beneath trees, behind bushes. Then I switch it off and stand still for ten minutes, straining my ears in case I hear something. Nothing. No one is here.

I slowly, slowly, tiptoe down the side passage. I need to check the front garden now. Slowly, slowly, I open the side gate. I hold my breath as it whines a little. I meant to ask the gardener to oil it last week. Into our paved front drive. I can't see anyone. I can't hear anyone. The ornamental gates are closed. The cars are just where I left them. Your Mercedes. My Range Rover. The nanny's Volvo run-around that no one is using at the moment. The Subaru BMZ. I get on my hands and knees and shine the torch under every car. No one is here.

I check where Hayley is on my iPhone tracker. Blue Bell Drive. Esher. Behind the Blackhills Estate, a mile or so from here. I imagine her curvy body snuggled up to her skinny green-haired boyfriend, and breathe a sigh of relief.

All clear.

189

Saffron

The alarm drills into the bedroom and wakes me up for my trip to Marazion House in Cornwall: 5.30 a.m. Too early for light to filter around the curtain edges. Waking so early has made me feel as if my body has been assaulted and I am in recovery. But I fight against the attack and force myself out of bed. I need to be sharp to check all Crispin Montague's tenancy agreements. A shower invigorates me. Now I feel awake and almost normal. I pull on the clothes I laid out last night, because at this time of day planning what to wear takes too much effort. Miles is still fast asleep. I lean down and brush a whisper of a kiss across his forehead, so as not to wake him.

My travel bag and car keys are waiting in the hallway. I press the control pad to open the gate, and get into the car. Start the engine. The brake warning light that usually comes on for a few seconds to let me know it's working doesn't show. The warning lights on this car are often a bit random. I'll get them checked at the garage, when I take it in for a service next week.

I set the sat nav. I should arrive by 10.30 if I blast down the motorway like I did last week. The gates open. I ramp up Classic FM and set off, Mozart's *Horn Concertos* resonating at full volume.

ONE YEAR LATER

190

Hayley

I'm hand in hand with the man of my dreams, walking, looking down on Lake Wakatipu. It's good to be home again, holding my breath as I admire the Remarkables, in awe of their beauty and their grandeur. Their rock-solid monstrosity. Back in my home country I have space and time. Time to think. Time to breathe.

My life has moved on, just as I hoped. I am marrying him. The man I fell in love with as soon as I saw him. A first marriage for me. A second marriage for him. It has been a struggle, a battle helping him come to terms with his grief, after his wife died in such a tragic accident. But now we are both moving on. I have a diamond engagement ring as big as a rock, and the wedding is planned.

We stop and drink coffee from a flask. He stands up. 'Come on, we'd better get a move on. I promised we'd meet her for a late lunch.'

191

Hayley

'So lovely to meet you at last,' she says through a turned-down mouth, as we join her at a table on the balcony of Jervois Steak House. Rugged mountain peaks jut above the rooftops in front of us. She has short steely hair. Her face is heavily wrinkled. Her brow is so furrowed it looks as if she has a permanent frown. She is wearing brown. Dark brown. Everything brown. Skirt, blouse, cardi. A human version of a prune.

I smile. 'Lovely to meet you too,' I reply.

'Why have you been keeping her such a secret?' she asks, giving Simon a look of vinegar.

Simon. My fiancé.

I look across at him. Physically he is so like you, Miles. But he is so much younger. And I feel so comfortable with him. There is no need to flirt or act up. When I am with Simon I am just me. We like all the same things. Plants. Walking. Paddle boarding. Rafting. Bungee jumping. We have just been living together in his apartment from the minute we met. We met on the plane on the way home. I finally earnt the money to fly back. He was returning from a business trip to London. Two Kiwis on the way home.

'Come on, explain why you've been keeping her a secret,' The Prune repeats.

'Well, Mum, you know after everything that happened, losing Veronica as I did, we just wanted to go carefully in private.'

Veronica. Losing Veronica. Simon has been so bereft. Imagine if I had been responsible for you losing Saffron, Miles. I would never have forgiven myself.

The Prune elongates her back and raises her chest. 'But I am your mother – I should always be in the loop.'

Simon reaches under the table for my hand, and squeezes it. He warned me she would be like this. He told me she had a difficult relationship with his father, and so always dwelt on him too much, in a way that was difficult to handle.

The waitress sidles over. 'What can I get you?' she asks.

'Simon and I will have our usual,' The Prune, aka Janet Wilkinson, barks.

The waitress turns to me. 'What would you like?'

'She can have a sirloin. Our usual is just for two,' Janet continues. 'Medium rare, please.'

'Please can I have medium. I'm not good with blood,' I interrupt. 'And no chips, just a side salad.'

Janet stares across at me. 'Sirloin's best medium rare. That is how it should be served.'

Oh my God, she's even more of a ball-breaker than I thought.

'Mother, let her have her steak how she wants it,' Simon says. He turns to the waitress, 'We will have the steak medium please, as requested with a side salad and no chips.'

The waitress looks at me sympathetically, gives me half a smile and scribbles down my order. She turns to go.

'What about asking us if we want a drink?' Janet says, voice raised.

The waitress turns around. She looks so young. About sixteen. A few tiny blisters of spots pepper her cheeks, carefully covered up with make-up.

'Sorry. I thought the drinks waiter had already asked you. What can I get you?'

'Sparkling mineral water with ice and lemon, pronto,' she demands.

'A glass of Merlot please,' I chirrup.

'This family doesn't drink at lunchtime,' she says, eyeballing me.

'If Hayley wants a glass of wine she can have one,' Simon says. He turns to the waitress. 'Two large glasses of Merlot.' He shakes his head and frowns. 'No actually, make that a bottle and two glasses, please.'

The waitress moves to take an order from the next table.

'Are you marrying an alcoholic?' Janet asks, under her breath.

'Having a few glasses of wine in a steak restaurant, on a special occasion, is not a sign of alcoholism.'

I sigh inside. Simon warned me she was difficult. I look at my watch. We've only been here twenty minutes, but I feel exhausted.

'Excuse me. I just need to pop to the toilet,' I say and stand up.

'Don't scrape your chair.'

I try not to scowl at her, but I'm not sure it works.

I walk slowly towards the ladies. I already need a break from her so I will prolong this as much as possible. I do not need to pee. I pull the wooden toilet lid down and sit, eyes closed. Breathing deeply. Trying to relax. Veronica's name spinning in my head. Thinking back to the night I could have killed Saffron. Seconds away from piercing the hydraulic feed to her car brakes.

What stopped me?

A feeling of foreboding. A sudden knowledge that Caprice was winding me up. That you and Saffron were good people. That neither of you deserved this. A darkness moved across my mind and I suddenly knew I must not do it. I got out from under the car and walked away quickly, closing the gate behind me. Body trembling, slowly, in the shadows of darkness I made my way back to the squat. Saffron must have had so much to put up with from Caprice. And now I am receiving my punishment. I have met Janet, or Janx, as Simon calls her behind her back. Janx sounds like an evil character in a sci-fi novel. She certainly seems evil, I'll give her that.

I force myself to stand up and walk back to the table. The wine and the food have arrived. We sit and eat in silence. As soon as his plate is empty Simon excuses himself to visit the bathroom.

As soon as she has me to herself, Janx leans towards me. 'I always hoped Simon wouldn't marry someone who was only a nanny.'

Only a nanny. Surely she wouldn't be so condescending and rude? I must have misheard.

I lean towards her. Our eyes meet. 'Say again? I didn't quite catch that.'

She leans forwards too and speaks succinctly in my ear, carefully enunciating every word.

'I always hoped Simon wouldn't marry someone who was only a nanny.'

'Only a nanny? Some people think childcare is the most important job in the world.' I speak stiffly, barely containing my temper.

That is it. The battle is on. Saffron, if I have correctly guessed the truth of your actions, I suspect one day I will need your help.

192

Saffron

Miles and I are finally clearing out your boudoir, Caprice. I will strip it of flounces and flowers and memories. It will be minimalistic and simple. A place of peace. Nothing to remind me of you.

So many clothes. Fifty pairs of shoes. So much to go to the charity shop. Make-up, straight into the bin – all the wrong colours for me to use. Perfume: Chanel, Dior, Yves Saint Laurent, I'll keep that. Then I shudder inside. No. The scent you wore will remind me of you. I'll give it to Julie and ask her not to wear it at work. Jewellery? I don't want to wear it. But some of it is valuable. I leave that for another day and ask Miles what he thinks about it.

Miles is sitting in the corner sifting through a box of old photographs, eyes watering, about to cry. I go and sit next to him. He hands me the one he was looking at. It's you in a white dress at your first communion. Smooth-skinned. Wide-eyed with innocence. Who would have known what a monster you would become? At the back of the box there is a pad of lined paper. I pull it out. The top sheet has been used as a blotting pad to write on. I can see indentations, in the shape of writing, but I cannot make out the words.

I am curious. You had so many secrets. So many different sides to you. Out of devilment I decide I would like to read what you wrote.

'I'll just go and make some coffee,' I tell Miles, removing the pad and taking it downstairs. Ben has a 'detective kit' with powder for deciphering secret letters. I pull it out of the kitchen drawer and spread the powder across your blotter, and vibrate it gently. The charcoal settles in the indentations.

Dear Hayley,

I left money to you because I know in the event of Saffron's death, you will be able to make Miles fall in love with you, and marry you. This way Miles ends up with the wife he deserves to spend his inheritance with. All you need to do is deal with Saffron, and my world is your oyster. I know you love him. Go get him. Please destroy this letter.

With all my love and respect,
Caprice

Oh my God. What is this?

I race upstairs. Miles is still engrossed in childhood photographs. I show him the paper.

'This is worse than I thought,' he says, going paler than pale.

'What does it mean? What did the will say? Am I in danger?' I ask, frantic.

He shakes his head. 'Not anymore.'

'What do you mean?'

He tells me the truth about the six-month condition on the inheritance. The huge motivation for Hayley to murder me. He takes me in his arms. 'I just didn't want you to be scared. I didn't want to worry you. It's over now. Hayley did nothing. Nothing. She just went back to New Zealand. Aiden and I watched over you like a hawk.'

I am trembling like a leaf, from top to toe. 'So Hayley didn't want to do me any harm, thank goodness. Despite all your mother's encouragement.'

'I'm so sorry, Saffron. So sorry I didn't realise how toxic my mother was. She did everything she could to fool me.'

'And Hayley is a better person than we thought.'

193

Hayley

My mobile rings, and I pick up.

'Hello, Hayley, it's Saffron Jackson here.'

I'm taken aback. 'I can't believe the coincidence. I was about to ring you. How are you all?'

'Good. Good. Listen, I'll get straight to the point, I just wanted to say thank you.'

'For what?' I ask.

'For not killing me.'

I laugh a nervous laugh.

'I've only just found out the truth about the conditions of the will. I was gobsmacked,' Saffron continues. 'And I discovered a copy of the letter Caprice sent to you, encouraging you to kill me.' There is a pause. Guilt at how close I came to doing exactly that coagulates in my stomach. My therapist's words twist and turn in my head. *The important thing is you didn't do it.* 'Thank you,' Saffron repeats.

I push my therapist's words away. I hesitate. I do not know what to say. Silence festers down the phone line. I cut through it. 'Saffron, I've met someone.'

'The way you say *someone*, with such strong emphasis, makes it feel important.'

I swallow. 'It is. I mean, he is. Important to me. His name is Simon. We're getting married.'

'Congratulations,' she says, and I wonder if she knows how I once felt about you, Miles. 'I hope you end up with a nicer mother-in-law than mine.'

I take a deep breath and admit the truth. 'She's the mother-in-law from hell.'

'There can't be two of them.'

'Come on, Saffron. Come to New Zealand and meet her. See for yourself.'

194

Saffron

I pick up the mail that has just thumped through the letter box. The usual junk. Pizza delivery letters. A free local magazine that no one reads. Bank statements. Bills. And a thick envelope from Queenstown, New Zealand. Marbled white paper. Gold-embossed lettering. I open it carefully. A wedding invitation. From Hayley and Simon, to me.

I pad around the house looking for Miles. The children are in their playroom, glued to a Disney cartoon. I find him in the kitchen unloading the dishwasher.

'Look at this,' I say, handing him the thick white marbled envelope.

He stands still and reads it. 'That's a turn-up for the books.'

'The fact she's getting married, or the fact that she's inviting me to the wedding?' I ask.

He passes it back to me and smiles. 'Both. I hope he's nicer than that dreadful Jono.'

'He's certainly more successful. He has an MBA from Harvard and he's setting up an adventure business in New Zealand; employing her father and brother apparently,' I reply.

He runs his fingers through his hair. 'How do you know that?' he asks.

'I've been in touch with her.'

'And I thought we were in the doghouse for sacking her.'

'She's forgiven us.'

Miles shakes his head. 'I thought we didn't trust her, after all the shenanigans with my mother. You shouldn't have been in touch with her. It's not a good idea.'

I step towards him and put my hands around him. 'On the contrary, I trust her now I know the truth of how far Caprice went to encourage my end. How calmly she ignored it.' I lock eyes with him. 'I want to go to New Zealand for the wedding. Hayley needs my help and advice, about dealing with a difficult mother-in-law.'

He frowns. 'What sort of advice?'

'Oh, just how to cope when you're constantly being minimised.' I smile inside. As if I could ever tell him the truth; the best thing to do with a difficult mother-in-law is to poison her, and make it look as if she poisoned herself.

I think about all the women who complain about not being made welcome into their husband's family. I guess there are millions, even hundreds of millions, of unkind mothers-in-law, all around the world. An epidemic of possessive jealousy.

And I know I need to go to New Zealand to teach Hayley what I learnt from Stan-the-man. The darknet expert. Expensive and discreet. The computer savvy, cover all your sins IT man. A daughter-in-law's dream.

Acknowledgements

First, I would like to thank my editor, Tilda McDonald, with whom it has been both a pleasure and a privilege to work. Next, the energetic team at Avon, HarperCollins. And then, my agent Ger Nichol of The Book Bureau, who supports me throughout. My husband, Richard, deserves a special mention. He is my first reader and sounding board; sad to say sometimes 'shrieking board' during these times of Covid-induced house arrest. Last, but by no means least, I want to thank the 'sisterhood' – my girlfriends, whose grievances and witty comments, added to my own, over many many years, have inspired me to write this book.

Don't miss Amanda Robson's #1 bestselling debut

'I absolutely loved it'
B A Paris, author of
Behind Closed Doors

The claustrophobic, compulsive thriller about the murder of a twin sister

'I read it over one weekend, completely enthralled'
Emma Curtis, author of
The Night You Left

A stalker. A secret.
Someone will pay. . .

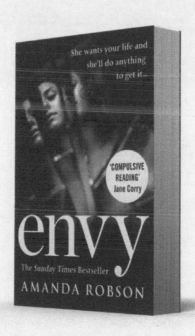

'Captivated me from the
unsettling opening until
the breath-taking finale'
Sam Carrington, author of
Bad Sister

A new couple moves in next door.
Nothing will ever be the same
again . . .

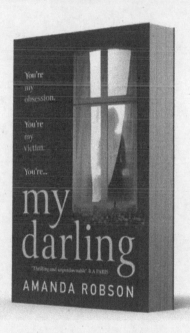

'Dark, gripping, brutal. I loved
every minute'
Jackie Kabler, author of
The Perfect Couple